duty

BETHANY-KRIS

Published by Bethany-Kris

www.bethanykris.com

ISBN 13: 978-1-988197-71-5

Cover Art © Mignon Mykel

Editor: Elizabeth Peters

For London. Who loves Andino more than even I, as if that is somehow possible. Ha.

CONTENTS

ONE

Godspeed to the men who plead.

Those words played on repeat in the back of Andino Marcello's mind as his cousin continued talking on the phone, and his attention varied between the conversation, and work. That was his life in a nutshell—mafia and family.

Nothing more.

Nothing less.

"Please don't ...*p-please*—"

Andino flicked a hand, and the enforcer who had come along for the ride with him that afternoon shut up the begging man who was currently battered and bleeding behind his desk. Andino had taken that lack of patience from his father—Giovanni Marcello had never been very gracious to foolish men who begged for mercy. He was actually quick to kill them for it.

"It'd be great if they just let me fucking *be*," John muttered. "All of them—they're suffocating me, Andi."

Yeah, he bet.

Between John being fresh out of prison, and everybody waiting for his next meltdown to come because some people in their family thought it was inevitable with John's bipolar disorder, it probably felt like he was a bug constantly being watched under a microscope. Nobody wanted that shit.

"Try to ignore it," Andino said to his cousin.

John sighed. "That's easy for you to say."

"They don't mean any harm."

"But are they *causing* it, though?"

Good point.

A lack of trust—or even the belief that someone didn't trust a man—could do damage like nobody understood in the world of Cosa Nostra. A made man was nothing when his word couldn't be trusted.

Andino knew that well.

It's why he made every effort to be an honorable made man. Even if that was a dichotomy.

A thump across the room drew Andino's attention back to the lawyer who had needed extra special Marcello attention that day. The enforcer had smashed the guy's head into the desk, and it made a hell of a mess of blood and broken teeth on the shiny surface.

Damn.

1

Usually, Andino would let his bookies handle someone like this—they owed money, the bookie would figure out a way to collect, so he wasn't in the red with the Capo who collected from him. Andino was that Capo; the bookie was fucking sick and tired of being skipped out on week after week.

It'd been a while since Andino got his hands a little dirty, and it was always good stress relief to beat the hell out of someone. Even if he was just watching.

John said something on the phone.

Andino missed it.

"Listen, I'll have a chat with my father," Andino said, "and see if he can make Uncle Lucian back off you a bit—Dante, too."

"Un-fucking-likely."

Truth.

"Still worth a shot," Andino returned.

John made a noise under his breath.

"What, cousin?"

"Nothing, I was just thinking ... you're good like that, you know? Always looking out for me."

Yeah ...

Andino had been on this earth for twenty-eight fucking years, and every single one of them had been spent looking out for John in one way or another. At the end of the day, next to his mother and father, Andino figured John was the only person he really gave a damn about.

"But when are you going to start looking out for you, huh?" John asked.

Andino laughed. "Probably never."

"You have to take care of you sometime, man."

It was the smash of the lawyer's head against the desk that drew Andino's attention again. Well, that, and the splatter of blood that hit the front of Andino's tailored blazer. He scowled, and gave the enforcer a look.

"Really, Pink?" Andino asked. "You know I have to have dinner with my mother tonight."

The enforcer—who refused to tell almost everyone how he got his nickname—shrugged. "Sorry, boss."

"Are you working?" John asked.

"Cleaning up a mess."

"Ah."

Speaking of which ...

The lawyer was pleading again.

Garbled.

Mumbling.

Bleeding.

2

"Godspeed to the men who plead," Andino murmured before giving the enforcer a nod. The lawyer was never going to pay; too much debt, and too bad of a gambling habit. That's why the bookie decided to come to Andino. "Finish it, Pink."

Turning his back to the scene behind him, he returned to the conversation with his cousin. Like nothing had happened. Nothing was wrong.

This was his life.

Business.

And family.

Only those two things.

Andino didn't know anything different.

• • •

"Evening, Ma," Andino greeted, bending down to kiss his mother's cheek.

Kim gave her son a warm smile and a pat on his arm. "Your father is tinkering in the garage."

"I didn't come to see Dad," Andino half-lied.

He had come to talk to Giovanni, but he always made time for his mother, too. Being an only child had allowed Andino all of his parents' love and attention as he grew up under their watchful eyes. His father had been easygoing and fun, as had his mother.

They made for interesting parents, if nothing else. Andino had been allowed to experiment with life without expectations or demands weighing him down. He'd always had a confidant in his father, should he need to talk. He'd always had a supporter in his mother, no matter his decisions. Judgement held no place in his parents' home and lives, and certainly not toward Andino or his choices.

Andino didn't even remember having rules.

"Was that a new Lexus I saw out in the driveway?" his mother asked.

Andino moved to sit beside her on the couch, grinning wickedly. He had a taste for expensive things, cars most importantly. "Yeah."

"You spoil yourself, Andino. Everybody always said we would be the ones to spoil you because you were an only child. I think they were wrong. You certainly didn't pick up your love of expensive things from your father and me, as far as that goes."

Chuckling, he rested back into the couch and let the familiarity of his parents' home soak into him. "I have to spend all the money I make in some way, Ma."

"How about on a girl?" Kim asked, smiling slyly.

"A girl?"

3

"Find one, marry her, and then you'll have lots more things to spend your money on, Andi. Things other than yourself. I think you'll find spending your money on someone else instead of yourself is rewarding."

"Ma—"

Kim clicked her tongue, stopping Andino before he could rebut her. "I want grandbabies someday, Andino. You're twenty-eight, it's time to settle down. Find someone to do that."

"I don't think you get it, Ma," Andino said quietly.

"Oh?"

"No. I haven't found anyone who makes me want to settle down. I won't force it simply because you want grandchildren to spoil rotten."

Kim smiled, but even the sight was sad. "I know."

Sighing, Andino asked, "Do you regret not having more children after me? Maybe if you had, you would have some *bambinos* running around or something."

"Not for a second."

Kim hadn't even hesitated before answering him. Her words came out frank and honest. Andino believed his mother. She had never even mentioned having more kids as he grew up. Neither had his father.

"Besides, your father would have lived his life in a constant state of panic had I birthed him any girls," Kim added, laughing softly. "When you came along, Gio might as well have skipped off to the doctor's office to make sure we wouldn't have any more."

Andino grinned, knowing that was probably true. "You're terrible, Ma."

"I only speak the truth."

Kim tossed the magazine she was reading on the coffee table and gave all of her attention to her son. While his mother's eyes were a slate blue, Andino's were a forest green like his father's. But in features, he knew he looked more like his mother. Where Kim was soft in her lines, Andino was the more masculine, sharper version. She often told him that he looked like his uncle Cody from Vegas.

Andino had never met the man, but it was only a matter of time before he eventually would. Cody Abella was the boss for the Vegas Cosa Nostra, after all. Giovanni was careful about keeping his son away from Vegas for as long as Andino could remember, although his father had never outright explained why.

He figured it had something to do with his mother. Like how she met his father. Andino wasn't stupid. He knew how that happened.

People talked.

"How is work?" his mother asked.

"Quiet, but busy like usual. Keeps me going."

"And John?"

4

Andino remained passive at the question. "Are you asking out of concern for him as an aunt, or are you trying to pry information out of me for Dad?"

Kim smiled. "You're too observant for your own good."

"No, I just know you, Ma." Andino shrugged, saying, "Dad can ask John how he's doing if he's worried about him. John was always closer to Dad than he was his own father, anyway. But honestly, he's doing okay. He's been home a few days and nothing has happened yet. He's working and whatever. He's got a lot to catch up on. Three years is a long time to be out of this game."

Kim's hand reached out and grabbed Andino's wrist. She squeezed him tighter than he expected her to. "Don't say that, Andi."

"Hmm, what?"

"A game. Don't call this a game. It has never been that, you know it. If you treat it like it is, then you'll lose like the rest who treat it like that, too."

Andino patted his mother's hand. She worried too much about him, and always had. Kim had never actively discouraged her son to join Cosa Nostra, nor did she say a bad word to him when he'd started dipping his hands in the family businesses and mafia. Kim simply let him live and grow to be whoever and whatever he wanted or needed.

He loved his mother more for it.

She still worried.

"I'm good, Ma," Andino assured.

"Good is not always safe," Kim replied.

She was right.

"Where is this coming from, huh?"

Kim glanced down at her hands, avoiding her son's gaze. "Nothing, Andino. Don't worry about it."

He wasn't sure he could do that, now. Especially not with the fact she seemed like she was trying to drop the conversation altogether, and she still wouldn't look at him. What was up with his mother?

"Ma?" Andino pressed. "What is it?"

Kim shook her head, looked up at him, and smiled. "Like I said, it's nothing. I just want you to know something, Andino."

"Sure, Ma."

"I'm so proud of you. I always am, no matter what."

Andino flashed her a smile. "I know."

"I want to keep being proud of you, Andi."

He straightened on the couch, surprised at her words.

"Why wouldn't you be?" he asked.

Kim reached out and patted his cheek gently. "Just remember to follow the rules, Andino. It might not be what you want right now, but it could be the best thing for you someday."

Andino blinked, more confused than ever.

"All right," Andino murmured. "Follow the rules. I got it."

"Good." Kim stood from the couch and brushed her pant legs down. "Go find your father and tell him supper is almost ready. I wasn't expecting you, but I'll throw an extra plate on the table. Is casserole okay?"

"Anything you make is *perfetto*, Ma."

Kim laughed. "You are just like your father. Too slick for your own good, and you know it, too, which only makes it worse. Why can't you find a girl with all that charm of yours, huh? Draw her in, Andino. It'll be worth it, I'd bet all my money on it."

Andino didn't think so, but he didn't correct his mother.

"You just want grandbabies," he said.

"I do," she agreed, totally unashamed. "So, get to work on that."

Probably not.

• • •

Despite having grown up with little rules and restrictions, when it came to Cosa Nostra and living the life, Andino never even tried to push the boundaries. He did what he was told, *when* he was told to do it. Even if it was something he disagreed with, or meant rearranging his entire schedule for a single meeting he'd been called to attend.

He was a good made man.

His father made sure of it.

So, when the boss—even if that boss was his uncle—called, and gave Andino a time and a place to be with no explanation, Andino made sure he was there. And he made it a point to show up early, too.

Maybe that was a fault of his.

Andino found his father and uncles in Dante's office by following the sound of their traveling voices. The topic of the conversation made Andino slow in his walk as he approached the open oak doors.

"It's time," Lucian said quietly.

"You could wait another couple of months, brother," Dante said. "Maybe even until after the next Commission meeting."

"Are you ordering me or asking me?"

Dante laughed dryly. "Between family, us being brothers, that's all. Not a boss and his underboss."

"I don't know, I get being over it all," Gio murmured.

Andino stopped his walk when his father joined in on the conversation as well.

"I mean, Lucian is sixty, you're fifty-nine, Dante, and I'm fifty-seven." Gio sighed heavily and added, "Dad stepped down at this age, too. It's not like we're talking about a premature thing here."

"I know that," Dante said gruffly.

"Let Lucian do it," Gio said. "In a few months, we'll look at someone for me. Andino can handle doing this for a few months. He'll have his hands accounted for. Trust that he can fill seats with the right men."

Andino felt a dead weight settle in his stomach.

He couldn't fill seats.

He wasn't the boss.

"I want to enjoy my time with my children and soon-to-be born grandchildren," Lucian said. "My oldest daughters are married, one is already gone, living in Chicago, and Cella is talking about moving to Florida with her husband for his job. Lucia just graduated, and she will be going to college in the fall out of state. And then there's John …"

"Give him time," Gio said.

Andino was grateful his father was taking his advice on that issue.

"That's exactly my point," Lucian replied. "I need to give my son time. Our entire life has been surrounded by Cosa Nostra. And that would be fine, Dante, if John was like I had been growing up, or even like how you and Gio were with Dad. But he's not, he's John. I can't expect my boy to be like we were when he's had an entirely different set of obstacles that he never asked for placed in his path. For once, I would like to have time with my son where I am not active in this thing of ours. Maybe then he can see me differently. Just a man, his father. Something. I'm ready to retire. I need to."

"Fine. Informally, then?" Dante asked.

"Informally works," Lucian agreed. "We can handle all the other nonsense when we need to."

"What do you think, Gio?" Dante asked.

"About what?"

"You know what. Andino."

"He's my kid," Gio said, chuckling. "He'll do okay. He's a damn good Capo, and he knows how to manage men just about as well as you do, Dante. Andino has been under our feet since he could walk. I have no doubt that he can run this family. He's your best choice for a successor, the entire family knows it. The whispers are already out there, you just have to listen for them. *La famiglia* wants Andino for the next boss."

"They do," Lucian agreed.

Andino was stunned. Nothing had ever caught him off guard quite as badly as this news had. It wasn't bad, not at all, but he wasn't sure if this was what he wanted. Being a boss had never been in his goals. Andino had focused on his crew, on being nothing more than a damned good Capo,

7

and that was it. He'd always seen John as his uncle's successor because he was the older Marcello between them, and John had always been included in more things than Andino.

What had changed?

He knew the answer, but he ignored it.

Would John understand?

Andino didn't have the answer for that.

Drifting out of his stupor, Andino's legs finally decided to work. He moved the last few feet between him and the open office doors. Standing in the doorway, his form caught the attention of his father and uncles.

Not one of them seemed surprised to see him there.

"Did you hear?" Dante asked from behind his large desk.

Andino nodded, but said nothing.

Gio stood from the couch. "This is good, Andino."

"Is it?"

Things were beginning to make more sense to Andino. The longer he considered it, the more he understood his mother's words to him about settling down and finding a wife. His father had likely known what was coming for him, and Gio probably took the news to Kim.

"Nobody thought to ask me?" Andino asked.

Lucian dipped his head down. "You should have known, Andino."

"I don't know that I should have, actually."

Dante sighed. "What is the problem?"

Andino didn't know if he was ready for this.

That was exactly the problem.

He was twenty-eight. Being a boss wasn't as simple as moving up in power when people retired in the mafia. There was a hell of a lot more to it.

His uncle—his boss—seemed to pick up on his inner thoughts.

"We're never ready, Andino," Dante said.

"I didn't ask for this," he said.

"No one ever does." Dante smiled. "We either take it, are given it, or are born to it. We don't, however, ask anyone for it."

"This isn't the kind of change that will be made overnight," Gio tacked on when Dante finished. "It'll be done over a span of time, Andino. Lucian is ready to step down, which will allow Dante to fill his spot. Lucian's position as the underboss will put you front row and center for the family first and foremost. You've acted as my middle man for years alongside being a Capo. You know how to do this, and it won't be a stretch to anyone who sees you in the position."

"Makes sense," Andino said.

It would work, and Andino understood his family's choice to advance him, especially if *la famiglia* was already looking at him for the spot. It was still a huge change. One he hadn't been expecting at all.

"Good," Dante said, smiling widely and clapping his hands together. "Then it's settled."

"You'll make a damn good boss, Andino," Lucian said.

"I agree," Dante said.

Gio passed his son a look that Andino didn't understand.

"You have a while to get everything sorted on the personal side of things," his father said. "No one is saying that you have to run out and get yourself settled with a wife right this minute, Andino."

That was that. Andino's future was decided and he didn't get a single say in it all.

Duty waited on no one.

"Now," Dante said, leaning back in his chair and steepling his fingers. "Onto other business."

Yes.

Other business.

Apparently, Andino's entire life could get upended just like that, but business still had to be talked about because this was their way. *This* was how they all lived.

"What business in particular?" Andino asked.

"You have a gun run coming up, don't you? You're handling the details of it—fill me in."

Andino held in the cringe fighting its way over his lips. "All is well on that front. It's a typical run. I don't expect any problems."

Except there was.

A lot of problems.

Their runner had been picked up on charges. He wasn't getting out. The run still needed to go through, and Andino was going to need to do what he needed to do to get those guns to the man who bought them. Otherwise, they'd have a hell of a lot more problems to deal with.

Thing was—he only knew one gunrunner able to do it.

A man his boss *hated*.

Cross Donati.

Dante's hatred of Cross stemmed back to something that happened between the gunrunner and Catherine—Dante's daughter, and Andino's cousin.

It didn't matter.

The guns had to be run.

Andino would just make sure his boss never found out who the fuck was running them—at least, not until *after*.

Yeah, that worked.

Andino nodded. "Everything is great, boss."

Dante smiled. "Make sure of it, Andino."

• • •

The best part of Andino's day was when nothing was happening at all. Usually, his life was busy because that's how he lived, always on some kind of go. He didn't take much time to relax, but his spoiled dog didn't give him a choice. There was nothing Snaps liked more than to chill.

Trailing his fingers through the pit bull's short-haired coat, Andino walked his dog through the silent park. Snaps was happy, content even. So was Andino.

Snaps took lazy strides, staying directly at Andino's side at all times like the dog had been trained to do. Thinking back, Andino hadn't wanted a dog, and certainly not one that required a lot of his attention all of the time. He didn't have the patience for that nonsense.

And then his father showed up at his door one day with a scarred puppy in his hands when Andino was just twenty-two. Maybe the little pup had reminded Andino's father of the rottie he'd had all those years ago before the dog succumbed to age and cancer. Andino wasn't really sure, but Gio hadn't given him a choice.

No, his father simply passed over the whimpering puppy and explained how he came about him. Snaps had been bred from a puppy mill, apparently. The fools who had been breeding the dogs did so with the purpose of using them to fight. Snaps had been nothing more than fodder to the dogs around him. If he survived, he would live to fight. If an older dog killed him during the period when the dogs weren't being watched, then so be it.

Another litter would be born.

Gio didn't like dog fighting—he wouldn't stand for it. When he'd found out his men were involved in it, he ended it, rescued the pup in the process, and brought it to Andino.

Now, Andino was grateful.

Then, he'd wondered what in the hell he would do with a dog like Snaps.

Running his fingers through the dog's fur again, Andino could feel the raised ridges of some of Snaps' old scars under his fur. No one could see them, but Andino remembered vividly what the marks looked like when his dog was just a pup, struggling to eat solid food and needing Andino to feed him liquids through a syringe. Yeah, Snaps had been that young. He wasn't so young or incapable anymore.

"Snaps," Andino said, noting the fact that the trail had cleared of people.

His dog's ears twitched, but Snaps never looked up.

"You ready?" Andino asked.

Snaps snorted, his nose pressing to the ground. Andino flipped the stick he'd been walking with. It was maybe six inches thick and a foot long. A broken tree branch that had fallen on the path and he picked it up as they walked.

"High," Andino ordered.

Snaps' head flew up, his gaze trained straight ahead. *Good dog*, Andino praised silently. All that time and training paid off. Snaps loved to learn.

"Get it," Andino said fast.

The stick flew from his hand in a flash of movement. Snaps probably hadn't even seen his master throw the stick, but the dog was already going after it. To most people, Snaps looked lazy as fuck. Andino didn't mind letting people believe that, either.

Snaps was twenty feet in front of the stick before it even began to drop from the air to fall to the ground. In a blink, the dog turned and charged forward. Snaps' two paws pressed hard into the paved walk and then the dog lunged into the air.

Six feet high, the dog caught the stick. Snaps' jaw clamped around the wood with an audible crunch. The stick splintered into nothing but scraps. Snaps landed to the ground almost silently, shaking his head at the same time. What was left of the stick fell from the dog's mouth to the ground before Snaps was back at Andino's side.

Chuffing, Snaps waited for his praise. He always waited. He never pressed for it.

"Good dog," Andino said.

Snaps pushed his large head into Andino's palm. Andino stroked the dog back.

When Andino's life felt like it was going too fast, Snaps always managed to slow it down. Today was no exception. But even worse was when Andino's life suddenly felt like it wasn't his own to control, as if he was now someone else's toy to command, Snaps was still the same.

His dog.

His companion.

After the news Andino learned the day before, he was still trying to adjust to what it all meant. A boss, that's what he was intended to be. He'd decided it didn't necessarily feel wrong, but the things he enjoyed most about his life, like being solitary, would have to change.

He wasn't ready for that at all.

"Whoa, that was crazy," came a soft, sensual voice to Andino's left.

He spun fast on his heel, alarmed that Snaps hadn't alerted him to the fact someone was around. Andino was sure he'd been alone.

Apparently not.

The woman, in her baggy tank and jogging shorts, stood at the mouth of a connecting trail. Her blonde hair, streaked with waves of teal and purple, was pulled into a loose ponytail. She had the lean, toned body of a runner and Andino found himself staring at all the curves of her body, from her hips to her waist, and up to her breasts. She was fit, tall, and by the expression she wore as he kept staring at her, fiery and feisty, too.

Andino liked that in a woman.

The woman put a fist to her jutted hip.

"Do you stare often?" she asked.

Andino smirked, amused at her candor. "I do when something deserves my attention."

The woman grinned. "That's what you got?"

Andino just shrugged.

What the hell else could he do?

"I only speak the truth," he said.

The woman looked him up and down. "Do you often wear a suit when you walk your dog on running trails?"

"Sometimes."

"Huh."

Andino cocked a brow. "Do you often question random people on the trails?"

"Sometimes. Is that a problem?"

A smartass.

Fantastic.

"Not a problem at all," Andino settled on saying.

"Good," the woman told him, her full lips curving into a smile and making her dainty features all the more beautiful, "because I was starting to wonder what kind of guy wears a three-piece suit, and walks a dog on the running trails."

"Were you?"

The woman stared Andino right in the face—it was the first time he got a good look at her eyes, and it shocked him. Bright blue like the sky, but stormy like the sea.

"Was I, what?" she asked.

"Wondering what kind of man I am," he clarified. "You know, because of the suit, the dog, and the walking thing."

She cocked a brow, but dropped her gaze to Snaps who had been progressively moving closer to her throughout the conversation. She didn't look bothered by Snaps even as he rubbed his muscular body against her legs, and sniffed her with his short snout. She petted Snaps' large head with her palm as she peered back at Andino.

"Bad things happen to people who aren't paying attention," the woman said.

Andino nodded. "That's true."

She gave him another look, adding, "I guess the bad guys probably don't wear three-piece suits, or walk their dogs in the middle of broad daylight."

Funny.

Hadn't he just killed a man a couple of days ago? Didn't he have a gun hidden at his back? Wasn't he just told he would be the heir to a criminal empire?

That all spelled bad guy to him.

Just in different ways.

"Life is busy," Andino said, whistling after for Snaps to come back. Unquestioningly, the dog left the woman's side, and came back to his master to sit patiently at Andino's leather loafers. "Too busy for me, maybe. I don't like change, but someone decided something recently that changed everything for me. Walking Snaps clears my head."

The woman crossed her arms over her chest, and it drew Andino's attention to the colorful artwork tattooed up her arms. Full sleeves on both arms, ink covering her throat, and traveling down to where the baggy tank top dipped low on her chest.

Damn.

He wondered what kind of stories her ink told.

Something amazing, probably.

"You should take a break, then, stranger who wears a three-piece suit to walk his dog." Her tone was half-amused, and half-teasing. "You looked happy right before I interrupted—I bet Snaps would like you to take a break, too."

"I—"

Andino's phone buzzed with a call—he cursed as he shoved his hand into his pocket, and pulled the offensive device out to check the call.

Dante.

The boss.

No shunning a boss.

It was a rule.

He turned slightly to make his shoulder face the woman as he picked up the call. "Yeah, boss, what can I do for you?"

"Nothing you can't handle, I am sure."

The *last* thing Andino wanted to do was handle business. Any kind of business. He thought of the woman, and her words. Maybe she had a fucking point.

"Actually, I need a couple of weeks," Andino said.

"Excuse me?" Dante asked.

"Yeah, I need a break."

"For …?"

"At this point, whatever the hell I want. And anything that is not in this city."

He needed to get away, and just … *relax*. Maybe then he wouldn't get so snappy when his mother asked about women in his life, or whatever. Maybe then he might start to feel better about this whole fucking *boss* thing.

"Is this about the business, and *la famiglia* again, Andi?"

"Do you really need me to answer that?"

"You're the *right* choice," Dante said quietly. "The best choice. And you know it."

"Fact remains. You've upended what I thought was my life. I need time to adjust."

Dante sighed harshly, and Andino knew then he was going to get what he wanted. After all, Dante would want to keep him happy.

This was a two-way street.

A give and take.

"Fine, but—"

"No buts," Andino interjected. "A break is a fucking *break*."

"Has your father ever told you that you're a demanding little shit?"

"Yes, and also that it suits me."

Dante grumbled under his breath, but Andino was pretty sure his uncle said, "He's not wrong."

"Yeah, well—"

"Take your break."

Dante hung up the phone without a goodbye. Andino wished he could say he was surprised. Turning on his heel to apologize and say goodbye to the woman who had been at the mouth of the connecting trail, he found the spot empty.

And the woman gone.

Fuck.

He hadn't even gotten her name.

Snaps looked up at Andino with his big, dark eyes—ready and willing to find yet another stick to be thrown for him, probably.

"Where did she go?" Andino asked his dog.

Snaps simply wagged his stubby tail.

Thanks for the help, buddy.

TWO

If it doesn't challenge you, it won't change you.

Haven Murphy had seen that inspirational quote on the office wall of a guidance counselor when she had been applying to college after college in high school, and it stuck with her.

That was eight years ago—when she had only been eighteen. Now, at twenty-six, not much had changed for her when it came to what she learned from that quote. She had taken those words to heart that day, and every single day thereafter, too.

It was why she jogged every single day. Eight miles, never failed.

She would jog until her lungs felt like they were going to give out; until the sweat soaked her clothes; until her legs just couldn't take anymore. And then she would stop for a breather, like she was doing right then at the same spot every time, turn around, and run all the way back home to her small Brooklyn bungalow.

That simple inspirational quote also cemented her decision right then and there that no matter what people were telling her—regardless of how much her father and mother wished she would travel or indulge her love of writing, or literally *anything else* but take over the family business—a business degree *was* the way to go.

It was what she had wanted to do, after all. Not travel to see a world that was falling apart at the seams, or write for decades upon decades only to have the gatekeepers of the publishing world tell her she wasn't good enough.

No, none of that appealed to her.

Haven was *responsible*.

Smart.

Practical.

And business was all of those things, too.

It worked out well for her—when her mother's health failed two years back, and her father needed to take a step back from the bar he'd been running for over four decades, Haven stepped in to keep *Safe Haven* running, and profitable for her father while he took care of her mother.

What she hadn't known at the time?

The bar her father had so dearly loved was suffering under crushing debt—a byproduct of her father trying to keep their head above water for years, pay for Haven's college, and then his wife had gotten sick, too. She wished Neil had said something; her father had always been too proud to ask for help.

Even now, two years after Haven had taken over the business, and bought her father out. She allowed him a safe retirement ... not to mention, *saved* Safe Haven from financial ruin. Neil was still too proud to admit anything had been wrong. He also hadn't come back to the bar since Haven had made a few changes to the place.

She didn't blame that one on her father's pride, though.

No, she blamed herself for that. Well, that and the fact that very little about the small bar was the same as it used to be. Where it had once been enjoyed as a quiet spot for a draft beer after a long day of work, it was now known for some of the most beautiful nude dancers in New York.

Or, *strippers*, if someone wanted to be particular.

Her father knew it was a good business to be in, and the cash was more than good, but he still didn't like it a whole lot.

Haven had been one of those dancers at first—she'd taken a pole dancing exercise class in college to keep fit, and challenge herself in a new way. She was always trying to find something to take her to the next level. Pole dancing fitness was certainly challenging, and fun.

It ended up helping.

She didn't need to dance now, though. Or at least, she didn't dance on a regular basis like she used to. There wasn't much need, frankly.

Bending over at the mouth of the running trail that connected with a main trail, Haven huffed hard as she tried to catch her breath. This was her turning point in her runs—the same place every day where she turned around, and headed back home at full speed.

Usually, she only rested long enough to take a drink of water if she hadn't already finished the bottle, catch her breath, and then she hit the ground running again. Today was a little different, though.

Today, she waited a bit longer than usual.

Took a seat on a bench.

Waited ...

Two weeks ago, in this very spot, she'd seen a handsome, dark-haired, green-eyed man with shoulders so expansive and wide, he looked as though he could play football. Haven was tall at five-foot, eleven-inches, but this man had been well over six feet. And yet, in his three-piece suit, he'd looked more like he would be appropriately dressed to sit behind a large desk inside an office rather than walking on a trail with a pit bull.

A ringing call had interrupted their encounter; his phone, not hers. It hadn't much mattered because Haven was already running a bit late, and made a commitment to pick up her friend's daughter from school since Valeria wouldn't be able to do it.

So, she didn't get the chance to say goodbye.

Or ... even ask the gorgeous man's name.

That bugged her.

She wanted to know his name.

And each day since, Haven had jogged at the same time every day—if she could manage it because sometimes she couldn't—just to see if the strange man would be back again to walk his dog on the trails. He'd made it sound like he walked his dog quite frequently, so Haven thought ... *maybe*.

This time, maybe didn't work out.

Like every other day for the past two weeks.

Sighing, Haven pushed up from the bench, did a quick stretch of her burning calves in hopes they wouldn't ache too badly when she slipped into bed later, and turned to head down the trail again. It usually took her a little longer to get back home than it did to run to her turn around point simply because she was winded, and tired.

Today, she made it with three minutes to spare on her stopwatch.

Damn.

Taking the steps to her bungalow's painted-red front door slowly, Haven took in the small potted plant Valeria had placed next to the welcome mat. Her place wasn't big—two bedrooms, one bathroom, a kitchen, living room, and a small back porch to sit on during hot summer days. It wasn't much to look at compared to some of the places on the block what with its red door, and beige siding. It didn't turn heads.

And she didn't care.

She paid for this house.

She earned it.

It was hers.

Haven loved it for no other reason than that.

Well, and something else, too.

Unlocking the front door, Haven opened it and stepped into the house to find Maria—her roommate and best friend's five-year-old daughter—hadn't bothered to pick up any of her toys in the hallway before she'd left for kindergarten that morning.

It made Haven smile.

For the year that Valeria and little Maria had been living with her, nothing was ever dull. Someone was always waking her up, or making a mess to clean. Her house was never quiet anymore, but she liked it that way.

They—and the strip club—kept her busy.

She didn't have to think about how lonely her life had seemed before a Latina woman had stepped into her club only a year after she took over, looking for a job, but being very clear that she didn't have papers. Haven had known that night, just with one look at Valeria, that the woman didn't have very fucking much at all.

She gave her a job.

And a place to stay.

The rest was history.

Haven didn't regret any of it.

Kicking her Nike sneakers into the corner with Maria's bright pink rubber boots, Haven didn't even get to the kitchen where her Bear Claw was waiting for her to devour it after her daily run. The ringing phone on the wall stopped her from getting her greatest treat.

Maybe that was why when she picked up the phone, she all but growled, "*What?*"

"Bad day?" a familiar voice asked.

Haven relaxed a bit at Jackson's question. "No, I just got back from running. Something up with the club?"

Jackson handled a lot of the club's business where the *personnel* was concerned—anything the girls needed, or the security. He kept their ship running smoothly whereas Haven handled all the paperwork, and making sure the business brought in a hefty profit.

She liked this arrangement.

It worked.

"Well, kind of," Jackson said. "That order you made last week for the liquor—they called today and said something was wrong with it."

"Nothing is *wrong* with my orders."

"Tell them that. You know they won't talk to me."

Haven rubbed at the spot of tension starting to form in the middle of her goddamn forehead. "It's supposed to be my day off."

She didn't get very many of those.

"Sorry—I'll buy you coffee and a donut to make up for it before opening tonight. We can go to the shop you like down the road."

She scowled.

Jackson thought he was sly.

He wasn't.

"No, I'm good."

"Come on, Haven."

"Your sneaky attempts to get me out on a date *still* aren't going to work, and you've been trying it for two years. I don't shit where I eat—stop asking me to."

"That's … a disgusting analogy."

"So be it; no dating employees. I'll be there in twenty."

Haven hung up the phone before Jackson could say anything more. She really wasn't interested in hearing him, yet again, miss the entire fucking point of her refusing his offer. Jackson wasn't a bad guy, and he was pretty harmless compared to some patrons that came into the club to watch the girls dance every night.

Still, he didn't take a fucking hint.

And that was a problem for her.

• • •

"For the *fifth* time," Haven said to the annoying man on the phone, "it's fifteen bottles of Patrón, and ten bottles of Jameson."

"Then why does it say—oh."

Haven felt her jaw click from how fucking fiercely she was clenching it. Two years of ordering liquor and doing the sheets the same goddamn way each time, and all it took was a change in staff at the warehouse for her liquor orders to be somehow screwed up every single time. It was getting to be a little ridiculous.

"*Oh,* what?" Haven asked.

"I was … okay, fifteen bottles of Patrón, and ten bottles of—"

"My order sheet was made out correctly, wasn't it?"

The man cleared his throat, and the volume caused the speaker to crackle in Haven's ear. "Well …"

Sitting at the desk in her small office, Haven rubbed at the even worse headache now starting to act like it might turn into a migraine if she didn't somehow handle it quick, fast, and in a hurry. She stared blankly at the wall with a large painting of the New York City skyline—something her father had left behind, and never asked for it back—as she willed the man on the phone to speak, and get this goddamn call over with.

"I may have been reading it incorrectly," the man finally admitted.

"You do realize that you just spent an hour of my time telling me I filled out the order improperly, and I was possibly going to see charges and fees because of it, right?"

"Yes, well, it was a mis—"

"And even after I repeatedly pointed out to you that my order was correct and done in the way it has always been done, you continued to press that I was wrong."

"I am very sorry, ma'am."

Haven gave a tight shake of her head, and rubbed at her forehead once more. "Listen, if this issue comes up again, we're going to have a problem, or I will find a new distributor to buy liquor from. I'm probably a drop in your bucket, but I'm going to make a safe guess here and say I am not even close to the only business you've pissed off lately. Have a good day, sir."

She cradled the phone on the base, and sighed.

"All worked out, then?"

Haven had all she could do not to roll her eyes at Jackson's question. He posed it from where he stood leaning in the doorway of her office—clearly he'd been standing there listening for a while. She really needed to start remembering to close the damn door.

"It's fine," she said.

"Ah."

At his knowing tone, she glanced up from her desk to find him frowning, but not looking directly at her. "What, Jackson?"

The blue-eyed, blonde man was tall, lanky, and by all accounts, handsome if you asked any of the girls who worked the poles. And frankly, a lot of women outside of the club, too. Jackson didn't lack where female attention was concerned.

He just … didn't interest Haven.

At all.

"You're still pissed at me about the coffee thing, huh?" he asked. "Sorry, H. I *do* know how to take no for an answer, but I just thought … well, it doesn't matter what I thought, right? I get it; no more. We good?"

Haven softened a bit. "It's not *you*."

"Don't pump up my ego, now."

She laughed softly. "Really, it's not you. This is just … work, Jackson. I'm not interested in it being anything else, and the more you ask, then the more I have to reject you. Stop being a glutton for punishment, all right?"

The man grinned. "Well, they do say no pain, no gain."

Haven cocked a brow. "And you're not my type."

Maybe that will do it.

Jackson came right back with, "Then, what is your type?"

Tall.

Dark.

Mysterious.

Handsome.

A guy who preferred a pet to people.

Not at all related to work.

Like the guy she met on the trail.

Except she didn't even know his name.

Haven settled on saying, "Not you, Jackson."

"Ouch."

"Yeah, I know."

The man shrugged. "Your loss."

Maybe it was.

But she doubted it.

The ringing of her desk phone saved Haven from needing to say something to Jackson that would likely hurt his feelings even worse. She reached for the phone, and flicked her wrist at Jackson at the same time to tell him to scatter.

"Before I go, the bookie called—said he'd be in tonight."

Great.

Haven wasn't entirely sure how she felt about Jackson giving the okay for an illegal bookie to use their club for his … well, whatever the fuck he did. The guy did keep a low profile—even if he had three different phones that never stopped ringing, and he also brought in patrons. She chose to turn her cheek.

"Yeah, thanks, and close the door," she told him as he turned around to leave. "Stop listening to my conversations—it's called *privacy*."

Jackson gave her a wide-eyed look colored with false innocence as he closed the door behind him. She just shook her head—over his nonsense—and picked up the phone with a short, "Yeah, Haven here. What can I do for you?"

Her office phone was a different number from the main club—it was used for business purposes, and the employees. Nothing more, and nothing less. She didn't have to answer the phone with an introduction to the club first, which she liked. And yet, she could still have main calls to the club transferred straight through to her number if needed.

It all worked.

"Haven, shit. I am so sorry."

Haven frowned at Valeria's tired, sad voice on the other end of the call. This was not who she expected, and her worry picked up a notch. "Hey, aren't you supposed to be sleeping right now? You've got a special on tonight."

"Yeah … about that, *amiga*."

Oh, no.

Haven knew what was coming, and she also knew it was sometimes unavoidable when it came to the girls. Things came up—unexpected shit.

Still, it made for a rough night.

"The school called—Maria was suddenly running a fever," Valeria said, "and then before I could even get over there, she puked all over the counselor. She kept vomiting, so I thought I should bring her into the clinic."

Haven chewed on her bottom lip. "Which clinic?"

"The one in Queens, you know."

Yeah.

The safe one.

They'd take Valeria's money, treat her daughter, and say nothing about the fact Valeria had no papers for her daughter, and no ID to go on record other than a clearly *fake* driver's license. Haven didn't know a lot about her friend's situation, but what she did know, it was more than enough to tell her it couldn't be good.

Valeria didn't talk about her time in Mexico, or what sent her running to the States. She didn't talk more than saying she had her daughter at seventeen, and now at twenty-two, the only thing she wanted to do was try to give Maria some semblance of normalcy.

Haven loved her friend.

And Maria.

She didn't ask *because* she loved them.

"*Lo siento*," her friend apologized. "I know you've been running the ads for my special all week, and it's supposed to be a big night for the club. I don't think I'll get out of this clinic anytime soon."

And even if Valeria did get out in time to make it to work, where would that leave Maria? Sure, Haven could and would look after the girl—she often did in the evenings when she was home, and Valeria danced. *But* not when the girl was sick. That was a *mother* thing; Valeria wouldn't want to leave her daughter, and Haven didn't need to ask to know that would be the case.

"That doesn't matter—I will handle it. I always do. No worries, Val."

Her friend let out a quiet breath of relief. "I am sorry."

"Just make sure Maria is good. That's what matters."

"Okay."

"Want me to bring home something greasy and hot?"

Valeria laughed. "My guardian angel, Haven."

She snorted. "Not even close to an angel."

After a quick goodbye to her friend, Haven hung up the phone. She stared at the flyer—one of many between online ads and personals—that had been put out for Valeria's special that evening. A well-known, popular New York DJ would be at the club in two hours to set up for the evening. Haven had paired him with Valeria for five dances choreographed to music he made specially for this event.

Now she had no dancer.

A *very* expensive DJ.

And soon, a club full of angry patrons.

Great.

This day couldn't get any worse.

Sure, any girl could get up and do their thing while the DJ played whatever music the girl asked for, but that's not how this night had been promoted. Valeria worked all of one night a week on the stage for *one* single dance, and for the rest of the time, she tended the bar and helped on the floor.

So, this was supposed to be a big night. Someone had to dance. Someone who didn't dance often, and who the crowd would love simply because it was them dancing.

That left one person.

Her.

Haven glanced at the black wig she used to wear to dance—it was her signature, in a way. Black hair, cream skin covered in ink, and a leather costume.

It had been a while since she danced.

Who cared?

It was the best way to get rid of a headache.

Win-win.

THREE

Strip clubs weren't Andino's typical scene—no judgement, he just tended to prefer his business to be done where distractions weren't present in every corner. It was easier to get right down to the nitty, gritty of things when he didn't have to worry about his associate being distracted by a piece of ass grinding her lower half against a metal pole while half naked, that's all.

But, he had also let this meeting with the bookie go for two weeks while he decompressed in New Jersey for his little *break*. So, he didn't have much of a choice but to get this done and over with as quickly as possible.

A strip club it was.

Safe Haven, actually.

Andino smirked a bit at the flashing neon sign above his head—Safe Haven was an interesting name choice for a business like this. He bet there were quite a few men who did find a safe haven within the walls of this joint. You know, as long as their wives didn't find out they were there.

The large man dressed in all black with the word SECURITY stretched across his T-shirt stepped aside as Andino came to the front door. As this wasn't one of his regular haunts, the security guard didn't recognize him, and so he was subjected to allowing the man to do a quick pat down before he opened the door. He muttered something about Andino keeping his hands to himself, and to have a good evening.

Right.

He wasn't here for the girls.

Andino did a lot of shit—mixing business and pleasure was absolutely not one of them. It never ended well.

All strip clubs tended to look the same if they weren't an absolute shithole. Dark walls, shiny floors, and raised platforms with poles. Tables, booths, and a bar typically decorated in the same color scheme. Dim lighting.

Andino was—maybe even *pleasantly*—surprised to find Safe Haven was none of those things. Oh, sure, the floor shined, but it wasn't simple tile or shined cement. Light hardwood, actually. The walls were covered in artwork, and neon signs that spelled out different names, places, and even the signature *Safe Haven* name of the joint.

The tables and booths were set just far enough away from the platforms for the dancers that there was no way a patron could possibly touch a girl during a dance unless he practically climbed up on stage. He bet the five bouncers he easily counted on the floor made sure that not one of the girls were bothered, either.

The lighting wasn't too bright, but it didn't give the appearance of shadiness, either. Chrome fixtures, and bare bulbs. Even the inverted lighting over the long, built-in bar with the gleaming bottles on the back shelves were bright overhead.

In the corner, a popular New York DJ had set up his booth and system, and was currently in the midst of finishing up a song Andino had heard the guy play in a hugely popular night club a month before.

Instead of a bunch of older men—oh, sure, there were a few of those here, too—it was mostly people in their twenties and thirties drinking, and watching the show. Nothing about the business gave off the *strip club* vibe.

Young.

Fresh.

Fun, sure.

Not dirty, seedy, or anything else someone might think when they were told women danced nude. One might think this place *was* just a bar.

If it weren't for the women.

Two girls danced on raised stages—one toward the far end with a pole, and one closer to the entrance without a pole where Andino had come in. He passed them a cursory look, but quickly searched the floor for the one man he had come here to see. It was just easier to handle this particular bookie when Andino went looking for him, and didn't demand the man clear his schedule for him.

Frankly, Andino would have the right to demand the bookie do exactly that, but ... Nathaniel wasn't so cooperative. He only let that shit pass because Nathaniel was a damn good money maker, and rarely had any problems.

Maybe that was why Andino had been so surprised two weeks earlier when he had to go in, and do a favor for the bookie by removing one of the guy's biggest debtors. That shit just wasn't common with Nathaniel, and damn, *every* bookie had one or two people who never seemed to fucking pay their debts when the time came.

Never this bookie, though.

Until the lawyer, anyway.

Soon, Andino found the bookie in question sitting at a small, single table in one of the only shaded areas of the joint. Beside him, a table full of twenty-somethings laughed over drinks, and swayed a bit to the fast tempo the DJ switched to in the next section. Really, the whole place was full of people—every table was at capacity, or pretty close to it.

He took it that Safe Haven was popular.

Good on them.

Given there was only one chair at Nathaniel's table, Andino grabbed the free chair at the table with all the people. "Just need it for a second," he told the guy who glanced at him. The bearded, ripped-jean wearing man narrowed his gaze. Andino laughed. "And now you can get it your-fucking-self when I'm done, asshole."

"Hey—"

"Yeah, you try it. You look like you could give me a run for my money outside."

Except he didn't look like that.

At all.

Swinging his back to the guy and not waiting for a response, Andino dropped the chair on the other side of Nathaniel's small table, and sat down with his arms hanging over the back. The bookie passed Andino a passive glance, and then went back to his phone call while his other two phones on the table randomly flashed and vibrated with texts.

In between the phones sat an open notebook with names, numbers, and other information scribbled in every line. How the bookie handled all of this information and numbers, Andino would never understand. But the guy did it—quite well, actually.

"No, for *you*," Nathaniel said to whoever was on the other end of the call, "because you catch an attitude every time I don't give you the answer you want, the minimum just went up to one G. Five to one on Macey—take it or fucking don't, that's up to you."

Hanging up the phone, Nathaniel dropped the phone on the table like he didn't give a shit about it at all. He passed Andino a nod, but his attention was on the changing lights up by the stage and whatever the DJ was announcing over the speaker. In typical Andino fashion, he didn't pay attention to that shit, but rather, the business that needed handling at the moment.

"Five to one—Macey. Is that the fight in Vegas?"

The bookie nodded. "It is."

"I heard those odds are actually *one* to five."

A sly grin spread over Nathaniel's lips. "You would be correct."

"You're purposely misleading a client?"

"I hate when he wastes my fucking time—minimum bet is actually three-hundred. Trust that in five minutes or so, he'll call back with a proper apology, I'll offer to halve the bet to five-hundred, and he'll pay with the odds I told him to. He'll lose, and it'll be a good lesson for him about how to speak to me the next time he calls. *And* ... he will call again. They always do."

Yep.

And this right here was why Andino let Nathaniel get away with some of his shit. The guy knew what he was doing, and he did it extremely well.

"And don't go starting shit with any of the fucking young ones in here, yeah?" Nathaniel said, nodding at the table where Andino had stolen the chair from. "I actually like this joint, Andi. I might want to come back."

Andino laughed. "Yeah, I'll try."

The bookie only sighed.

"On your issue—the lawyer—I cleaned it up. I was able to retrieve seventy percent of the debt through other means."

For the first time since Andino sat down, Nathaniel's cool demeanor cracked as his gaze narrowed, and a scowl fettered over his mouth. "That so?"

"It is. It's not like you to get mixed up with someone who can't pay their debts. What happened there?"

"He developed a habit, I guess."

"That all?"

Nathaniel sucked in air through his teeth. "Favor to a friend, maybe."

Ah.

"That makes more sense," Andino noted.

"Lesson learned."

"You know the deal, huh?"

The bookie shrugged. "If you have to step in, and you don't retrieve one-hundred percent of the debt, then my cut drops back to ten percent. Yeah, I got it, Andi."

"You do good business, Nathaniel. Keep doing that."

Nathaniel didn't even seem to hear Andino—his attention was focused on something else over Andino's shoulder, and the widening of his eyes before a low whistle split through his lips cut through the noise in the room.

"Damn, girl," Nathaniel muttered appreciatively, "it's been a hot minute since you danced, hasn't it?"

What in the hell?

Turning to see what had the bookie distracted was probably Andino's biggest mistake of the evening. He couldn't afford to be off his game when he was doing business, even if it was with someone he trusted, but the second he saw *her* on the stage dancing, that's exactly where Andino found himself.

Off balance.

Stunned.

And entirely stupid, too.

He hadn't seen the woman since that day he walked Snaps in the park. And she certainly didn't look like she did that day, either.

Then, she'd been wearing running clothes, with her blonde hair streaked in bright colors pulled up into a pony, and little makeup.

Tonight, she wore a black leather body suit that was made out of criss-crossed strips that covered her body from her ankles to her neck. The strips of leather strategically covered any part of her that someone might *really* want to see—but it still left enough to look at that there was nothing for the imagination to wonder about.

As she did a quick spin around the pole by using one hand to keep herself steady against the metal, he got a peek at how the strips of leather fell below the curves of her ass, and the G-string she wore under it. And the colorful spread of multi-colored stars tattooed across her back, and down her spine.

Jesus.

He suddenly found himself to be ridiculously interested in just how many stars he might be able to count on her body if given the chance.

Those patent black pumps on her feet had to be at least six inches tall, but every step she took made her body sway in the *best* fucking way possible.

She was soft curves.

Toned lines.

Creamy skin.

Covered in ink.

Black hair pin-straight down to her sexy-as-fuck ass.

The black hair was new.

Andino hadn't known what to expect, but the moves the woman made on the pole were not it. She didn't grind, and shake her ass, but rather, used a mix of acrobatic moves and dances in such a way that he barely even noticed she *wasn't taking anything off.* Not that she needed to with how much skin that damn outfit—if you could even call it that—was showing, but still.

His daze was only broken away from her when during a move where she swung around the pole while upside down using her fucking ankles and feet hooked one over the other to keep her on the pole, Nathaniel chose to do that goddamn whistling thing again.

A hot shot of *something* hit Andino in the gut hard, fast, and entirely unexpected. He gave the bookie a look, and snapped, "Would you knock that the fuck off?"

Nathaniel's gaze widened. "What—do you know how often she dances? *Never*, Andi. Not anymore. Mind your own, and let me enjoy the show."

He had a good mind to punch Nathaniel in the mouth, but he glanced over his shoulder instead. The woman was back on her feet, and winking over her shoulder like she hadn't just spent twenty seconds upside down and swinging around a pole.

There were cherry blossoms tattooed on the side of her neck.

A crown in the middle of her chest.

Waves on her arm.

And *so much more.*

Damn, she was beautiful.

Her gaze drifted over the people slowly, and then *finally*, landed on Andino and where he sat with Nathaniel. He didn't miss the slight widening of her eyes, or the way she hesitated in her next step.

Still, she kept moving.

She kept dancing.

And she kept looking back at him.

Well, *damn*.

• • •

Andino slipped into the back hallway when the security's back was turned—although he was pretty sure the guy still saw him, anyway. It wasn't like the guy could have missed how Andino followed the woman who got off the stage, and headed for the back.

He just caught sight of black hair slipping into the room at the far end of the hallway before he heard the door close behind her.

Shit.

What was that—a changing room, or something?

Andino was going to find out.

Not that he had any business to—or that he should. Because the answer to both of those were a big, fat *no*. It didn't matter; he was still going to talk to the woman because he *wanted* to, and Andino wasn't very damn good at denying himself things he wanted.

He blamed that on being an only child who had always been given whatever the hell he asked for, whenever the fuck he asked for it. Or, that was the excuse he chose to use when someone asked.

Andino quickly realized this hallway was not for changing rooms, or anything of the sort. He passed storage rooms, and an exit door that led out to a back alley. At the end, he found the door he had seen the woman disappear into just as he slipped into the hallway. He didn't even think about it—he just knocked.

"Just a sec," called a sweet, familiar voice.

Andino heard the click of heels approaching the door, and then it opened. It was like every fucking time he got a glimpse of this woman, something changed. Something made him blink, silenced him, and he had to take her in all over again.

Gone was the black hair from when she had been dancing on the stage, and back was the blonde with teal and purple streaks from the jogging trails. She'd tossed on a silk robe over the leather ensemble, but Andino still couldn't control his fucking gaze from wandering *all over*.

Christ.

What was wrong with him?

"I figured you would follow me back here," she said quietly.

Andino's gaze jumped back up to meet the woman's. "How did you know I was following *you*? I might have been coming to ask for the manager … or owner."

Yeah, that worked.

Andino mentally patted himself on the back for managing to not look and sound like a complete fucking *cafone*. He certainly didn't think this woman would appreciate him saying that yes, he followed her because … well, he didn't really know why.

He wanted to.

That was it.

Kind of made him sound like a *creep*.

Andino didn't chase women.

It wasn't his style.

Yet, here he was.

The woman offered him a simpering smile. Her painted-red lips curved in the sexiest way as she did a little twirl right there on the spot, faced him again, stuck out her hand as if to shake his, and cocked an eyebrow in challenge.

"Nice to meet you. I'm *Haven*. Haven Murphy. The owner."

Andino blinked.

And then blinked again.

Just like a fucking *cafone*.

Well done, asshole.

Somehow, Andino managed to save himself from looking like an even bigger ass. Although, he wasn't quite sure how. Honesty was the best policy, or so the saying went.

"Sorry," he murmured, "I was actually coming to talk to you."

Haven—the name of the joint made more sense now—nodded. "Like I said, I figured."

"Took me off guard to see you … up there, I guess."

"Stripping, you mean?"

Andino made a noise under his breath, and shrugged one broad shoulder. "You weren't actually stripping, though, were you? I didn't see you take anything off, or … *strip*."

Haven smiled in that teasing way of hers again. "Yeah, but I really don't need to, either."

His throat tightened.

So did his fucking slacks.

"No, I suppose not, Haven."

She put a hand to the swell of her hip where the robe was opened, and tipped her head to the side a bit. Andino couldn't help but follow the expanse of her toned stomach up to pert breasts, and then the colorful ink tattooed along her lower throat.

"Was there something you needed?" she asked.

His gaze went back to hers.

She was grinning.

Like she *knew* he'd been looking.

Fuck, he really needed to get control of that.

"Maybe," he said. "Do you really own this place?"

"I do. Why is that surprising?"

"It's not. I was just curious."

"It used to be my father's. After my mom got sick—and then got better—I bought it from him, and he took my mom and moved to Florida, so they could both retire. He's not been back."

Andino cleared his throat, and chuckled. "Is that maybe because his daughter dances on stage while wearing ... that?"

He gestured at her with an opened hand.

"Possibly."

"I can't say I would blame him, then."

Haven made a face. "Never said I did, either."

Yes, she was still a smartass.

She was still a little feisty.

Just like that first day.

Andino liked that *a lot*.

"We never got to finish that conversation on the trails," he said, "You took off."

"And what, you thought now would be the right time?"

"I don't walk those trails very often. That day was a random pick. Snaps decided to go a different route, and I just follow him."

Haven nodded once. "I noticed."

Andino stilled.

Had she?

And how had she noticed that at all unless she went back to ... wait, had she gone back looking for him?

"What does that mean?" he asked.

Haven's pretty blue eyes darted away from his, and her grip on the door tightened a bit. "Doesn't matter. So, hey, I didn't take you for the type—is that like your thing, or something? Illegal gambling to relieve the stress of working nine-to-five in an office every day? The three-piece suit makes more sense, I guess. Let me guess ... some higher up job in a company; high-rise, likely. Corner office?"

It took Andino a second.

And then *two*.

She meant Nathaniel.

Because he'd been sitting *with* the bookie.

"No," he said.

Haven's stormy-blue eyes darted back to him. "Pardon?"

"The bookie—he works for me, not the other way around. I don't *do* office work, and that is not why I wear a three-piece suit. Not even close."

"Oh." Haven's brow knotted together in the cutest way, belying the way she looked in that fucking outfit—like sin poured into leather. "What kind of job do you have that you're the boss of an illegal bookie?"

"A little of this, a little of that," Andino said, waving a hand and grinning devilishly. "Nothing that'll be interesting to you, I promise. But hey, I like that you wonder."

A sweet pink climbed high on her throat, and colored Haven's cheeks, too. "I wasn't wondering—"

"It's good. Why do you think I came back here? I wondered about you, too, *donna*. My name is Andino, by the way."

She blinked, and then those long, dark lashes fanned her gaze as she stared up at him. She was tall for a woman—he still had a good four inches or so on her. Compared to his large, muscular build, this woman seemed small.

And yet, there was a fire in her eyes.

A curiosity, too.

Andino liked that she didn't know him at all. That she could only *guess* things about him, and he had the option to confirm, deny, or lie altogether. It wasn't very often that someone didn't recognize his face. That was just a byproduct of being a Marcello in New York.

But this woman …

Haven didn't know him at all.

Not that he was a Marcello—a made man; a capo for the mafia, and now, a fucking Cosa Nostra *boss* in waiting all because someone decided he was the right fucker for the job. She didn't know his family, or the crushing weight that currently sat on his shoulders.

She didn't know anything.

He liked that.

Haven was still staring at him even as Andino inched a little closer in the doorway, asking, "By the way, just how many stars *are* on your body? I got to twenty."

She wet her lips.

Smiled.

Gave him *that* fiery look.

It made his dick hard.

"You must have been looking terribly close to count that many," she murmured.

"I think some might be covered ... even with that outfit. So, how many? Care to let me count them sometime?"

He wasn't even playing now.

Andino wanted to get to the fucking *point*.

Haven shook her head, and nipped on her bottom lip. How this woman could seem innocent wearing the ensemble she currently wore, he didn't fucking know. But she made it work, and he liked it far too much for his own good.

"You are something else, Andino."

"I'm glad you—"

The ringing phone on the desk stopped Andino from saying more. Haven gave him an apologetic look, and then left him standing in the doorway and she moved to pick up the call. She didn't tell him to go, though, so he stayed right where he was.

"Yeah, Haven here." A beat of silence passed before worry colored her next words, "Oh, no, really? I thought you said Maria was doing better?"

Andino tipped his head to the side, and let his gaze travel along the curves of Haven's thighs, and how that robe fell just high enough on the swell of her ass to show off a bit. He had missed two stars—the points of the stars peeked out just beneath the straps of the black leather curving around the bottom of her ass.

Twenty-two, then.

So far.

"The fever has gotten that high?" Haven asked.

Andino's attention went back to her in an instant.

"Okay, no ... don't panic, I'll come help. It just needs to break ... no, I know you can't go into an emergency room without paperwork, and ... yeah, I'll be there. Try to relax, okay? Give me twenty or so. Bye"

Haven hung up the phone, and didn't even pass Andino a glance as she grabbed the jeans and sweater that had been tossed on the chair next to the wall. She was dressed in a flash, and grabbing the messenger bag hanging from a hook next to the door before she finally spoke to Andino again.

And it was only to say, "Sorry, I have to run. Maybe I'll see you around, Andino."

Damn.

Why was his luck so shitty lately?

• • •

"You better have a box of leftovers in the fridge," Andino grumbled, passing his cousin by where John had stretched over the couch. Snaps trailed behind Andino, but was quick to go greet John who already had a piece of crust ready for the pup.

"Left you three pieces, asshole," John replied. "You act like I always forget about you."

Andino grumbled under his breath. "Good."

He headed for the kitchen while John stayed put on the couch—probably watching that show he liked so much with the dragons and fire and *craziness*. Sure enough, he found the leftover pizza waiting for him on a plate, and not in the pizza box. That was typical John. The man couldn't stand to have things be dirty or disorganized.

Throwing his plate in the microwave, Andino waited for the pizza to heat. By the time it was done, and he was back in the living room with his cousin, the television was playing commercials, and John had finished his pizza.

"You're back late," his cousin noted.

Andino fell into the recliner, and sighed. "I was out."

"*Famiglia* business?"

"Sort of, and ... not really."

John lifted a brow. "Really, *you* ... Andino, who only ever works and never does anything else ... were doing something other than work?"

"I do other things, man."

"*Rarely.*"

"Mind your own, John."

John grinned from his reclined position, and tossed an arm behind his head. "Seriously, what were you doing?"

"I had to chat with a bookie."

His cousin pointed a finger at him. "*See*, I told you that you weren't out doing something for you. It's always about work, Andi. You're predictable."

"And then I met someone."

John stiffened on the couch. "Wait, like *met* a woman?"

"Something like that."

"Listen, either she *is* a woman, or she isn't. And you need to update me on your preferences because I didn't know that kind of thing could change."

Andino didn't even think about it—he whipped the small decorative pillow behind his back, and hit John square in the face with it. "There's your fucking update, asshole."

John only laughed as he pushed the pillow away. "So, you met someone?"

"Maybe. It's not Marcello business. Just ... something to do."

"I get that."

And maybe he needed to tell someone.

John was good for that.

Andino gave his cousin a look. "You know, I think I might miss coming home to see your ass stretched out on my couch every day."

"Don't be like that. I'm looking forward to moving into my new place tomorrow."

"Yeah, I know you are."

John looked like he was waiting for Andino to say something—like everybody else always did to him. People voiced their concerns, or bothered the hell out of him to make sure he was doing everything he needed to do. Like he didn't know how to take care of himself, or some shit.

Andino wasn't one of those people.

He had his cousin's back.

For *everything*.

"You need help tomorrow?" Andino asked.

John nodded. "I could use an extra pair of hands."

"I'll be there, then."

FOUR

"How did the meeting go?" Haven asked the second Valeria walked through the door.

Her friend passed a look to her daughter, and then to Haven she replied, "Well, *someone* didn't tell me the whole story about what went on."

Five-year-old Maria huffed in her pretty pink dress, and crossed her arms over her chest as she glanced away from her mother with a *humpf* under her breath. "I was *right*."

Haven had to force herself not to grin—as she was learning from Valeria, it was never good to let a kid think bad behavior was acceptable just because an adult found their antics cute. Give a kid an inch, and they would undoubtedly take a mile.

For the most part, Maria was a good little girl. Sweet, and cute. Loud a lot of the time, but quiet when it counted. She listened, and behaved when told. Haven had very few problems with Maria since she and her mom moved in with her.

"*Anyway*," Valeria said, "The *niñita* here thought it was okay to tell her classmate that the way she ate her fruit was stupid."

Haven literally had to press her lips together for that one to stop the laughter or smile. It made her words come out in a mumble. "Oh?"

Maria sighed loudly, and threw her tiny hands in the air. "She doesn't even put sauce on it like my *mamá's*! It's *gross*."

"Well, hot sauce on fruit is a little yucky," Haven told the girl.

"Is *not*!"

"I kind of think it is."

"Is not, Haven!"

Putting her hands on the countertop, Haven stared Maria down. "See, you didn't like it very much when I said what you eat is wrong. Right?"

Maria quieted, and considered what Haven had said. Valeria, on the other hand, shot Haven a wink and a grin.

"Well, that's not nice," Maria eventually said.

Haven nodded. "And it's not nice for you to say those things to someone else. Food is food—sure, we can make it better or worse, but it's still food, and everybody likes their own kind of food at the end of the day."

"Still think it's gross with no sauce."

"But?" Valeria asked.

Maria let out another one of her loud, child-like sighs before saying in a monotone voice, "We don't tell other people that."

"That's my good girl." Valeria patted her daughter on the top of her black curls, and then added, "Take your backpack to your room, and I'll be in to start your homework with you."

"Okay, *Mamá!*"

Just like that, the issue was done and resolved. Maria was quick to skip off out of the kitchen with her sparkly pony backpack on her back, and her pretty white shoes clicking against hardwood the whole way.

Haven gave her friend a smile. "Kids?"

It was their way of explaining things that sometimes didn't need much more of an explanation other than a single word to say it all. A lot of the time, that's how it was with Maria and any issue that came up.

Kids were kids.

And kids did kid-like things.

Valeria nodded. "Yeah, *chica*, kids."

Haven laughed. "You hungry?"

She gestured at the spread of food she had made for supper—porkchops, mashed potatoes, and mixed vegetables with gravy. It wasn't much, but it was the best she could pull off after a run, and little time.

"I could eat," Valeria said. "But you're not dressed for home—more like the club."

Haven glanced down at her skin-tight black leather pants, the flimsy crop top that showcased the tattoos on her stomach, and shrugged.

"Got a call earlier. Rita had an emergency. I need to go in and handle the bar since she won't be in, and no one else can take it ... unless *you* want to, of course?"

Haven put that offer to her friend as though she were dangling something sweet and juicy. It was the look on Valeria's face that told her the answer.

"I would, but ..." Tipping her head toward the door, Valeria said, "I have to take my days off for her when I can get them."

"Yeah, I know."

And it wasn't like Haven would ask for anything different, either. Not from her friend. Valeria was a good mom that way.

Valeria made a face. "Sorry."

"It is what it is, right? Hazard of being the owner and manager. I need to step up where others fall short, or plan for this."

"*Chica*, you don't even take days off," Valeria replied, grabbing plates from the cupboard, and setting them on the counter. "Like ... *ever*."

"I *try* to take days off. It just rarely ever works out that way for me."

"You should let Jackson hire another manager so you can step back a little from everything. Or even a *temp* one, Haven. Anything."

The thought of that actually turned her stomach. It made her sick, and anxious, and nothing fucking good. What if they screwed up? What if her lack of attention and care for the business her father had struggled for years to maintain crumbled because she needed a *break*?

No way.

Not going to happen.

Haven decided to change the topic, and fast, because this just wasn't something she even wanted to discuss. No one would truly understand how important it was to her that she keep Safe Haven successful, even if that meant she worked herself into a grave to do it.

She was fine with that, too.

"So, I forgot to mention something, by the way," Haven said.

Valeria was busy piling the two plates with food, but still asked, "Oh, what's that?"

"A few days ago—I ran into Mr. Three-Piece again."

Her friend all but dropped the plate onto the counter, and her gaze cut to Haven fast. Curiosity and a sly grin stared back from Valeria. She'd told her friend about Andino—although at the time, she hadn't known his name—shortly after their first meet. Valeria thought she was crazy to keep looking for the guy on every run.

Apparently, Valeria had been right.

It wasn't another run where they ran into one another again.

"Did you now—*where*? Oh, wait, let me guess. Probably on the running trail again, right?"

"No, the club actually. The night I had to do your special."

Valeria whistled low. "*Damn*. Bet that was not what he was expecting to see, huh?"

Haven laughed. "He wasn't what I expected to see, either. To be fair."

"Was he wearing a suit again?"

She smiled slyly. "He was."

"Still gorgeous?"

"Very much so."

Valeria grinned, and arched one perfectly manicured brow high. "Now, for the better question—did you get his number?"

"Didn't get the chance."

Her friend cursed. "Shame on *you*."

Haven laughed, and shrugged. "I expect he'll be back."

"Oh?"

"I mean, he did seem to like what he saw."

"On stage, or off?"

Haven smiled a little at the exchange she had with Andino *after* she'd been on stage, but also the way he'd watched while she was on stage as well. "I'd say both, actually."

"Well, then. You do you, *chica*."

That was usually the plan, yep.

• • •

Haven took the tip a customer slid across the counter to her, and put it in the jar while she wiped down the bar with a rag. She didn't keep the tips when she helped out at the bar, instead saving them up, and then dividing them between the servers for the night. What the usual bartenders did with their tips was up to them, though.

Once the bar gleamed again, and the stools were cleared of patrons, Haven went to the next task of putting the liquor bottles back in their rightful spot.

She couldn't say she was a *great* bartender, but she was decent enough. She could pull off about twenty drinks, and those were the most requested at the club. Should someone come in wanting something she hadn't heard of, a simple app on her phone could give her all the ingredients and direction she needed to make the drink happen.

She still preferred to be in the office.

Or even … sometimes … on the stage.

"No dancing tonight?"

Haven felt a warm sensation slide down her spine at the familiar, dark tone. Like brown sugar, she thought. His voice was rich, and candy to her senses.

Andino.

She had been right.

He was back.

Turning around, Haven found Andino approaching the bar. He didn't take a stool, but rather, stood on the other side of the bar with a grin that said he was happy he found her there.

"No dancing," Haven returned. "I'm filling in elsewhere tonight."

"That's the mark of a good boss, then."

Haven shrugged. "You could say that."

"You work often, don't you?"

"Never stops."

"I know that life." Andino muttered, glancing away.

Haven was quick to search the floor while she had the chance to. Surprisingly, she found that Andino's bookie friend—or employee, or whatever the hell he was—wasn't in the club. The bookie sat in the same spot whenever he came in, and currently, that table was empty.

That told her two things.

Andino hadn't come for the bookie.

He *had* come for her.

Maybe she liked that a little bit.

"Twenty-three," Andino murmured.

Haven glanced back at him at the sudden drop in his tone when he spoke. She realized then that he had been looking at her again while she searched the floor, but she had been too distracted to notice.

Huh.

"I beg your pardon?"

"Twenty-three stars so far. I missed one behind your ear."

Her heart stopped for a split second—she swore it did. How was he still keeping track of how many stars she had tattooed on her body? Hell, *she* had stopped counting four years ago when she got her twentieth.

Subconsciously, she moved to tuck a strand of hair behind her ear, but forgot she had pulled her hair up into a high, messy bun to work the bar. Which explained how he had seen the star behind her ear, considering the last time they met, her hair had been down.

Andino grinned lazily.

On another man, she might think that cocky look wasn't her thing. On him, though? It looked *divine*.

"You could save me the trouble," Andino said, "and just tell me how many stars there are."

Haven *really* shouldn't be flirting while she worked. It was a rule she had for all the girls that worked the place—it was fine to smile, and whatever else, but lap dances, private rooms, and meets outside the club were strictly forbidden. They weren't *that* kind of joint, and she didn't even want to give the appearance that they were to begin with.

And yet, all she wanted to do in that moment was play with Andino—tease him a little, and give it back to him just as much as he was giving it to her. He made it easy, and fun. God knew it had been a long damn time since a man came around to perk her interest.

Haven always had too much to do.

Too much work.

Too much responsibility.

Too much *everything*.

Valeria was always telling Haven to take a break, or do something fun. To try something new, and get out of her comfort zone. Maybe this was something she could do that with—what would it hurt?

"Where's the fun in me telling you how many stars are tattooed on my body," Haven asked, "when you seem quite intent on finding them yourself, Andino?"

The man across the bar flashed his teeth in a wickedly sinful smile, and let out a husky laugh that made her wet between her thighs from the sound alone. It rocked through her body, and touched every single one of her nerves.

Jesus fucking Christ.

The man was several feet away.

A bar separated them.

He wasn't even touching her!

And he made her wet.

Yeah, this could be fun.

"I mean," Haven continued, shrugging her dainty shoulders, "your way seems a hell of lot more fun than just telling you. The game ends once you know."

Andino shoved his hands in his pockets, and rocked back on his heels a bit. He turned his head to the side, giving her a glorious view of his strong jaw, green eyes, and all the hard lines of his face. The man really *was* beautiful. He looked like he hadn't shaved in a couple of days what with the dusting of facial hair covering his jaw and cheeks. She bet that scruff would feel some kind of good between her thighs.

Wow.

She went right to that place fast.

The man had to be at least two-forty or even two-fifty in weight, if not more. And yet, he didn't look *bulky*. Fit, strong, and dominating. She hadn't noticed before, but he had a tiny cleft in his chin, and a dimple in his left cheek when his grin deepened just enough.

Yes, with his suit tailored to fit his large frame, and those looks of his, he was every woman's walking wet dream come to life. Sex in the flesh, if there was such a thing. Tall, mysterious, handsome, and a whole lot of trouble.

Andino peered at Haven through the corner of his eyes, and she swore she could feel the wheels in his head turning. "So, is that what this is, then? Have you decided?"

She cocked her head to the side a bit. "You're going to have to be clearer."

"*This*," he said, gesturing between them, "you and me, and whatever this little chase is I seem to be doing with you. You've decided it's a game, then?"

Haven wet her lips, and smiled. "I didn't know you *were* chasing me, Andino."

"Me either … until now. You know, though, so tell me." He edged closer to the bar, and pressed his hands to the top. Leaning a little over the counter, he came close enough that she could smell the cologne he wore—a strong, distinct musk that made her think *leather*, *smoke*, and *man* all rolled into one. Somehow, Haven had moved to creep a little over the bar, too. Both of them were close enough that all she could see was his handsome features, and the darker green flecks inside the lighter greens of his eyes. "Is it a game you want to play?"

"Is there going to be a winner?"

Andino laughed, nodded, and slapped the bar before pushing away. "You bet your pretty ass, *donna*. There will most certainly be a winner."

He gave her a wink, and just like that, turned away from the bar. Haven thought to ask where in the hell he was going after that show he just put on, but one of the girls serving people came up with a new order at the same time.

Damn.

Why were people and things always getting in the way with Andino? And why did she care?

Well, Haven didn't need someone to answer that question. She knew exactly why she cared—the man himself was the answer, and the way he was still looking at her with that intense gaze even as he settled at a table near the entrance. He didn't watch the girls on stage, and he didn't even look at the server when she came up to take his drink order.

No, he just watched Haven.

Somehow, Haven managed to get back to work even feeling like her fucking skin was tingling because she just *knew* Andino was still staring at her. She didn't know how long it was before the tingling stopped.

But when she looked for him again, he was gone.

Well, then …

Who won that round?

• • •

It was nearly three in the morning before Haven was finally able to close the bar, and lock up. Last call came at two, and the final dance was over by two-thirty in the morning. All the patrons had to be gone and tabs paid within ten minutes after the final dance. The bouncers always made sure that everyone followed the rules.

It made work easier, anyway.

Georgie—the last security guard to always leave every night—waited with Haven as she locked the entrance doors to the club, and then turned to face the darkness of the parking lot. There was a very large part of her that was entirely unsurprised to see Andino leaning against the side of her black Cadillac SUV, and looking like he had all the time in the world to stand right where he stood.

She might have grinned.

May have liked to see him there.

Possibly got a thrill from it.

Haven wouldn't admit it.

Jesus.

Who was this man?

At his side, the dog—Snaps, she thought Andino had called him—sat next to his master, but his behind wiggled when he saw Haven. As though he recognized her, and was excited to see her. It was cute—such a big, nasty looking dog, and he seemed *joyful* to see her.

"That a problem?" Georgie asked, nodding in Andino's direction.

Haven laughed a little, and shook her head. "Definitely *not* a problem, but thanks for looking out for me, Georgie."

"That's my job, girl."

The security guard gave her a wink, and a smile before he took the steps two at a time, and headed for his truck parked at the far end of the lot. Haven didn't miss how Andino's gaze narrowed on the man after the whole wink thing, and didn't move until Georgie pulled away.

"Did you just glare at him for winking at me?" Haven asked.

Andino's piercing green gaze turned back on her in a blink as she approached. "Yes, I did. Is that a thing?"

"Who, Georgie?"

"Who else?"

"He's an employee. I don't fuck my employees."

Andino chuckled and straightened a bit, so he wasn't leaning against her vehicle. His hands stayed firmly stuffed in his pockets, still giving off that don't-care-about-a-thing aura. "Good to know; I don't like to share."

"You can't share something that isn't yours, Andino."

"We'll see about that," he murmured.

She pretended like she didn't hear that comment, *and* that she liked it. "You know, we have security for men like you—anyone waiting outside after closing gets the cops called on them."

Andino shrugged. "Cops won't even touch me. And very little scares me, *ragazza.*"

"And just what does that mean, now?"

Because he was full of those vague statements.

"I waited hours just to ask you to do something with me tonight, Haven, so are we going to sit here and have a conversation in an empty parking lot, or do you want to do something?"

She pretended like she was considering his offer. "It's three in the morning. What could we possibly do at this time?"

"I know places that are open all night."

"Oh, you do, huh?"

"You could use some fun, couldn't you?" he asked.

"I definitely could." She glanced at Snaps who was still wiggling his backside that rested on the ground. "Is he coming?"

"Snaps usually follows me along everywhere. Someone is always willing to keep an eye on him, or take him for a walk. You know, as long as he hasn't bitten them yet."

"That's a joke, right?"

Andino flashed a grin she thought was predatory.

And *entirely* sexy.

"Not particularly," he murmured.

Well, then.

"Would this be like a date?" she asked.

Andino shrugged. "Call it whatever you want. Care to join me?"

"Yes, I think I would."

He gestured at a black Lexus across the lot. "Then, allow me. Ladies first."

FIVE

"Here we are," Andino said, pulling his Lexus to a smooth stop in front of the club's entrance. Despite Snaps jumping forward to rest his big ass body on the middle section between their seats—he always got excited whenever he was able to come to one of the clubs—Andino still saw Haven's eyes widen. "Something wrong?"

"That line, I guess."

Ah, yeah.

The line of still-waiting people—despite the time, they were always itching to get a look inside the popular nightclub—stretched halfway down the block.

"I can't believe you think we'll actually get in with a line that long," Haven said, shaking her head. "The sun will be rising before we get in."

Andino chuckled loudly. "I don't wait in *lines*."

Ever.

Saying nothing else, Andino cut the engine, and opened the driver's door. He waited as Snaps quietly followed behind his owner, and his metal collar clinked with every step of his paws. Haven glanced back at Andino with a furrowed brow before she finally got out of the car, too. He'd drop his keys with the security at the front, and they would park his car. Simple.

Dragging the tips of his fingers along the short, stiff hair of Snaps' head, Andino joined Haven's side. She said nothing even as he put a hand to the small of her back, and gestured at the club waiting in front of them.

"Ladies first," he urged.

Haven peered over at him with a sly smile. "Who owns this place, anyway?"

"Me, actually."

"I wish I was surprised."

Andino grinned sinfully. "What gave it away?"

"Oh, I don't know. Different things."

"Mmhmm. Does that change things, then?"

Haven cocked a brow. "What would it change?"

"I suppose owning a club—though, technically, I own five clubs between here and Chicago," Andino said, "would make me your competition in a way, wouldn't it?"

Her laughter came out almost *challenging*. And damn the woman because the sound alone was enough to make Andino respect her, and harden his cock at the same fucking time. Where had this woman been hiding, anyway?

Haven leaned closer, put a hand against Andino's broad chest to pat the spot directly over his thundering heart, and then her mouth came close enough to his ear that her soft lips grazed his skin as she spoke. "Oh, I don't think we're competing, Andino. At least, not in *this* sense."

She didn't give him the chance to respond before she stepped away from him altogether, and headed for the club's entrance. Andino rocked back on his heels—admiration and lust spinning through his bloodstream—and watched the way Haven's ass swayed in those tight-as-fuck leather pants of hers as she walked away from him, not to mention the peek of creamy, tattooed skin her crop top showed off.

And would you look at that.

He found another star.

A pink one this time.

"Twenty-four," he murmured to himself.

Snaps chuffed beside him as though he had spoken to his dog. Andino, on the other hand, was still interested in memorizing the shape of Haven's body and how it moved. It was quite a sight—who could blame him, really?

Jesus.

This woman was something else. His dick was already trying to punch through his fucking slacks it was so goddamn hard.

It was going to be a fun night.

"Are you coming?" Haven called over her shoulder.

Those blue eyes of hers glittered.

Stormy like the sky after a good rain.

Crazy beautiful.

Andino darted forward, saying, "How could I say no?"

● ● ●

Music pumped.

Lights flashed.

People danced.

Drinks flowed.

Andino took it all in with the keen eye of a business man appreciating his hard work.

Haven, too, took in the filled-to-capacity club with an appreciative eye as she said, "Maybe I should up my game in this business, huh?"

Andino smirked. "What, open a few clubs?"

"The idea *is* appealing, but, maybe not."

"Why is that?"

"The club scene is a risky business. There's a lot of variables. I prefer a sure thing when it comes to making business decisions. I've worked incredibly hard to be where I am right now, and I don't want to ruin it by making the wrong choice simply because something seemed like a good idea at the time."

She was right.

He respected her opinion.

"I don't tend to have that problem," he admitted.

Haven gave him a look. "Consider yourself one of the lucky few, I guess."

Yes, it was that, or the fact that Andino kept his many businesses very rich through his other illegal ventures. Of course, he wasn't about to mention that to Haven.

"Care for a drink?" Andino asked, putting a hand to Haven's back as he guided her toward the bar. "Whatever you want, they can make."

"Actually, just a whiskey would be great."

Andino couldn't stop the groan that came out of his fucking mouth. "A woman after my own heart—*damn*."

Haven's laughter came out sweet, high, and all too goddamn sexy. "I am full of surprises."

"So I am learning."

One of the two women—and one man—working behind the bar smiled widely when Andino and Haven approached. The woman tossed down the rag she had been using to wipe down a bottle, put her hands on the bar top, and lifted herself high enough that she could peer over the other side. At the sight of one of his favorite people, Snaps' stubby tail wagged again.

"And there he is," Candace said, grinning. "Guess what I've got for you, Snaps? Guess."

The pit bull answered the bartender back with a loud *woof*. It sent a man sitting on a stool a few seats down jumping out of his seat with wide eyes. The sight made Andino laugh under his breath, but just as quickly, he glanced down at his dog.

"Like you're not spoiled enough, huh?" he asked Snaps.

The dog was quick to scoot around the side of the bar when Andino jerked his head to the side—one of his few commands of *go ahead*. Candace already had the door open for Snaps, and had one of his favorite freeze-dried meat treats in her hand.

Candace fed Snaps a treat as she looked back to Andino, asking, "Working tonight?"

Andino shrugged. "Something like that."

The bartender's gaze drifted to Haven who was currently watching the DJ dance behind the safety of his glass-encased booth. "*Ah*. Do you want me to call a girl off the floor to make sure you're both happy, or ...?"

"Not tonight. Just keep an eye on Snaps for me."

"Will do."

"And two whiskeys—have someone find us on the floor."

Candace nodded. "You got it, boss."

Now that his pup was handled, Andino put his attention back where he really wanted it to be for the evening—on *Haven*. She was still watching the DJ, though, and he wasn't sure he liked that too much. He would much rather have her looking at him.

Stepping in behind her, Andino slid a hand around Haven's waist, and grabbed tight. He felt the way her muscles jumped at the unexpected touch, and how she shivered when he leaned in close, and murmured in her ear, "Have you found something you like?"

"Is that jealousy, I hear?"

Andino grinned. "You should answer my question."

"He's got a great ear for a good beat."

"Mmm, and a drinking problem."

Haven made a face. "Yeah, that kind of ruins it."

"Would you like me to introduce you, or—"

"Stop being a shit, Andino."

"Most people call me Andi," he said.

Haven glanced at him from the side, and her teeth cut into her lip. "Do they?"

"Everyone who knows me well enough—unless they work for me, I suppose."

"I like Andino."

"Oh?"

"Mmhmm," she hummed with a sexy grin. "*And*, you didn't see me asking about your bartender there, and how much she loves your dog."

Christ.

She was beautiful.

Cutting.

And quick.

All the things Andino liked.

"Fair is fair," he admitted.

Haven winked. "Exactly—I want to dance. So, let's do that, Andino."

"Demanding, too," he murmured.

"Only when I'm not on my knees."

Yep.

I am so fucked.

"Let's dance, then," he said huskily.

He chased after Haven's laughter as she led him out onto the floor. He was beginning to find he liked the sound of her laughter as much as he liked all the many different facets of her. And he was only starting to learn things about this woman—what was he going to think when he knew *everything?*

Andino figured that didn't matter.

Not now, anyway.

He found it hard to focus on anything but the way Haven's tight ass fit perfectly against his groin once they were on the dance floor, and the music turned up a notch. Under the flashing lights, she looked like a sinful angel swaying and grinding to the beat of the song, her lips moving to sing the familiar tune.

There was no hiding how fucking hard Andino was. No pretending he didn't want this woman—preferably, bent over some flat, sturdy surface as soon as he could possibly get her there. Was he asking for too much? He sure as hell didn't think so.

The closer he pulled her, the more she grinned. The more he let his hands wander over her curves, and sneak up under her crop top to find the lace of her bra meeting his fingertips, the darker the blues of her eyes became. She was soft silk under his hands, and warm, too.

He bet she was wet somewhere else.

She watched him under dark, long lashes. Danced without missing a step. Whispered in his ear when he brought her closer.

She was a teasing *minx.*

A siren, maybe.

Too sexy for her own good, and it kept pulling Andino back in again. He didn't mind—at least, not for tonight.

Haven's laughter colored up his senses with something thick, and promising when her ass grinded against his groin again, and Andino groaned. His fingers dug in tight to her hips, promising something of his own if she kept that fucking shit up.

"Don't pretend like you can't *feel* my cock," he murmured against her neck.

She shuddered. "That's why I keep doing it."

Of course.

Haven tipped her head sideways just enough for Andino to catch the shape of her pretty mouth curving into one of those sly grins—that was enough teasing for him. He wanted a *taste*, and so he took it. Pressing his lips against hers, and moving forward at the same time Haven turned to face him completely. Her hands fisted into his silk shirt as he dragged her flush against his body. She wasn't shy—her lips parting for him the second his tongue struck against the seam of her lips with a silent demand to *open up.*

Christ.

She tasted like mint.

Heat.

Sex.

At least, the promise of it.

He heard the club around him, and felt the bass of the music thumping against the soles of his shoes, but none of it really mattered. None of it seemed important next to the way this woman kissed him like she needed nothing more than to taste him on her tongue.

Andino finally broke their kiss when the song changed. Haven's pink tongue peeked out to lick him from her lips—and fuck him, his dick *ached* from the sight.

"Still want that whiskey?"

"I don't think so," Haven said. "I'm in the mood for something else now."

Fucking *yes.*

He was up for that.

All of that.

• • •

If Andino thought Haven had tasted like sin when he kissed her on the dance floor, he had been mistaken. She *truly* tasted like candied sin when he had her sitting on the edge of his desk in the club's office, and was peeling those leather pants off her shapely legs one slow fucking inch at a time all the while kissing her. Finally, he had those pants of hers off, and tossed away to the floor somewhere.

He swore she was taunting him with those challenging grins, and the way she licked her lips when he pulled away from their kiss. Not to mention how she fucking looked just *sitting* there waiting for him to do something.

Legs spread.

Black lace panties on display.

Not the least bit shy.

Andino grabbed the top of her bare thighs with his hands, and squeezed roughly as he leaned in close enough to feel the warmth of her breath on his face. "You're a dangerous fucking woman, do you know that?"

Haven's tongue swept her bottom lip again.

Jesus.

If she kept doing that, he was going to need to fill her mouth full of something else. *Focus, Andino. One thing at a goddamn time, man.*

"How so?" she whispered.

Airless.

Hot.

Ready.

"You're just ... too much of everything," he said, the words rumbling out of his chest.

Haven blinked. "What?"

"Too confident. Too beautiful. Too *you*. It's unsettling as much as it's amazing, but you don't even realize any of that, do you? Most women need a man to hold them up in some way—stroke their fucking egos, keep them entertained, or cater to their insecurities. You don't give a single shit about any of that noise, do you?"

Haven grinned widely. "Why would I need you to stroke my ego or take care of me? I know what and who I am, Andino. A man didn't make me this way—*I* did."

Exactly.

And that's why she was perfect.

"Don't change that," he told her.

Haven shrugged. "Wasn't ever planning on it."

"Good."

That was quite enough talking for Andino. Especially when Haven reached between them, and stroked the outline of his hard cock through his slacks, eliciting another one of his gruff moans.

"*Fuck*," he muttered.

"I bet you'll like when I suck you off, too," Haven said, her words nothing more than a soft whisper against his skin. "Don't you want to see me on my knees for you, Andino?"

Hell yes. That and more.

She palmed him with a firm enough touch that he was pretty sure he could come like that if she kept it up—that was not in the plans, though. He closed the distance between them again, and slammed his mouth down on hers. He couldn't get enough of the way this woman kissed him; entirely wild, and unashamed. Like she couldn't get enough, and he was the air she was trying to take into her lungs just to breathe.

Between her thighs, he found her pussy warm and damp overtop of those lace panties. She sucked in a ragged breath when his knuckles grazed along her slit, and then she released the sexiest moan when he let two of his fingers slip beneath the lace to find her sex.

Wet.

Silken.

Hot.

Tight.

Her hips bucked forward into his hand the second he thrust those fingers into her cunt—her walls clamped down around him, and a shudder raced through her body. And *Christ* ... those blue eyes of hers flew wide, and he was kind of struck at how amazing she looked staring down between her thighs to watch him fuck her pussy with his hands.

"Damn, you're soaked," he murmured.

"Do you like that?"

Fuck.

Andino leaned forward, and kissed her three times to punctuate each one of his words. "So. Fucking. Much."

"Show me, then. *Taste me.*"

Her words came out so fucking high and breathless, sounding like the best kind of music to him. He wondered, and leaned a little closer, making sure all Haven was looking at then was him, and nothing else ... "How will you sound then, huh? When my face is between your thighs, and I've got that sweet pussy in my mouth? Are you going to scream for me?"

This woman never failed to stun him.

It's just who she was.

This was no exception.

"Depends on how talented that mouth of yours is," she countered.

Damn.

"Challenging me is dangerous, Haven," Andino warned.

She cocked a brow. "Who said I wanted *safe?* I'm pretty sure if you don't have me pinned to this desk, sore all over, and unable to speak by the time we're done here, I'm going to be sorely fucking disappointed, Andino."

Well, then.

"Ask and you shall receive, sweetheart."

He kissed her one more time—harder and longer. Before he pulled away from that candy-mouth of hers, he bit her bottom lip hard enough to make her gasp. Fire flashed in her eyes, but Andino only winked, and kept stroking her wet pussy alive with his fingers all the while. She was shaking now; trembling from the tips of her toes, and it was only spreading more the longer he kept his fingers moving inside her cunt.

Haven didn't have the chance to react when Andino reached up and grabbed her throat. In a flash, he had her back pushed flush to the desk, and forced her to stare up at him. That fire in her eyes only intensified as her hands came up to encircle his wrists tightly. She grinned, flashed her teeth at him, and wiggled her hips as his fingers slowed a bit inside her pussy.

"*Ask me* to taste you," he said.

Haven let out a soft moan. "That's not—"

"Ask me, or you get nothing."

"*Andino.*"

His fingers slowed more—she'd been close to coming before. He'd felt it in the tightening of her inner muscles, and how wet she had become. She wasn't going to get that orgasm until he got what he wanted first.

"All you have to do is say one simple sentence, Haven," Andino taunted. "*Please taste me*. That's it, baby—easy."

"I—"

"Say it."

Haven whined when her grinding hips couldn't get his fingers back to the speed she wanted them inside her pussy. She even had the audacity to glare at him when he removed his fingers from between her thighs altogether. *Poor thing*. Her gaze was back to that wildness again. All raw, and unbidden. Fuck him for wanting more of that look on her, too.

It was enough to test his control.

Every last bit of it.

"Oh, my God," Haven gasped, "*Please* ... please, just taste me. Get your mouth on my pussy, and—"

"You got it, love. See, now wasn't that simple?"

Andino kept a tight hold on Haven's throat, making sure she wasn't able to move while he got his first taste of her pussy. Moving between her opened legs, he glanced up to see her watching him from his position between her thighs.

"Lift up," he ordered as he fisted the gusset of her panties. She did, raising her backside off the desk just enough for him to yank those panties down her legs, and toss them aside. He leaned closer, then, his nose skimming the side of her thigh as he got a whiff of her unique scent, and eyed the slit of her pussy. His groan came out thick, hard, and *wanting*. "Fuck, you look good like this."

Good enough to eat, really.

So, he did just that.

And sweet Christ, she was hot, sweet, and fucking tart on his tongue. His first taste of her was like a shot of heroin right to the vein, and all he'd done was drag his tongue from the slit of her pussy right up to her clit. She was soft against the roughness of his tongue, and her flavor flooded his mouth like nothing else ever had.

But it wasn't just her *taste*.

No, it was her, too. The broken moans. The shudders. Her hand coming to tangle in his hair, and pull him back to her pussy for more. How she wrapped her thighs around his head, and he could feel her heartbeat in her throat racing against his fingertips. Everything about her was fucking addictive.

Andino went back in for more—a fast beat of his tongue against her most sensitive spot that was unrelenting, and sure to give them both what they wanted. His fingers slipped into her tight cunt at the same time he sucked hard on her clit. The wet sucking of her pussy taking in his fingers, while he licked up every last drop of her arousal that he could, filled his ears.

And so did her words.

"Jesus Christ, *yes* … don't fucking stop, please."

He couldn't talk like this. Didn't really want to, either. Now, he just wanted to know what she sounded like when she came. He added a third finger to her pussy, and sucked on her clit one last time just to push her over the edge.

Haven didn't disappoint, either.

Loud, breathless, and shaking, she sounded like an angel coming undone for him. Her skin heated, her pussy got even wetter, and Andino was damn sure he could listen to the sound of her shouting his name while the taste of her cunt still lingered in his mouth for the rest of his days. He'd die a happy fucking man that way, surely.

"Fucking hell," Andino grunted, feeling his dick trying to punch a hole through his slacks with every pulse in the shaft. What he needed now was to be buried nine-inches deep inside her pussy, and getting Haven to make those sounds again. She hadn't even finished shaking by the time he'd shuffled his pants down around his hips, and fished his length out of the confines of his boxer-briefs. She watched him with lust-filled eyes as he rolled a condom down his length. "Next time, I want you playing with yourself while I jerk off."

Haven laughed breathlessly. "*Next* time, huh?"

"It can't be just *one* time."

"Good point."

Andino winked. "Now bend the fuck over."

He reached for her, and had her spun around on the desk in a flash. Haven's feet hit the floor at the same time Andino bent her flush over the desk again. One of his hands pressed firmly at the back of her neck, keeping her pinned down, while his other held onto his cock so that he could drag the tip down her ass, and through the lips of her wet slit.

He didn't give her a warning—just thrust in.

All the way in.

"*Fuck.*"

Haven let out a gasping breath. "*Shit.*"

Andino wasn't a small man by any means—and his cock was fucking proportionate to that. And yet, this woman took every thick inch of him in, and then she *pushed against him.* Like she was trying to fucking get more.

Good God.

"Twenty-five, and twenty-six," he said, punctuating each word by pulling out his cock, and thrusting back in again. Hard enough to send Haven up on her toes. "How many more am I going to find when I pull that shirt off you?"

Haven laughed in that high, spun way again. "The dimples on my back?"

"Yeah, baby. Blue stars."

"My first tattoos—sixteen years old, and my parents *cried*."

Andino chuckled. "Poor them."

"Shut up and fuck me."

He did—rough, and raw, and *hard*. Every thrust sent Haven slamming into the desk over and over. He was sure she was going to have marks on her thighs and stomach, but she didn't seem to care. If anything, she only urged him on, and held tight to the edge of the desk when his pace came even faster, and more brutal.

There was nothing like sex.

The sounds.

The smell.

The *feel*.

It was all unique, and addictive. Sex with this woman, though, was something else entirely. From the way she said his name, to her soft pleads when he knew she was close to coming for a second time, it was all glorious.

She reached back with one hand, and held onto his wrist when he fisted a hand into the hair at the back of her head, and pulled firmly. He was caught between the feeling of being buried inside her while watching the sweat slick the ink on her skin.

She came fast when he slapped her ass hard enough to leave a red imprint of his palm behind. And then she came *harder* when he stuffed two fingers up her ass, and called her a slut. Shit, she got *off* on it.

Andino loved that.

It was only when she could barely speak, he knew she was aching, and she begged for him to come that he finally let go of that control he'd been holding onto. He pulled her off the desk, put her to her knees, and yanked off the condom before Haven had his dick all the way down her throat. She sucked him dry—until his balls hurt, and his spine turned numb from the sparks flying behind his eyes.

She was teeth, tongue, and lips on his dick.

Using all of it.

And he heard *nothing* but blood in his ears when he finally came. She took every drop from him, too. Took it all in, and swallowed it down.

Andino was *just* catching his goddamn breath when the noise started outside the office. Swearing, and shouting. Something heavy being thrown around, and groans of pain following right behind. Haven's eyes widened as she looked up at him from her knees.

He wanted to comfort her—tell her it was okay.

Problem was, he knew those voices.

Enforcers.

Marcello enforcers.

This was business, and he couldn't say a thing. Maybe he could make it quieter, though. That was just about the best he could do.

"Is someone getting beat up? Go help them!"

"No, and also no," Andino said quickly, tucking himself back into his pants. Haven was still on her knees when he stepped away from her, and headed for the door. He opened it just a crack to see some of his guys beating the hell out of a dealer who had been sliding in on Andino's business at the club—it was an on-going issue. "Hey!"

The enforcers stopped.

Andino cocked a brow. "Take that shit outside, *cafones*. Business like this doesn't happen in the club. You know the fucking rules."

Neither of the two men questioned Andino. The bloodied man on the ground looked like he probably couldn't even see out of his swollen eyes.

"You got it, boss."

Andino closed the door.

Haven was already getting dressed when he turned around. "I should go."

"Don't let that bother you," he said.

She shook her head. "It didn't."

Except it had.

He could see it.

Fuck.

• • •

"Fucking *finally*," his boss—and uncle—grumbled as Andino strolled through the office doors of Dante's home, "he decides to roll his ass out of bed, and come see little old me when I call on him. Good morning, Andino. Take a seat."

Andino passed his father in the corner a nod, but gave Dante the majority of his attention. Clearly, he'd pissed his uncle off in one way or another, and that wasn't good for business when it came right down to it.

"Sorry," Andino said, "long night."

It wasn't a lie. He hadn't stopped moving in almost two weeks. Business picked up, and between shit he was trying to handle—like a gun run, and keeping the details well hidden from his uncle lest Dante find out it was a man he *despised* running them for their family—and the fact he had a whole host of new responsibilities for Cosa Nostra, it just never ended.

Hell, he hadn't even seen Haven since that night at his club a while back. He didn't have time, and he couldn't seem to make it. It was the end of fucking August now, and the woman probably thought he didn't give a shit about her.

Giovanni perked his head up at that statement. "Work?"

"It's always for work; don't worry about it."

His father cocked a brow, but said nothing.

Dante, on the other hand, frowned. "It's not like you to ignore my calls."

"I didn't ignore it. I didn't *hear* it."

Christ.

He'd only gotten three hours of sleep.

"Just … cut me some slack this morning," he mumbled, running a hand down his unshaven jaw. "Won't happen again."

Dante nodded. "Good—to business, though. I have questions, and you have answers. So, I'm going to need you to give them to me, Andi."

Andino blinked. "What?"

"John."

"What about John?"

Because as far as Andino knew, his cousin was doing fine. Keeping his head down after being released from prison like he was told to do, managing his capo duties just fine, and managing his meds and life without trouble.

"There's no problem with John," Andino said. "He's doing fine."

Dante cleared his throat, and passed Andino's father a look. "On the surface, it certainly seems so. That's what everyone keeps telling me, anyway."

"So, then leave him be."

"At the moment, I can't do that."

Andino groaned, and tipped his head back to stare at the ceiling. "I am too tired for this shit today, okay?"

"I beg your pardon?"

Fuck.

There was *that* tone.

The one his uncle was known for—it was cold, and harsh, and biting. It promised violence without actually having to threaten at all.

"Andino," Giovanni warned quietly. "Try again."

Andino sighed, straightened in the chair, and gave Dante his attention again. "My apologies."

"Thank you."

"I just think—"

Dante pointed a finger at Andino, and narrowed his eyes. "I don't care what you *think* right now, Andi. I care that you listen, and do what you're told until you sit your ass down in my seat. And considering your newfound position as the boss who will take over after me, I expect a hell of a lot more out of you, now. You're a good made man—don't get fucking lazy with me. Got it?"

Jesus.

"Yeah, I got it. What's the problem with John?"

"He's seeing someone. Or he might be. We're not entirely sure at the moment."

Oh, *that.*

Dante nodded. "By the look on your face, I can safely assume you already knew this, and it's not news to you."

"If you mean Siena Calabrese, then yeah, I knew *something* about it. Not a lot, mind you, but just enough to mind my fucking business. Kind of like everybody else should do."

Dante's gaze narrowed. "Watch your step, now."

Andino had another thought.

"Wait," Andino hedged, "how do you know about Siena and John?"

Because he'd only run into Siena once at her brother's restaurant the other day, and she asked about John. His cousin hadn't even told him he was involved with someone yet, let alone Siena. Andino didn't even know if someone could call it a relationship.

Andino doubted his cousin *offered* that information freely to his uncles, or even his father. John just wasn't the type; he didn't like people in his business.

"Well, I needed to keep an eye on him, as you can understand, to make sure he's following the rules I set out for him," Dante started to say.

Oh.

Andino got it.

"You're following him? Because that will not end well for you."

Dante leaned back in his chair, and steepled his fingers. "Is that a threat?"

"No, it's a warning. You know how John is. Just let him figure out shit on his own. Don't step in on his personal business. That's all he asks."

"I can't do that in this case—the Calabrese woman isn't acceptable for a man like John, and you know the history between our families. Bad blood, Andi. We can't trust them; we never have, and for *good* reason, too. So yes, information. I need it. Hand it over."

"I don't have any."

Dante sighed heavily, and stared him down. "If you're trying to protect your cousin—"

"Listen, I don't need to lie to protect John, but I don't *know* anything about the Calabrese chick. Not yet, anyway."

"Well, when you do, I need to know."

"It's probably harmless. He's been in lockup for years. Let him get his fucking dick wet."

"Andino," Giovanni murmured from the corner of the room. "Come on, now."

"It's true. All the man thinks about is staying under the radar, getting work done, and taking his fucking meds at the right time. This is *harmless*. She's a woman. Let him have his taste of her, and move the hell on. I would stay out of it."

"Not possible," Dante said simply. "And now we move to the topic of *you*."

"What about me?"

Giovanni cleared his throat, bringing Andino's attention to his father. "Your personal affairs—it's time to considering getting things in order, or at least, start planning for it so the move from Dante's underboss to acting boss won't be challenged by anyone."

Andino heard what his father didn't say.

Personal affairs.

A boss needed a wife.

Cosa Nostra rules.

Andino felt suffocated by it all. "It can wait."

"Not for much longer," Dante countered, "and if you want, we can start the process for you."

"What does that mean, exactly?"

"We could find you an appropriate wife," his father explained, "if that's what you would prefer."

Jesus Christ.

Not likely.

"She has to be appropriate for your standing, and for *la famiglia*," his uncle reminded him. "I can't give you much longer to figure this out on your own, Andi."

Yeah, shit.

Probably not.

With a flick of his wrist, Dante dismissed Andino from the meeting without a word. Andino just wanted to get the hell out of there, and get back to his bed as soon as possible. He didn't say goodbye as he left the office and found Snaps patiently waiting for him at the end of the hallway like he always did.

Giovanni followed Andino out. "Don't stress over the semantics, son. Dante is on edge lately, that's all."

"Mmm—heard through the grapevine that Catherine is fucking around with Cross Donati again. How much truth is there to that?"

Because ... that spelled bad news for Andino, in a way. Andino might have been able to keep his business with Cross quiet when Dante wasn't keeping an eye on the man since he wouldn't be anywhere near Catherine. But if Cross was screwing with Dante's daughter, it wasn't likely that their deal for Cross to run the guns would stay secret.

Didn't he have enough to worry about where his boss was concerned without adding that to it, too? Andino fucking thought so.

"Quite true, from what I hear," Giovanni said. "And you know, from the way Dante's going on about it. Like I said, don't stress over all that shit. You're doing you, and taking care of your business like you're supposed to. That's what matters."

Right.

Like he was supposed to.

Not that he was working with a man who his uncle hated just to make sure a deal went through. That wouldn't matter *at all.*

Right.

Andino bent down to pet Snaps—his one source of calm in his life right now. "Kind of hard not to stress, that's all."

"You could let us look for a wife, if—"

"Just ... don't bother right now," Andino muttered.

"Dante is right, though. She does need to be appropriate for your standing. Italian, Catholic, preferably *in* the life, or from a similar family. A good reputation. A respectable wife for a *boss.*"

Andino scoffed, and under his breath, said, "I suppose a non-Italian white girl who occasionally dances on a pole and is tattooed all over won't fit the bill, huh?"

"What?"

He glanced up at his father.

Shit.

He really thought he said that quieter.

"Nothing," he said. "I need to take Snaps for a walk."

"Yeah, all right, son. You do that."

SIX

"*... to see what she could see, see, see ...*"

Haven smiled down at the black mane of thick curls bobbing along at her side. Valeria's daughter kept a tight hold on her hand as she skipped on the sidewalk, and sang the song her mother had taught her the day before.

She figured her friend needed to keep an eye on this kid—Maria didn't miss a click, no matter what the situation was. She was smart as hell, picked up on just about anything quite fast, and ran with it.

"I don't think you missed even one *see* that time," Haven said.

Maria beamed up at her. "No?"

"Nope—got 'em all."

"Yay!" Maria pumped a small fist in the air in triumph, and did a tiny jump at the same time. Still, she didn't miss a step beside Haven as they continued their walk. "You'll tell Ma for me, won't you?"

"You bet I will."

"Awesome."

Usually, Valeria would walk Maria to school in the mornings. She tried her hardest not to miss a day, but occasionally when she had to work a long shift at the club the night before—*especially* if she had to dance—then Haven didn't mind stepping in to help her friend. Today was one of those mornings.

Maria never complained, either. Haven always suspected that was because Maria *did* have such a good mom—Valeria was hands on, and never stopped being involved in anything and everything her daughter wanted to do. Even if there wasn't a father figure in the picture, Maria was getting on just fine with her mom.

Haven stopped in front of the gate to the school where Maria attended—a public school that didn't require very much documentation, and apparently didn't ask very many questions. Or, that's how Valeria explained it. All the school was worried about was that every child that needed to be educated, got their education. Permanent residency or immigrant status be *damned*.

As it should be, Haven thought.

"Okay," Haven said, bending down to be at eye level with Maria. The sweet five-year-old beamed in that way of hers, and held on tight to Haven's hand. "You have a good day, and be nice to everybody."

Maria nodded firmly. "Even if they're not nice to me."

"And why do we do that?"

"Kill 'em with kindness."

"That's right."

Maria let Haven kiss her on the cheek, and only then did she let go of her hand. Haven stood as Maria darted beyond the safety of the playground gate, and headed for the waiting teachers supervising the incoming children. She didn't turn around to leave until Maria was safely inside the school, and gone from her view.

It was a twenty-minute walk back to the house, but Haven took her time. She didn't exactly have anywhere to be until around noon when she needed to go into the club, and do the paperwork she had been leaving to the wayside for longer than she should have.

Well, about two weeks.

That's how long she'd been distracted.

Ever since—

"No run today?"

That voice.

Haven recognized it even as it traveled over the light early September breeze to carry his words to her. She hadn't heard him talk in weeks—since that night at the club when she left him standing in his office with his fly still undone and the assurance she would get herself home just fine without his help.

Andino.

Haven looked up from her feet—when she was running, she always looked straight ahead so she didn't miss a step, or stumble over something she didn't see coming in plenty of time. But when she walked? She enjoyed looking around, or even staring at the ground.

Clearly, that was a mistake today.

She hadn't seen Andino coming *at all.*

Shit.

It would have been better if she had.

Haven found Andino leaning against the side of his black Lexus that he'd parked *in front of her fucking house.* She was momentarily distracted by how relaxed he looked in nothing but dark slacks, a silk dress shirt rolled up to his elbows, and black leather loafers on his feet that he'd crossed one over the other.

Cool.

Calm.

Collected.

His silk shirt was tight to his chest, and showed off all the hard lines of his muscles. The definition of his body really was something else. Did he know how fucking good he looked when he didn't even *try?*

In his hand, he held a pair of aviator sunglasses, and wore a smirk that could melt the panties off any woman he turned it on. Probably her, too, if she let him.

Like sex on a *stick*.

Sin walking.

And he was waiting for her.

Haven didn't know what to do about that—never mind the way this man left her confused. Something about Andino screamed bad news, but she couldn't quite put her finger on exactly what it was. She did know that the whole club incident hadn't helped.

A man had been beaten.

Beaten.

And Andino barely blinked about it.

In fact, he told the people to take it elsewhere. As though they were being a nuisance to his evening, and not like he was surprised it was actually happening. They called him *boss*, because yeah, Haven had heard that little tidbit, too.

So, what did that tell her?

People worked for him—an illegal bookie who occasionally visited her club, and others who beat people up. That was just on the surface. She wasn't sure she wanted to dig deeper because she didn't think she would like what she found should she try.

Oh, yeah.

He had that dark, handsome, and mysterious thing going on. That was also a huge part of Haven's problem because she didn't know this man at all, and some of the things she did know, she wasn't very fond of.

Haven crossed her arms over her chest as she came closer to the car. In that second, Snaps jumped up to the passenger window, and stuck his big head out. His pink tongue lolled out of his mouth, and he panted happily as he stared at her. She didn't even think about it—just reached out to pet him because he looked so fucking happy to see her, and it was cute.

"Hey, there," she murmured to the dog.

"At least *he* gets a greeting," Andino grumbled.

Haven passed him a look. "How do you know where I live?"

"I looked you up."

"*How?*"

"I have my ways," Andino returned easily. "You have a roommate, huh?"

Haven stiffened. "Pardon?"

"I saw her come out to get the paper, and put the Barbie bicycle away."

Oh.

Haven nodded. "I guess you could call Valeria a roommate. Her and her daughter have lived with me for a while. She also works at my club."

Andino turned his head a bit, and Haven *swore* she could feel his eyes drinking her in although he didn't say a thing. For a long while, the two of them stayed silent like that, and she kept petting a very happy Snaps.

"Why are you here?" she asked, finally breaking the silence.

"I wanted to see you—I actually got a minute to get away."

"What, from work?"

"Work, family ... life," Andino muttered. "It's all the same to me now."

"Andino—"

"Did the club thing scare you off, was that it?"

Haven let out a heavy sigh, and finally looked at the man. Looking at him, she found, was bad for her body in a multitude of ways. He was still staring at her in that intense way of his. As though for the moment, he couldn't and didn't want to see anything but her.

It was enough to make her skin heat up, and her heartbeat race out of control. It was enough to send memories of the way he felt fucking her rushing through her mind, and setting her nerves on *fire*.

Damn.

Get ahold of that, girl.

"It was more than the club," Haven admitted.

"What, then?"

She shrugged. "I just ... don't get involved with people I don't know, *and* despite what you may think because of my job and my appearance, I don't do the casual sex thing. Jesus, Andino, I don't even know your last name."

Andino chuckled. "Is that all?"

Haven's brow furrowed, and her gaze narrowed. "Don't *dismiss* my concerns just because you might think they're silly. I'm allowed to have them."

"I didn't dismiss them. I don't assume anything about you because of your job, or appearance. *I* don't mind casual sex—I actually tend to think that's an easy way to handle something like sex when you just don't have the time to get involved. I *never* said I wanted casual sex with you, though. And it's Marcello. My surname, I mean."

Haven blinked.

That name.

Why did it—

"Like the Marcello Complex?"

A huge, towering building in the middle of upper Manhattan. It was just one of several buildings in the city with the Marcello name on it, if Haven was correct.

Although, something else prickled at the back of Haven's mind—another reason she should recognize that surname, but it just wasn't coming to her. The more she tried to remember what it was, the less she actually knew.

Andino smiled. "Yes, that's my uncle's building, actually."

"Huh."

"I would like to take you to breakfast," Andino murmured, "if you have time, and would like to join me. Snaps would be happy about that, too."

"Don't manipulate me with your *dog*, Andino."

He grinned. "Where was the lie, though?"

Because Snaps *was* happy, and every fucking time she stopped petting his head, he leaned out of the window, and bumped her hand with his nose to make her start up again. Cute dog—even if he did look like he might kill somebody.

"Just breakfast, though," Haven said. "Nothing else."

Andino smirked. "Not today, anyway."

Jesus.

This man was something else.

• • •

"I take it you own this place, too," Haven said, cutting into the waffle dusted with cinnamon and confectioner's sugar. "Right?"

Andino smiled across the table. "What makes you think that?"

Haven nodded in the corner of the private dining area where Snaps slept on *his own bed*. Yeah, he had his own pillow that was big enough for a dog his size, and that's right where he had gone after they entered the business through the back.

"I figured it out when Snaps went to his *bed*," she said, giving him a look.

Andino laughed. "Yeah, he's not really supposed to be in here. They call him a health hazard."

He scoffed.

"He's actually really well behaved."

"I know," Andino replied. "So, I bring him in through the back, and he sleeps on his bed in here when I'm doing business, or he'll sleep next to my desk in the office."

Haven popped a bite of the waffle into her mouth, and considered his words until she was free to speak again. "So, I take it you do quite a bit of work here, then?"

"Mostly, yes."

"For the restaurant?"

Andino lifted a brow. "Yes, and no."

"What does that mean?"

His husky laughter filled up the table, and the rich sound was enough to make Haven's stomach clench in the best way possible. He looked damn good no matter what he was doing—laughing, though?

Christ.

Andino looked sinful when he laughed.

Reaching for the cup of coffee in front of him, Andino lifted it for a sip, and then stared at her over the rim of the mug. "The restaurant is a hub of sorts for a lot of my business—look at it like that."

That told her nothing, and left her with more questions. This man had a way of doing that with every single thing he told her, but Haven didn't quite know what to make of it. She just wanted a straight answer, and yet, she also found she didn't care.

Why?

She liked his company.

Talking to him.

It was all easy.

Or ... it seemed to be.

"Your parents must be incredibly proud of you," Haven said, smiling. "You're a successful businessman, you've got your shit together—"

Andino barked out a laugh. "I *do not* have my shit together. Far from it, actually."

"Oh?" Haven arched a brow. "Do tell."

"Just ... duty waits on no one," he said cryptically. "I wasn't expecting a whole legacy worth of duties to come falling on my shoulders, but here I am. It's certainly reminded me that in fact, my life is just as much a mess as anyone else's is—simply in different ways."

"I don't—"

"Understand, yeah I know. I'm glad you don't, though."

Haven frowned. "Why?"

"Because none of that matters when I'm with you."

Oh.

"But my parents," he added after a few seconds, "well, they're a different story."

"Why is that?"

He shrugged. "Kim and Gio—that's my mom and dad—they would have been proud of me, regardless of anything else. I could have flipped burgers on the side of the road, and they would have told me to go ahead and live my best life, as long as I was happy."

Haven laughed softly. "Really?"

"Really, yeah. They ... I'm their only child. My mom had a rough time after I was born, I guess, and she was scared to go through it again, so they didn't have more kids. I think that really affected the way they chose to raise me in a lot of ways."

"And how was that?"

Andino made a noise in the back of his throat—amused and contemplative at the same time. "Freely, you could say. They didn't hover. They didn't make choices for me, or put down very many rules … if *any*. They just let me go, and followed along for the ride. Yet, I never really went wild, or found myself in too much trouble. I had fun, took some risks, and always had a safe place to fall back on. I learned a lot about who I am and who I wanted to be because of the way my parents stepped back and let me figure it out on my own. Most people can't say the same, you know? I was lucky."

Haven could hear it in his voice …

"And you love them for that," she said.

"I do," he admitted. "I love them for that the most. And what about yours, huh?"

Haven widened her eyes. "My, what? Parents?"

"Mmhmm. What are they like—or *were*, when you were younger?"

"Uh, typical, I think."

"You think?"

Haven grinned. "I mean, they didn't want me going crazy, but they let me stay out until one, and Dad let me help at the bar from the time I was fifteen. Couldn't make drinks or serve them, though."

Andino chuckled. "Sounds decent."

"And then I wanted a tattoo once; they said no, and I went and did it anyway. First time they ever grounded me, but what were they going to do?"

"The tattoo was already there, I suppose," he said.

"Exactly. And I think my mom helped with that, too. She's an artist; paints for a living, but it's more a hobby now that they're retired."

Not to mention she doesn't get around as well as she used to.

Haven didn't bother to mention that.

"Anyway, my mom explained despite the fact they didn't like or agree with it, this," she said, gesturing at her colorful ink marking up a good portion of her visible skin, "was a way of expressing myself, and expressions of one's self shouldn't be contained or controlled. The only thing they asked was that I didn't tattoo my face or hands."

"You haven't, either."

"Nope," she agreed.

"Why so many stars?"

Haven cleared her throat, and glanced down at the waffle she'd forgotten about in their chat. It was so easy to talk to Andino that she even forgot to feed herself. How strange was that?

"My first tattoos were a pair of stars—the ones on my lower back, you saw them. My best friend—Mari—committed suicide when she was sixteen … she was just sick, you know. Screaming for help, but nobody heard her, I think. Or we weren't listening close enough. Anyway. She loved stars. She loved a lot of things, but especially stars. We were planning to go and have matching stars tattooed on our wrists."

Haven laughed, but even she could hear how sad it sounded. "You know, like best friend bracelets, but less juvenile. She hung herself two days before the appointment that we'd lied about, and snuck around to get done. It was her funeral that day—I couldn't go, so I went to the parlor instead for the appointment. It was for two stars, so I got two. One for her, and one for me. Now, whenever I get the chance to do something she never will, I add a star for her. Travel, turn eighteen, or drive a car. And it's a good reminder for me, too. Look how lucky I am, I guess. Look at what I have, and all who love me."

"That's—"

Snaps lifted his head, making Haven realize in that second the dog hadn't actually been sleeping at all, but only pretending to be. His dark eyes darted to the doorway, and his stubby tail wagged. It was only his sudden movement that stopped Andino from finishing his sentence.

They didn't have to wait for very long to see what—or rather, *who*— had caught the dog's attention. A hazel-eyed gentleman with salt peppering his dark, slicked back hair strolled into the private dining area with two men trailing close behind him. The other men stayed at the door, while the man leading them came closer. His three-piece suit was tailored perfectly to fit him, and just the way he carried himself screamed *money* to Haven.

Not once had their breakfast been interrupted. Not even a server came back after they'd gotten their food. Andino made it clear not to allow anyone back—unless, he'd said, it was certain people. This man must have been one of those *people*.

Andino's gaze landed on the man, and his shoulders stiffened as his stare darted back to Haven just as quickly. The unknown man, on the other hand, smiled widely.

"They said you were back here, *nipote*."

"Uncle Lucian," Andino greeted, standing from the table to greet the man. He took the quick hug his uncle offered, but Haven didn't miss how Lucian's gaze drifted to her, and lingered for a second or two. Not in an uncomfortable way, but more … she didn't even know how to put it. Andino sat down, but Lucian stayed standing. "I didn't know you were coming over this way."

"Last minute thing," Lucian murmured. "Who is this? I didn't know you had a friend—does your father know? Or … *Dante*, Andi?"

Andino cleared his throat, and glanced back at Haven. She could tell just by the way his mouth settled into a grim line, and the hardness of his jaw that he didn't like where this was going. And all of the sudden, Haven wished she wasn't there at all.

This breakfast had started so well.

Why was it ending like this?

She was missing something.

Haven was sure of it.

"Haven, this my uncle—Lucian Marcello. *Zio*, this is Haven."

"*Haven*," Lucian repeated as though he was trying her name in his mouth.

Haven stared the man head-on. "Haven *Murphy*, actually."

Andino kept that same blank expression. "Yes, Haven. A friend."

"Oh, I figured that much out," Lucian said, looking at Andino, "the better question is what kind of friend? Safely assume that's what your boss is going to ask, Andino, and you better have a good answer."

What?

• • •

"Thank you for letting me take you out to breakfast," Andino murmured.

He pulled the Lexus to a smooth stop in front of Haven's house. On the porch, she could see Valeria reading on her e-reader, and drinking a coffee. Her friend pretended like she *didn't* see a car drive up with Haven inside, but she knew that was just Valeria's way of giving her some sense of privacy.

"Yeah, sure," Haven replied.

"I don't know when I might be back around, but—"

Haven had other things to ask, and talk about, actually. "So, we're just going to ignore the awkward and strange conversation that happened when your uncle showed up? And how he left right after, but barely even spoke to me?"

Andino sighed in the driver's seat, but kept his gaze firmly stuck on the road ahead of him through the windshield. She didn't think she had ever met someone who was as in control of himself and his emotions as Andino Marcello. He could seem cold even when she could plainly tell he was also frustrated.

It was disconcerting.

To say the least …

"There's nothing to talk about," he said, shaking his head and tightening his grip on the steering wheel. "Just business that doesn't concern you."

"Business."

"That's what I said."

"How does taking a woman out to breakfast fall into *business*? Or why is it any of your family's business?"

Andino laughed dryly. "Because, Haven, to a Marcello ... family and business is one in the same. I don't expect you to understand, all things considered."

"No, I guess not."

He glanced over at her. "I'm sorry?"

"I don't know anything about you, really. Who are you, Andino?"

His eyebrow lifted curiously. "You still haven't figured it out, yet?"

She felt like he was telling her something. Maybe she just liked living with her head in the sand. Who fucking knew?

"Maybe a part of me doesn't want to know what you're hiding," she said.

Andino smirked. "That part of you is *smart*."

SEVEN

Four days.

It took his boss *four days* before Dante finally called Andino in after the run-in with Lucian at the restaurant. Andino was impressed that his uncle had that kind of restraint—Dante Marcello wasn't known for his fucking patience.

He got that from his own father.

"Boss," Andino greeted from the dining room entryway.

Dante had swung the captain chair around, so his seat at the head of the table faced the large window overlooking the grounds. On either side of him sat Andino's father, and his uncle. Lucian gave Andino a look. One that clearly said, "You should have told him yourself."

The problem with that?

There was nothing to tell.

Giovanni, on the other hand, let nothing slip on his expression. He was a mask of cool, and calm; nothing was going to break him. Andino could tell that just by looking at his father, and he wasn't about to try his luck, either.

"Would you like to sit or stand for this conversation?" Dante asked.

He never turned his chair around, and didn't even look over his shoulder to glance at Andino. He didn't really need to—Andino could hear in his uncle's tone just how pissed off the Cosa Nostra boss was with him.

First time for everything, huh?

Dante—along with every other man in that dining room—was probably just as surprised at this turn of events as Andino was, really. Andino wasn't the man who caused problems in *la famiglia*. He played by the rules, and stayed the fuck away from anything that might get him knee-deep into shit. He lived honorably, or as much as a made man could. He was just here to make money, do his thing, and make sure he was home every night to take Snaps on his walk.

Nothing more, and nothing less.

He spoke his oath to the life.

To *the family*.

And he meant it.

"I think I'll stand, actually," Andino settled on saying.

"Your choice," his uncle returned dryly.

"I'm surprised you waited four days. Or rather, that you made it this long before calling me in."

Dante chuckled, but the sound was hollow. A look passed between Andino's father and his other uncle—a stare he couldn't quite decipher, but that shit wasn't anything new. These three brothers had long mastered the ability to have silent conversations with one another by simply giving each other a nod, stare, or some other fucking gesture that no one but them could understand. It was annoying.

"I had to do my homework," Dante said, sighing a little. "I'm sure you expected that, Andino."

Andino cocked a brow. "Homework—as in, *Haven?*"

"Who else?"

"You looked into Haven."

It wasn't even a question.

Giovanni cleared his throat, and drew Andino's attention for the moment. "There's always something to be said about a man who feels the need to see someone, but doesn't also feel a need to share those details when he knows they are important."

Lucian made a sound under his breath. "Not in every case, brother."

"You did not have the standing Andino does, either," Dante muttered. "There was not a whole host of problems that would be waiting for you—and the family—because you chose a woman that was outside of the standard for Cosa Nostra."

Lucian quieted.

What was Andino missing here?

Giovanni—who seemed entirely unbothered by the conversation happening beside him—nodded but was still looking at his son. "And there is where you differ, Andi."

"Because I took a woman to breakfast?"

Dante slowly raised from his chair, and turned to face Andino. He had been right; his uncle did look pissed off enough to scare the Devil himself, but Andino wasn't the Devil. And he didn't frighten easily.

"I know what I know about her," Dante said, "but I'm going to give you the chance to tell me what you should have told me from the start, Andino. Go ahead."

Andino arched a brow. "Haven Murphy—twenty-six, owns a strip club in Brooklyn, and jogs every day. That's how I ran into her the first time; the second was at her club when I had business to handle with a bookie who enjoys the place. Quite a successful business, actually. I took her to breakfast. Anything else?"

Dante sucked air through his teeth, and set the coffee mug down that he'd been holding. "You tell me if there's anything else I should know."

Andino didn't even have to think about it. "Nope."

"No?"

"That's what I said. I don't tend to stutter, you know."

"Andi," his father warned.

He ignored Giovanni.

Andino was getting tired of being the fucking doormat someone thought they could walk over just because he played by the fucking rules of this family, for the most part. He was nobody's goddamn doormat.

He hadn't done anything *wrong*.

"How about the fact she *strips*?" Dante asked coolly. "Or that she's not Italian. And oh, we can't forget the most important part—literally everything about what and who she is will never be appropriate as the wife of a boss, present or future. You would not find another man heading a family with a seat at the Commission who would take a look at that woman and what she offers, and have them say she is acceptable as a boss's wife. So, yes, let's not forget that bit. I think it's important."

Amusement flitted through Andino.

Fast, and fleeting.

It walked hand in hand with his irritation over this whole thing. Because all of it was fucking nonsense, and nothing more. His uncle was making a mountain out of a stupid mole hill. Dante *assumed*, and didn't think to ask.

Boss's right, sure.

Andino didn't care, either.

"Because I took her to breakfast," he said.

Dante's jaw stiffened—a sure sign of his anger if there ever was one. "How many times are you going to say that this morning?"

"Until you realize how fucking ridiculous it is."

"I beg your—"

"I took a woman to *breakfast*," Andino said, "Lucian interrupted it by showing up, ran to you with the information—"

"I didn't *run* to him with it," Lucian grumbled.

Andino ignored his uncle and continued on with, "And now you've somehow decided she's more than what she is."

"No one would have to assume anything, Andino," his father pointed out from his chair, "had you just spoke up in the first place about what you were doing."

"Because it's none of your business who I fuck when I feel the damn need!"

Dante cleared his throat, and brought all the attention back to him. The only boss in the room—even if Andino was the boss-in-waiting, and the only man to have the floor to speak when he wanted it. So was their ways and life.

"It is my business—that's where you're wrong," Dante said simply. "It will always be *my* business. I am the boss of this family, and I have chosen for you to take over and sit in my seat once I am gone. And so, everything you do needs to reflect well on me, this organization, and the family. From the point you left my office the day we told you what would be happening, you no longer got to make your own choices, Andino. Not when every single choice you make won't only affect you."

Andino clenched his teeth so hard that his molars ached.

Goddamn.

"And you know this," Dante continued on as though he couldn't see Andino's anger vibrating through his tense body just ten feet away. "You know this is how it works, and why that is. You know that if you want to have a relationship—or a casual thing—with someone that the family or other organizations won't approve of, then you do so quietly and privately."

"I was," Andino snapped.

"By taking her to your restaurant?" his father asked. "Where anyone could walk in, and where you do business every single day?"

Dante tipped his head in Giovanni's direction. "Exactly that, yes."

"It was *breakfast.*"

"You keep saying that like it shouldn't mean something, but we both know it does."

Okay.

Fuck this.

"Why can't she be *nothing?* Why can't she be a bit of fun I'm having while the rest of you fucking upend my whole goddamn life?" Andino clenched his fists, but shoved them into his pockets to try and keep some semblance of composure even while he was raging pissed. "Why can't she be a break from every other thing I have to deal with? No—she can't be any of those things. She has to be something else entirely because you *think* she is."

Dante straightened a little taller on the spot. "And is she nothing, then?"

Andino hesitated.

Not one man missed it.

His father's ridged posture softened, but Giovanni said nothing. Across the table from his brother, Lucian's gaze drifted to the floor.

Dante, though, only nodded. "I see."

"Don't do that," Andino muttered. "Don't make that in to something."

"I didn't. Your lack of a response did."

"It wasn't anything. It was breakfast."

"Except you couldn't answer my question, Andi."

"Because it doesn't matter."

Dante tipped his chin up. "Excuse me?"

"Just what I said—I know what I have to do, and what's expected of me. So, yeah, it doesn't matter what she is, or what I want, I still know where this is going to end up, and what I have to do at the end of the day."

"This family is a legacy," Dante murmured.

"I know."

And *he did*.

He knew how hard his grandfather had worked to build the Marcellos into the empire it was, and how much effort and pain his uncles and father had gone through to keep that stronghold through the decades. It was supposed to be Andino's turn now—his uncle chose him. Dante was passing off that torch, and the legacy was now on his shoulders to keep going, and hold strong. To grow, and to keep it thriving.

Dante sighed, and stared at Andino like he could read the thoughts going through his mind. "The legacy has to live on—you have to make sure it does. It's your duty like it was ours to carry on before you. We sacrificed in our own ways; you will, too."

"It was just breakfast," Andino repeated again.

"Except it can't be when you are who you are, Andino," Dante replied. "Remember that for the next time."

"Sure."

But probably not.

"I won't keep you longer," Dante added, gesturing at the door behind Andino. "I know you've got that gun run coming up to oversee, and of course, keeping an eye on John for us."

"Of course," Andino echoed.

Just not the way they wanted him to. Andino needed to start taking care of himself first—nobody else seemed to be.

• • •

"Pink."

The enforcer currently checking out the backside of a server as she passed him by glanced back at his Capo with a raised brow as if to silently ask, *Did you see that ass?*

Andino shook his head, and chuckled. "Do me a favor?"

"What do you need, boss?"

He nodded at Snaps who was currently sitting at his feet. "Take him for a walk, or something. He's being good, but I don't want him to get restless."

"Sure thing." Pink whistled, and patted his thigh. Snaps darted away from Andino without a look back mostly because the dog liked this particular enforcer. "We'll be back."

75

Andino waved a hand, and went back to his cousin sitting at the table with him. "Plan still the same?"

John nodded, and leaned back in his chair as he surveyed the VIP section of the club. "Still the same, yeah. Make sure the gang leader knows the deal with our territory. Get our product in his hands. Keep the bloodshed at a minimum."

Andino smiled.

He didn't fucking know what everybody was worried about where John was concerned. All the men of their family kept voicing their opinions about watching John, and making sure his mafia business was on the up and up as a Capo, but it was un-fucking-needed. John knew what he was doing, and he was damn good at it, too.

Like tonight.

Andino *had* to be here.

He had to watch his cousin.

He had to *hover.*

It wasn't necessary at all. John had this meeting covered, and handled. It was going to go off without a hitch whether Andino was there to supervise, or not. John didn't need someone babysitting his ass, regardless of what Dante and the rest of them thought.

At the same time … well, Andino didn't want to upset his cousin, either, so he didn't bring any of that up, or his own issues that he had going on. John probably didn't need that shit piled onto all the rest of the crap he was already trying to handle.

No one did.

"You're quiet," John noted.

Andino shrugged. "I can't be quiet?"

"You usually *aren't.*"

"Fair," he murmured.

"Is it this meeting?"

Andino passed his cousin a look. "When I say this meeting and how you choose to handle it is the last thing on my mind, that's exactly what I mean. I'm not worried about it, and you shouldn't be, either."

"You're the only one who isn't worried about me."

He did worry about John.

Just not for this.

There was a difference.

"Dante still riding your ass?" John asked.

"Don't be worrying about—"

"Shut up and answer the question."

Andino let out a dark laugh. "Fuck you, man."

John grinned. "What—hit the nail on the head, did I? I knew there was a reason you were quiet."

Yeah, he did.

John had a way like that … or, at least when it came to Andino. Maybe it was because the two had been looking out for one another since they were kids. Maybe it was the fact they could be brothers if not for the whole different mothers and fathers thing. Maybe it was just their life that made them this way.

Who fucking knew what it was, really?

Who cared?

As long as they were tight, nothing else mattered.

Not for him.

He'd look out for John.

John looked out for him.

"It just … the control is getting to me," Andino admitted. "This whole boss-in-waiting thing, I mean. Every step I take, someone is there to fucking correct it. I can't breathe without someone telling me I did it wrong. I didn't even ask for this—I never said I wanted to be the head of this family. Wasn't it supposed to be *you*?"

John smirked a bit. "Man, they can't trust me to have a meeting with a gang leader, and you think they ought to let me have control of a whole organization? Fuck that noise."

Andino grunted under his breath. "Point remains the same. I was happy doing what I was doing. I was a fucking good *Capo*. And now, they've shoved something else on me that I didn't even want, but they still expect me to take it with a smile and a thank you."

John cleared his throat. "Damn."

"Yeah."

"I guess now you kind of know how I feel with them all hovering over me like I do."

Andino sighed heavily. "Sorry."

John shook his head. "No, it's all right. I mean … you do sound a little bitchy, though. *I* expected this because you're the right choice."

Yeah, his cousin told him that once.

Andino still wasn't sure he believed it.

"Point is—suck it up," John murmured, standing from the table as the gang leader they'd been waiting for was led into the club. "So what, Andi?"

His cousin glanced down at him, waiting.

"Pardon?"

"*So what*," John repeated, smirking in that way of his again, "if they make you the fucking boss—take it, and don't let them control how you sit your ass down in that seat, or what you choose to do with it. They want a boss, then *be* a boss, Andino. You can do that—you're just too stuck in your fucking feelings to figure it out right now."

Was he?

Was *that* what it was?

Andino stood from his chair as the gang leader approached. "I would kind of need to be the boss to handle myself and the family without their input, John."

John laughed. "Do that, then."

Do that.

How easy that fucking sounded.

Was it, though?

That was the question.

Andino didn't particularly have an answer. At that moment, he didn't have the time to think it over, either. Not with the gang leader now standing three feet away, and looking like he would rather be anywhere else.

It was time for business.

Andino loved business.

"Maverick, right?" John asked.

The tall, dark-skinned man nodded. "It is."

"I have a proposition for you."

"And you'll want to take it," Andino added. Then, he gave his cousin a pat on the back. "I'll go grab you a drink, John."

John passed him a look, but Andino didn't return it, or pretend he had even seen it, for that matter. His cousin had this meeting handled— Andino was not going to sit there and babysit. Absolutely *not*.

Andino took his sweet time on the bottom level of the club; he made sure it was more than long enough for his cousin to handle the meeting with the gang leader without him hanging over his shoulder the entire time. He grabbed a vodka, and tossed it back, before getting a glass of water for John.

That would only *look* like vodka.

No need to go messing with John's meds.

By the time Andino got back upstairs into the VIP section, it looked like the meeting was just about done, and as he thought, *without* issue. Andino gave John his drink with a nod as if to silently tell him it was only water—he knew the deal. John took it with a nod of his own.

The gang leader took the second glass Andino had brought up that *did* have alcohol. "Thank you."

Andino waved it off, and took a seat at the table with the other two men. Maverick and John clinked their glass together—a peace offering, if Andino ever saw one.

"Pleasure doing business with you, Johnathan," Maverick said.

John took a drink, and smirked. "And you."

Once the drinks were finished, it seemed like so was the meeting. Clean, simple, and easy. As business should be.

"So that's settled then," John said to the man.

Maverick stood from his seat. "Seems so. You'll supply, and I'll buy from only you."

"Keep that agreement, and you won't need to see us again."

"We wouldn't be as nice the second time," Andino added.

It was a good reminder.

The gang leader gave a nod in response and then held up two fingers. His men waiting at other tables stood, and waited their leader out as the three men said goodbye.

John and Andino's two enforcers who had been waiting in the shadows throughout the entire meeting only came closer the second the gang leader and his men were gone. The empty glasses on the table were removed, and the enforcers made their presences scarce.

"Thanks," John said.

Andino grinned. "For what, man? You handled that on your own. I don't know what the hell Dante is worried about with you. I wasn't even needed here tonight."

A quiet laugh echoed from his cousin. "Tell him that."

"I will."

And he would.

"I meant, thanks for the water," John said.

Andino shrugged, and shoved his hands in his pockets. Didn't his cousin know? "I've always got your back, John. Even when you don't know it."

"Not really your job, though."

"Still going to do it."

Till the day one of 'em fucking *died*.

"What about when you don't have the time anymore, huh?"

Andino's gaze turned into slits at that statement. "Like fucking when?"

"How about when you're the boss, and have a whole organization to manage? You don't need to be worrying about me when that happens, Andi."

"Yeah, sure, but—"

"No buts. You work on you—make sure you are where you need to be in this organization, Andino. I'll handle me."

Andino scoffed, but clapped John hard on the shoulder as the two stood from the table. "Man, even when I am looking out for me, I am still going to be looking out for you. I don't know how to do anything different. Not after everything. Speaking of looking out for you ..."

John glanced at his cousin. "Pardon?"

"I ran in to somebody—looks like she listened to me."

"What are you talking about?"

It was like this—Andino might have gotten refused something he wanted, and his life might have been on fucking display for the men of their family to pick apart, but he wasn't going to let them pull all that same kind of shit on John.

John wasn't Andino.

At least one of them would get what they wanted.

Tonight, anyway.

Andino pointed over Johnathan's shoulder, and grinned slyly when his cousin spun around fast to see Siena Calabrese being escorted across the floor by an enforcer. John stiffened, and Andino chuckled.

"I figured that was fucked—finished," John said faintly.

Andino arched a brow. "What—her? I ran in to her when I had to handle some business with the Calabrese brothers. I hate them fuckers."

And he did.

So damn much.

But business was business, and he had to handle whatever business he had with other families and organizations even when it was the last thing he wanted to do. It had been just shit luck that Andino ran into Siena at one of her brothers' restaurants, and that she dared to utter John's name in his presence.

She worked at her brother's place—ran numbers, apparently. Andino respected that, really. He got why she might have caught John's eye being she was smart, pretty, and everything he probably wasn't supposed to have.

Yeah, Andino *got* that.

Except his *do-not-touch* thing was a woman covered in tattoos, and on the other side of Brooklyn. Funny how that worked.

His first reaction when the girl asked about John had been to protect his cousin—every man in their family thought this female was some kind of bad news because of her last name, after all.

Andino wasn't every man, though.

And apparently, this woman had caught his cousin's attention for whatever reason. Andino didn't see the issue in helping it along if there was no harm done on either side. Who fucking cared what the rest thought?

"Yeah, but no. I meant, I kind of ducked out on her," John said quietly. "What did you do?"

Andino clapped his cousin's shoulder. "She asked about you when I ran in to her. Kind of figured you must have made ... an impression."

John cleared his throat. "Not really supposed to be dating."

"Who said anything about *dating*? Have some fun, John. That's all."

His cousin deserved it after everything. Lockup wasn't easy on a man in that way. Pussy was not accessible. Fun was nonexistent.

John grinned when Siena came closer.

Andino figured he'd done his job.

For one of them, at least.

• • •

What the fuck are you doing here?

Andino ignored his inner thoughts as he parked his Lexus, and tipped his head to the side to see the flashing neon sign above the door of Safe Haven.

Girl is going to send you out on your ass, Andi.

Man, his head was a special breed of hell tonight.

He had no business being here—it wasn't even about Haven, and yet it was at the same time. He'd dropped off her radar for two weeks, and not by his fucking choice. It just was what it was, in a way.

Andino figured if he gave it enough time, then he wouldn't keep thinking about the next time he might be able to squeeze in a visit with her. He wouldn't be wondering how many fucking more stars there were to find on her body.

He wouldn't want to fuck her again.

Talk to her again.

See her again.

Something.

And all because of what?

Because she was a woman outside of everything else—something untouched by his life, and unknowing of the crown he'd been handed, but didn't quite know what to do with. She *was* fun; hell, he hadn't lied about that.

She was someone he was told he couldn't have. Andino had been an only child. He didn't do well with being told no, so fuck it, he might as well blame it on his parents.

Except he couldn't.

Andino *liked* that Haven was an outsider, didn't know a thing about him. Thing was—the longer he kept involving himself with her, and coming back for one more round, the more of his life he was going to bring with it.

And thus, his problems, too.

She didn't ask for that.

She didn't even know it.

He knew that.

He still got out of the car, and headed for the club.

EIGHT

Safe Haven was packed—it was probably over the fire code for maximum occupancy allowed inside the venue, actually. Filled to capacity, and it was only a little past midnight. The club still had several hours to go before closing time. Normally, Haven wouldn't mind this at all. A lot of people was good for business, and she did like money. She liked when the work kept her busy, and moving from one thing to another.

Tonight was not quite the same.

Running short on staff with two call-ins, Haven was just now realizing she needed another person—or even two—on call just in case. A bartender that knew how to work a bar, and a girl on the floor.

She made a mental note as she poured a line of whiskey shots for the frat boys still trying to get her attention with their polo shirts, and dimpled smiles. For another woman, these frat boys might have been a welcome reprieve to a busy night. Some harmless fun and flirting, but not for Haven.

Not my type, sorry.

At least, they weren't being pushy or overbearing. Nothing she couldn't handle, anyway. Just a little drunk, and having some loud fun while she poured their drinks. That wasn't anything new for Haven.

"There you are, boys," Haven said, flipping the whiskey bottle around in her hand before sliding it under the bar. "Enjoy your drinks."

"Have a shot with us!"

Haven eyed the blond frat boy at the end. "Don't drink on the job, sorry."

"Awe, come on, don't be like—"

"Yo, Haven!" came a shout from down the bar. "I need another one of these."

Max—a regular—was already pointing at his empty drink, and looking right at her. It didn't matter that he wasn't even in her section of the bar, and the other girl serving drinks was closer to him, he seemed to prefer to have Haven serve him.

"Sorry," she told the frat boy, "another night, maybe."

But unlikely.

She left the group of frat boys to their whiskey shots, and slid down the bar, grabbing bottles to make Max's specialty drink as she went. She chatted with the regular—despite his interest in her, he was harmless for the most part—as she mixed his drink. She barely finished with Max before she was pulled to someone else, and then again for three servers who came up to the bar with their own drink orders for the floor.

Yep, definitely need an extra person or two.

Haven wasn't complaining. This was a sign that her business was doing well … more than great, even, but that didn't mean she wouldn't like a breather. She *would*. Five minutes off her feet to recharge would do her wonders, but she couldn't even afford to take that little bit of time.

"Yo, Haven!"

Max, again.

Haven just turned away from the patron she was serving to tell Max to chill out for a minute while she finished at the other side of the bar, but a familiar voice calling to her from down the way silenced her instantly. And also made her blood heat up, not to mention the way her pussy clenched at the same goddamn time.

"I got it—no worries, *bella*."

That voice.

That Italian.

That *man*.

She found him already behind her bar, reaching for bottles like he knew exactly what he was doing, and not the least bit uncomfortable by all the people, never mind the fact he was wearing a three-thousand dollar suit and serving drinks in a strip club. Just standing there like he was, doing what he was doing, seemed like a giant contradiction. Then again, everything about him kind of felt like that at one point or another.

His grin deepened.

His green gaze darkened.

She smiled at the sight of him. "Andino—you mix drinks?"

He shrugged. "My father taught me. He owned a bunch of clubs, although he sold most of them about a decade ago when he stopped being so involved in the business, and didn't want his name attached to any that might fail or whatever. Anyway, that's what I used to do with him on the weekends when he had to work in the club."

"Ah."

"You looked like you could use a hand," he added.

Haven hesitated on pouring the shot of vodka into the shaker. Just how long had he been in the club, and watching her from afar? She didn't have time to think on it for very long—the chick waiting for her drink was huffing and side-eyeing Haven like she thought the liquor was never going to come.

"Thanks, Andino," she said.

He gave her a nod. "Don't mention it, my girl."

My girl.

Haven didn't miss that. She was just too fucking busy to respond. It was another two customers, and the lineup of frat boys back for another round of shots, plus a server with ten drink orders before Haven passed Andino by again, and got a chance to speak to him again.

He'd taken off his suit jacket, and tossed it somewhere else. His blood-red vest and tie was a bright contrast against the black silk shirt he had rolled up to the elbows. She was caught for a minute staring at those arms of his—muscular, strong, and defined. Every large vein bulged with his muscles each time he moved.

He was something else.

Too good looking.

A little too arrogant.

Every woman's wet dream when he tossed on a suit, that smirk, and very little effort elsewhere.

Mix all of that together, and it made for one hell of a dangerous combination in a man. And that was before Haven even got in to his tall, dark, and mysterious appeal. That was a whole different monster when it came to Andino Marcello.

He knew it, too.

Probably.

"Something on your mind?" Andino asked.

Haven's gaze darted up from where she'd been staring at his arms to find Andino was smirking at her. *Asshole.* Except ... she kind of liked it. Maybe something was wrong with *her.* Because what kind of normal woman lusted after a man she didn't know, but who still managed to show time and time again that he was probably bad news, and a bit of a fucking flight risk considering how often he took off?

It had to be her—she was the broken one.

Yeah, that sounded right.

Maybe.

"Well?" he asked.

Haven reached for the bottle of cotton candy flavored liquor behind Andino to make the sweet drink that would have someone's teeth aching, and asked, "Do you do this often to other women you're fucking?"

He missed his pour into the shaker of whatever drink he was mixing, but recovered quickly enough. Not that she missed the look he shot her— she didn't. He didn't even offer an apology to the man waiting for his drink, but at that point, Haven didn't care.

She just wanted an answer to her question.

Not a rebuttal.

Not a denial.

Not a deflection.

No, a *real* and honest answer.

Was she asking for too much?

"I beg your pardon?"

Haven went back to her spot, but talked all the while. "You know, *this*, Andino. Drop of the radar for two weeks, and come back into their life like you weren't gone at all. Barely give them any information about you or your life, but make yourself right at home in their business and life. Do you do that with whoever else you're dating? Besides me, I mean. Or am I just a special case?"

"The truck is in!"

Jackson's shout from the back hallway reached Haven's spot at the bar. She found her floor manager waving to her above the heads of the moving people, and raised her own as a signal that she had heard him.

With that, the conversation with Andino was finished. At least, for now. She had other things to do—other business to handle. Andino would have to wait. It wasn't like she was purposely trying to get out of having this conversation with him. It was quite the opposite, actually. She felt like this conversation between the two of them was a long goddamn time coming, all things considered.

Shooting Andino an apologetic look over her shoulder, Haven said, "Guess that conversation will have to wait, huh?"

Andino's cocky smirk was gone. "Haven, wait—"

"Have to go help Jackson unload a truck. Thanks for helping with the bar, though. I appreciate it, Andino. And if you do want to finish this conversation I started, then you should stay until I close up."

There.

She gave him a chance.

He could be a coward and run, or he could stay put and wait for her to finish with work for the night. She still had a few hours left to go before the bar would close, but that didn't matter. A huge part of her *wanted* Andino to stay—to let her give him that opportunity to correct her misconceptions and the conclusions she had come to about him because he didn't offer her anything else.

She wanted him to stay.

"Stay," she told him again.

Andino only nodded.

Haven left the bar.

• • •

"Yep, no worries, I have the rest handled," Haven said, waving Jackson out the door. "One last sweep of the floor, and locking up. That's it."

"If you're—"

"I'm sure."

Usually, Haven wouldn't be so quick to refuse help when one of her employees offered to stay late, but she really just needed five minutes alone to breathe after a night like tonight. Once Jackson was fully out the door, Haven locked it behind him, and then closed the large, steel door behind it before pulling the deadbolts on that, too. She'd go out the back way later.

Passing by the tables, Haven snatched up a crumbled piece of paper on one of the tables, and shoved it into her back pocket. One last sweep of the floors to make sure the place was all picked up, and she was good to go.

On one of the raised platforms—the one with the middle pole— Haven saw a hair tie on the floor. Likely from one of the dancers. It wasn't unusual for them to lose something small when they were dancing. Jewelry was most common, but they almost always found it and picked it up before getting off the stage.

Hoisting herself up onto the stage to grab the hair tie, Haven felt his eyes on her the moment she stood up straight again. Of course, she hadn't forgotten that he was there—watching her all night from afar.

How could she forget?

She *felt* him when he watched her. His presence was a tangible fucking thing to her—real and vibrant and *terrifying*. Yet, not in a bad way. It didn't matter how busy she had gotten with work because she still knew Andino was there somewhere watching her in the background.

Never failed.

"Are you going to do a little dance for me up there?"

Haven leaned a hip against the gleaming, silver pole as she turned to find Andino sitting on the bar. He nursed a lowball glass of something— she couldn't tell what kind of liquor it was from thirty feet away.

But fuck him.

Because *damn* he looked good sitting there like that—tie undone, his hair slicked back like he'd been running his fingers through it, and those sleeves rolled up to show off his strong arms. Despite the busy night, and the fact he'd jumped in to help her and the other employees, he didn't look any fucking worse for wear.

Cool.

Calm.

Collected.

That was Andino.

"Do you *want* me to dance for you?" she asked.

Andino tipped his head to the side, and grinned sinfully. "Well, there isn't any music."

Haven wet her bottom lip, and slid her palm along the cold metal of the pole before she did a quick spin on the stage. She'd put on ballet flats since she was going to be on her damn feet all night, but that just made it easier for her to lift off the ground, do a flip on the pole mid-spin, hook her leg around the metal, and then hang suspended upside down with only her knee and calf keeping her steady.

She peered at Andino, aware of just how close her head was to the floor, and knowing that if she even let go of the hold she had on the pole by a fraction, she would crash. And crash *hard*.

"I'm sorry," she said, smiling as she ran her fingers through her loose hanging hair, "you thought I needed music to dance?"

Andino's husky chuckles as he pushed off the bar and landed soundlessly to his feet made her fucking stomach clench. With every step he took closer to the stage, a blazing heat started to travel over her entire body. Deep in her bones, and raging through her sinew. Thickening her blood, and making her nerves snap.

There was something about this man.

Something ...

"Haven," Andino murmured.

She blinked.

He was standing at the edge of the stage, now. His palms lying flat to the LED lights lining the stage as he leaned over, and his face came to a stop just a few inches from hers. Upside down, and suspended like she was, the only thing she could see was him.

And it was all she wanted to see right then.

"Yes?" she whispered.

"That conversation—would you like to finish it now?"

Haven laughed. "*Right* now?"

"You could get back on your feet, if you want. I mean ... I'm not going to tell you to stop dancing, or whatever. I do like that."

She grinned. "Of course, you do."

He just shrugged. "Why deny it?"

Haven winked, and then quickly lifted her upper body, grabbed the pole with two hands, and let go with her leg. She landed gracefully to her feet, and then turned around to face Andino once more. He wanted to have this conversation, so she was ready to talk.

"Are you going to come down?" he asked.

She stared down at him. "No, I think I like it up here right now."

"Lady's choice."

"Talk."

"Counteroffer," he posed, pointing a finger at her and twirling it in a circle, "you dance, and I keep talking."

"Oh, is that how this is going to go—you'll make sure I'm distracted enough not to hear what you have to say to me?"

"*Dance*, woman."

Haven pursed her lips, and started to move toward the edge of the stage to get down. "Hmm."

"I hadn't had sex in two months before I fucked you at the club that night."

Haven hesitated. "Really—*two* months?"

"I have dry spells."

He said it so defensively that she had to laugh.

"Is that what you're calling it?"

Andino sighed. "I get *busy*. My life is chaotic."

"I understand that."

"Do you?"

Haven nodded once. "It's like … everything starts coming at once. It all piles up, and for a while, you forget that you're even a real person with needs and wants to take care of, too."

Andino let out a breath. "Exactly like that, yeah."

"So, two months before me."

"Two, yep. And my last relationship? Didn't exist."

Haven cocked a brow. "What does that mean?"

"If you consider the girlfriend I had in high school for a total of three whole weeks—before I decided teenage girl drama wasn't for me—to be a relationship, then that's your opinion. I don't, though."

"That was your last relationship? And I mean, a *real* relationship, Andino."

His broad shoulders lifted. "That was it."

"So, casual sex is—"

"My thing when I feel the need. I don't have time for more."

Haven openly frowned. "I don't want casual sex, Andino."

"I know you don't."

"Then, why—"

"I haven't been out with anyone. I don't have girls on the side. I'm not fucking somebody else when I'm not around for you to see me. I'm sorry that I have to come and go because my life is a mess, and I'm trying to get it figured out. But *here I am*. I'm here—right now, Haven. Here with you because I want to be, and because I like you. You don't want casual sex, then fine, we won't do casual."

"I'm not asking for the whole titles and that bit, either."

Andino laughed. "I get it—you don't want me sticking my dick into somebody else while I'm fucking you. It's fine, girl. I *get it*."

He was crass.

Brash.

Kind of fucking terrible.

She liked it, though.

"What about the rest?" she asked quietly.

"What else is there?"

"*Everything*. You, mostly. There's a lot I don't know about you, and I feel like you're keeping things from me."

Andino cocked his head to the side, and let out another one of those hard breaths. "Can't this be enough for right now—what we're doing together? Let it be enough, okay."

"But—"

"Please, let it be enough."

A part of her wanted to keep pushing. At least, until she got what she wanted, and he gave her something more than *nothing* in this regard. But he had given her more in a way. He'd given the honest conversation she asked for, and answered some of her questions. It was better than absolutely nothing.

The part of her that didn't want to say a thing, and just keep enjoying this man while she had him decided to keep quiet.

And she didn't mind.

"Now," Andino murmured, his tone dipping lower and his lips spreading with that sexy, signature smile of his, "dance for me, Haven."

"You're still on that, huh?"

Andino pushed away from the stage, and grabbed one of the chairs resting against a table. He swung it around, and set it in front of the stage before he dropped his body into the seat. Folding his arms over his broad chest, he stared at her.

And waited.

"Dance," he said.

She only had one question.

"With clothes on, or—"

"Definitely clothes off. Or you can strip while you dance. I'm not fucking picky."

Jesus Christ.

His voice was enough to make her wet.

"You got it," Haven said, turning to move for the pole again.

She was quick to kick off those ballet flats, and then shrug off the tight, dark-wash skinny jeans, too. There was nothing sexy about trying to strip jeans off—it didn't matter how good a girl could move. She was just bending over to throw the pants aside when Andino made a dark noise under his breath.

Sexy.

Thick.

Harsh.

"Christ, you've got a beautiful ass."

Haven grabbed the pole, and tossed him a simpering smile over her shoulder. "I know."

The crop top Haven wore fluttered around her chest as she did a slow spin around the pole using her hands to keep her steady while her feet lifted from the floor. In nothing but a thong—and a small lace bralette under the crop top—her body was mostly on display as she did a dance that was familiar, and fun for her. A few tricks on the pole, her ass high in the air, and her hips rocking to a soundless beat when her feet were back on the floor.

She *did* have to remind herself to strip the remaining clothing items from her body when she had a chance to do so, and while she wasn't doing a trick on the pole just because she was so used to remaining in one of her leather get ups when she danced.

It was only when Haven was naked in nothing but her skin, and on all fours down to the floor with her back curved inward, and her ass arched high that she felt him touch her. She hadn't even realized Andino had moved from his chair—he'd never said a word.

That warm palm of his cupped the curve of her ass, and slid lower to the back of her thigh. She sighed when his hand grabbed tight to her leg, and then his other one grasped tightly to the other side, too. She barely had time to catch herself when he pulled her back.

"No more," she heard him say in a husky grunt that whispered along her exposed skin. "My turn, now."

She felt his breath first—washing across her backside, and then along her slit.

"This *pussy*," Andino groaned, his nose skimming the inside of her thigh. "This fucking pussy of yours drives me crazy, *donna*. Every fucking day—I'm thinking about it. I want to fucking eat it, and fuck it. All the goddamn time."

His thumb had slid down her ass, and she felt him press the digit into her wet slit. Slow at first, pushing a bit to stretch her open as it slid inside her cunt. He used that thumb of his to massage along her inner walls in just the right spot to make her *shake*.

"Oh, my God."

"So fucking *wet*," he muttered. "And hot, too. Christ, is it dancing that gets you wet, or dancing for me, baby?"

"You."

Definitely dancing for him.

Anyone else, and it was a job.

It was something else right then.

"I want a taste, girl," Andino said.

Haven's hands curled into tight balls against the floor. "Do that, then."

He did.

God, he did.

She couldn't have prepared for it if she tried. His mouth was on her pussy before she even got the chance to take in a proper breath. His thumb stroked her inside while his tongue worked against her clit, and he palmed her ass hard enough to leave his fingerprints behind.

He groaned.

And she whined.

There was nothing sexier than the sound of man enjoying the taste of your pussy—nothing hotter than hearing him get off just by having your come in his mouth.

Andino squeezed her ass harder, and pulled her back into his mouth and thumb even more. She wiggled her hips, just to get more friction. That first orgasm came on strong, and fast. She hadn't even felt it building until it was already there, and throwing her off the cliff of bliss.

Damn, was it a good cliff to jump from.

His name fell from her mouth.

Echoed all around.

He didn't relent even a little bit. No, he just slipped that thumb from her pussy, and circled it against the tight ring of her ass as his tongue kept working her already sensitive and throbbing clit. One circle, two, and then three. On the fourth, his thumb slipped into her ass as his lips encased her clit, and he sucked hard enough to send her spiraling again.

Grasping for air.

Gasping for breath.

Gone.

Entirely.

Andino only pulled away from her once she had stopped shouting his name, and shaking. His arms circled her waist, and he pulled her down from that stage fast enough to make the fucking club spin around her. Her hair was in her face, and she couldn't even think.

Yet, she didn't mind.

She wanted *one* thing.

To get on him.

To have him.

Right fucking now.

Andino had Haven turned in his arms easily, and she wrapped her legs around his waist. He fell back into the chair as her hands worked the buttons on his vest apart, and her mouth slammed against his. She could still taste her pussy on his lips—tart and hot and *good*. That only made her wetter; it made her cunt clench all over again with the need to have him inside her, and fucking her like he did.

Haven lifted from the chair—straddling overtop Andino—just long enough to help him get his fly undone, and his cock free. She stroked his length in her hands while he got the condom ready. All thick, hard nine inches of him that had her stomach twisting with want and need.

Fuck.

Cocks were cocks.

They weren't particularly beautiful, or anything of that sort. They served a purpose, and got the job done. And yet, she *loved* Andino's cock. Every single inch—soft velvet against her fingertips, and wet on the tip where his precum was starting to leak. She could feel his heartbeat pulsing in the shaft, and his dick jerked in her hands when she stroked him tighter.

"Fuck," he snarled, "let me—"

His hands replaced hers. That condom was on. Then, he was pulling her into his lap again. One of her hands pulled open his dress shirt, uncaring that she popped three buttons, and they hit the floor somewhere. She just wanted to touch him; have her hands on his chest, and his mouth on hers while he filled her full.

She got exactly that, too.

Skin on skin.

His tongue warring with hers.

And *Christ*, it felt like heaven when he slid inside her. Filled her full, and stretched her open. She was so wet that his cock made the most delicious sound as he grabbed onto her hips, and started fucking her hard.

A fast rhythm.

Hard, and brutal.

Every drag of his body against hers had her clit rubbing against the hard muscles of his body. Added friction that drove her fucking insane. Like the way his fingertips dug into her ass, and stung. Yet, that pain only felt *good*. It melted into her nerves like someone had poured liquid gold down her spine.

"There—you feel that cock, baby?"

"Y-*yeah*."

"You better come for me again, Haven. Fucking give it to me—I want to taste that pussy of yours after I've fucked it raw, my girl. You gonna let me do that?"

Jesus Christ.

She'd *beg* him to do it.

His lips brushed against hers with every word he spoke. And then he bit her bottom lip, too, making her hiss when he yanked her down even harder on his cock again.

Fuck, there it was.

That orgasm on the edge of her senses.

That bliss again.

She came so hard.

Her vision blurred, and her voice went hoarse. She swore she saw God somewhere between the feeling of Andino's cock in her pussy, and his teeth cutting into her lip again.

And he just *chuckled*.

He chuckled as he stood them both up, then put her feet down to the floor before turning them around, slammed her hands down to the chair, bent her over, and fucked her like that, too. Only that time, he pulled her hair, spanked her ass, and called her a slut.

She loved that, too.

Too much, maybe.

It was only when she was sitting on the chair again, and watching Andino jerk himself off to a finish that would paint her throat and chest with his come while she played with her wet pussy with her legs wide for him to see that she thought …

Not too much.

It wasn't nearly enough.

She was never going to get *enough*.

NINE

"That little *shit*," Andino heard his uncle hiss. "After everything, Gio, don't you think he should know better than to be messing around with my daughter? And after that show at the restaurant—how can I keep letting that fucker walk around like he's done *nothing*?"

Andino heard his father chuckle. "Yeah, so glad I wasn't there for that."

"Fuck off."

"Just saying."

Dante sighed heavily. "Cross Donati is a *problem*."

Great.

His uncle was back on that fucking shit again. Andino knew there was a whole bunch of things happening in his family that didn't involve him—he tended to keep his nose in his own business, and for good reason. He found less trouble that way.

If only his cousin hadn't gotten mixed up with Cross again ...

"Lucian thinks you should back off on Catherine and Cross," Giovanni said.

"Lucian thinks a lot of things."

"I think he's ri—"

"Say it," Dante urged, "I dare you."

"Listen, I know you've got issues with Cross," Andino's father said, "but you need to work through it, Dante. Figure something out. Your daughter is going to do whatever the fuck she wants to do—you *and* her mother raised her that way. Hell, she's still dealing drugs for Andino on a regular basis and doesn't even tell you that, either. You think she cares what you think about whether or not she's dating Cross Donati again? Catherine *doesn't*. She's just really fucking sneaky, and she'll simply get sneakier about it the louder you become in your anger. Trust that."

"I still want him handled. I'll send a goddamn message—it's not like the men of the family aren't already in an uproar about him attacking me at the restaurant a couple of weeks back. A little word from the boss could send them—"

"Don't play with that kind of fire."

"*I* am not playing with anything. Cross started this."

"You sound foolish."

"So says—"

Andino decided he had enough of eavesdropping—for one, the conversation was boring, and for another, this was something else that often got men like him in trouble—and headed into the private dining area. His uncle and father didn't notice him at all at first, but the enforcer manning the door gave him a respectful nod as he entered.

His mother, on the other hand, smiled widely at the sight of her son coming to have dinner as he'd been *told* to do. Despite the conversation that had been going on around her at the table, his mother hadn't joined in at all.

So was Kim Marcello's way.

It wasn't that his mother was a wilting flower—she was far from it. Kim just didn't like to involve herself in other people's drama, and figured it was for others to figure out before she ever needed to put her two cents in.

Smart, really.

"*Mio ragazzo.*"

Andino smiled at his mother's greeting, and ignored the fact that his father and uncle were only *now* starting to figure out he was in the room. Apparently, this Cross Donati problem his boss was having with his daughter was quite a fucking distraction.

He didn't even want to *think* about how pissed Dante would be if he found out Andino had Cross running their guns. He doubted it would be a situation that ended in his favor, at the moment. *Damn.*

"Hey, Ma."

He bent down, and kissed his mother on the top of her head. Kim beamed up at him with the kind of smile a mother reserved only for her child. He loved her for, that—loved that she loved him unconditionally.

Kim reached up, and cupped Andino's cheek with a warm, soft palm. "You're so busy lately. I never get to see you."

Not a lie.

It wasn't even a fucking exaggeration.

"I know, Ma," he said. "I'll try to come around more."

"Good, you do that. Breakfast with me this morning is a good start, though."

"Not *too* busy, I hope," Dante grumbled.

Andino passed his boss a look. "What was that?"

"I hope you're not so busy that you've let anything slip, Andino. I know you've got a lot going on with *la famiglia* and business, but—"

"Nothing is slipping," he said firmly.

Dante arched a brow. "*Nothing?*"

"No."

"Don't act offended just because I asked a question," Dante said. "I have a right to ask. You've got a hell of a lot of responsibilities on your shoulders, now. I want to make sure you're keeping up with it all."

Andino started listing things off just because he could, and because he felt like being a fucking shit for once. "Business is good—up by ten percent this month, but I'm sure you'll see that come tribute. John is minding his own, and doing his thing as he's *supposed* to be doing, but you know that, too, considering he's been looking for his sister for weeks now with his father. How in the hell is John going to find himself in some kind of shit when he's not even here to *get* in fucking trouble?

"There's not been one issue between Capos or in their territories between crews; I've made sure to step in and keep peace whenever something came up, so *you* never even had to hear about it. Just like a good underboss should even though I don't have the title just yet. But you don't know that, right?" He smirked, and shrugged, adding, "Everything is fine, *boss*. Just as you would want it to be. Or do you need me to fill you in on every little step I make?"

His mother glanced down at the table, likely hiding a smile. Giovanni, however, didn't even bother to hide his smugness as he gave Dante a look from across the table.

Dante, though, simply stared at Andino. "And what about you, hmm—are *you* following the rules?"

"What rules are—"

"You know exactly what and *who* I am talking about, Andi."

Kim's brow dipped as she glanced at her son, but Andino was a little too busy playing a game of *fuck you* with his uncle at the moment to answer her unspoken question.

No, he wasn't following those *rules*.

Yes, he was being quieter about Haven, though.

"I'm doing what you want me to do," Andino said, offering nothing more. "What more do you want?"

Dante's gaze hardened, and he turned to Gio. "Why is everyone in this family testing my good graces and patience lately? *Why?*"

Andino's father laughed. "Wouldn't our father say that's a good sign it's time to pass the torch to someone else in this life—when you've clearly had enough?"

"Yeah, well …" Dante scowled, and gave Andino another look. "I'm trying."

But was he *really?*

That was the better question.

•••

The enforcer who regularly kept watch over Andino while he worked in the restaurant popped his head in, saying, "Hey, boss, Cross Donati just pulled up to the front of the joint looking fit to fucking kill somebody."

Andino pursed his lips. "Why?"

"How would I know?"

"Because I *asked.*"

And that should be good enough to warrant an answer.

"I don't know why the man is pissed," the enforcer said, "but there was word making the rounds today that the big boss isn't happy about Cross, and all that shit he pulled a couple of weeks back, you know, with the restaurant thing. Anyway, it had some guys in a fit, and they were talking about—"

"Ah, *fuck,*" Andino muttered.

He would bet every dollar in his overseas bank accounts that his uncle had decided to send the message to Cross that he overheard Dante talking about with his father. Even being told it was a bad idea, when Dante got something in his head, he went ahead and followed it through. One could count on it.

It also made another problem for Andino.

One he didn't *need.*

"Something wrong?"

"No, just … get out of my face before Cross gets in here," Andinio said, gesturing for the man to scram. The enforcer did what he was told without Andino needing to tell him again, thankfully. Small miracles. "And you be good, too."

He'd offered that order to the dog resting beside his desk—Snaps peered up at his master with his big, dark eyes as to ask, *Who, me?*

"You heard what I said," Andino muttered.

Snaps huffed, and rested his big head back down on his paws. Andino went back to the papers in front of him. He heard the rumbling, low growl that promised someone was going to get hurt echoing from Snaps long before Cross even came within five feet of Andino's office. He reached down to trail his fingers through the dog's fur to calm him, but went back to his work.

There wasn't much else he could do.

"You couldn't let me know they were planning something, asshole?"

Cross moves fast, I guess.

Andino found Cross standing in the doorway of his office looking— as the enforcer had stated—fit to kill someone. He didn't come further, though, and Andino suspected that was because Snaps was still lying next to Andino's desk but now he had his teeth bared in a silent snarl, and his dark eyes were pinned right on Cross.

"I beg your pardon?" Andino asked.

"Marcello enforcers. Following me. Cornering me in my territory. Ring any damn bells for you?"

"Not really," Andino lied.

He *hadn't* known that up until a few minutes ago, but hey. Cross should have known better than to mess with Dante Marcello, or the man's daughter. Cross came from a neighboring New York mafia family—one similar to the Marcellos, but not as big.

Nonetheless, Cross was spoiled because he'd been the *principe* of his family, and never had very many rules keeping him in line when it came to his own father, another boss. He knew what the rules of this life were when it came to other families, and how to *be-fucking-have*. Andino couldn't help the man if he didn't want to follow the rules.

"But hey, Marcello men are vicious, Cross. You made a scene with Dante, and nobody wants to take that shit lying down. I'm surprised even one man in the family let you walk around this long without some kind of action, to be honest."

"Fuck you all," Cross muttered.

Andino shrugged, but yeah, that right there was about half of the reason Dante took issue with this man. "I'm just saying."

"Listen, you make sure that shit never happens again."

How is this my problem?

"I don't even know what happened in the first place."

"I told you," Cross said. "A group of Marcello enforcers cornered me in my territory coming out of a meet with some of my guys. Mind you, this was after they tailed me for days. Add in the fact Calisto got a personal warning from Dante for me to stay the hell away from Catherine, and I don't think those fools came up with this idea on their own. They weren't the brightest fucking bunch."

Andino let the man's words sink in before he finally replied with, "I mean, I can't really help you, Cross. None of us are supposed to be working with you, or any Donati man, for that matter. I'm not going to go around sending out warnings, and raising somebody's alarm bells. I need my guns run."

"Holy shit, your fucking guns." Cross groaned, and shot Andino a glare that could have killed him on the spot had his eyes been made of fire. "I am going to get those guns down the Gulf regardless, you piece of shit. But I won't be able to if one of those assholes puts me in a grave."

Snaps growled.

Cross stiffened, and shot the dog a look.

"Hush, Snaps," Andino said quietly, passing the pup a look to make sure he was going to stay in his spot for the time being. Sometimes, it was hard to say with Snaps. He was well-trained, but he also didn't like a threat against Andino. Right now, he was absolutely taking Cross to be a threat. "Maybe you should heed the warnings, and stay away from my cousin."

"Maybe you all should mind your business."

"You have a death wish."

"They've said that about me for my whole life," Cross barked, throwing his arms wide. "I am still here. Somebody better make sure what happened yesterday doesn't ever happen again, or none of you will like what I do."

Andino frowned. "I'll see what I can do."

"Good."

Cross turned to leave.

Andino figured he owed the man some kind of warning. "Next time, don't rush my office without knocking first. I was kind enough to stop Snaps today from reacting how he's been trained—I will not be kind again."

The man in the doorway nodded, but he was quick to leave after that. Andino didn't really blame him.

It didn't matter.

He had bigger problems.

"*Pink!*"

The enforcer from earlier popped his head in the office doorway thirty seconds after Cross had vacated, and gave Andino a cocked brow. "Yeah, boss?"

"Find out who the fuck was involved with confronting Cross Donati today, and let me know if even *one* of them was a man of mine."

Pink cleared his throat. "I can do that."

"Hurry it up—I've got business to handle."

The enforcer disappeared, and Andino glared at the wall as he tried to relax in his chair. It didn't work; he ended up folding his arms over his chest, and trying to ignore the building headache starting to throb in the base of his skull. He needed to keep Marcello men away from Cross Donati, at least until those guns got down to the Gulf, and also, keep Cross far away from the boss ...

There was no way in hell Andino was going to let any of his guys go off half-cocked just because someone else was in a bad mood, and ruin the shit he was doing—they were not going to cause him those kinds of issues.

Not now.

Not ever.

Fuck what Dante thought.

• • •

"Nick," Andino said, letting the bat in his hand swing back and forth like a pendulum. The enforcer's gaze didn't want to move away from the bat for even a second—smart man, really. "Let's go over this again. What did you do, and why was it wrong?"

The enforcer swallowed hard, saying, "I d-don't know."

Andino sighed. "Wrong answer. Try again."

"Cross. Cross Donati."

"Getting warmer."

Nick glanced away from the bat for a split second. "I just thought— he went after the *boss*, Andino. We were supposed to let that go unanswered?"

Andino tipped his head to the side, and pretended like he was actually considering the man's words. "*No*, but you do come to me before you do something fucking stupid."

The man blinked.

Andino smiled.

"See, you're setting a dangerous precedent for me," Andino murmured, crouching down so he was eye-level with the man tied to the chair in a warehouse where no one was going to hear the guy screaming once this really got started. "People already think I'm the fucking *easy* one, Nick. I won't push back—I follow the *rules*. See the problem? You didn't even *think* to come to me first, and ask if you could go after Cross."

"But ... but—"

"Do you know what that tells other men—or *made* men?" Andino asked.

"N-no."

"It tells them that they don't have to come to me for anything. Not a request, not for permission, and certainly not for business. That's a fucking problem. You made a problem for me. *You're* a problem. Get it now, you stupid fuck?"

Nick's eyes went wide, but Andino's point was made. Sure, a large part of this was making sure nobody messed in Andino's business. Then, the guns he needed run would go off without a hitch, and with Dante still unaware that his Capo had used a man he hated to do it.

It was more than that, too.

Andino wasn't going to be anybody's pushover.

Not their punching bag.

Or their fucking doormat.

All it took in this life was one man stepping out of line to make it seem like the man above him was weak. Given his fucking status, and what was coming for Andino in this family, he couldn't afford for him to be *that* kind of man to the rest of the organization.

John had said it.

Don't let them control how you sit your ass down in that seat, or what you choose to do with it. They want a boss, then be a boss, Andino.

Andino had to start taking care of his own shit, and worrying less about the problems of others. It started here.

It started with this.

And any other fucker that thought to step in his way.

"I'm sorry," Nick mumbled, "please—"
Godspeed to the men who plead.
Andino stood, and swung the bat.
Bones crunched.
A man screamed and begged.
Blood splattered.
Andino just kept swinging.
Let this be a fucking lesson.
One of many, he was sure.

• • •

Andino shrugged off the bloody, ruined dress shirt, and shoved it into the trash. All the while, Snaps passed his master by, and headed for his empty food bowl. Sitting by the bowl, the dog stared at Andino with big eyes.

Begging without actually *begging*.

"You can wait five more minutes," he told Snaps.

Snaps' ear flicked.

Andino laughed. "You're fine."

More big eyes.

More silent begging.

Everybody who had ever seen Snaps in action gave the dog a wide berth of space just because they didn't want to be in his line of fire when he attacked. Andino, on the other hand, got to see his dog act like a giant baby because he thought he wasn't going to get fed like he didn't get fed *every single fucking night.*

"Five minutes," he repeated to the dog.

Andino headed for the kitchen sink, and turned the taps on. Once the water was hot enough not to scald but still sting, he grabbed the bar of soap on the side, and got to work on washing away the dried blood on his hands and arms. Killing someone with a bat could be a messy business, but he figured it was worth it.

The lesson would be learned.

The water circling the drain faded from a rusty red to a light pink the longer Andino scrubbed. He was done with washing the proof of his crime away, and onto pulling the raw strips of meat prepacked for Snaps' meals from the fridge when he heard the front door of his house click shut quietly.

Snaps didn't react.

Andino *knew* then.

There was only one person Snaps didn't alert for.

"Hey," Haven said, strolling into Andino's kitchen, and patting Snaps' bobbing head as she passed him by to come to Andino first. She dropped her bag on the island counter, and then pulled Snaps' bowls up from the floor to help Andino. He didn't even have to ask, or explain what he was doing. She just jumped into his life to *be* there and help, for fuck's sake. She wasn't even supposed to be around—he *should* be keeping his fucking distance. And yet, he liked getting five minutes with her when he could manage it. He enjoyed having her show up at his house in the evenings when the day was done, and it was just them.

Two weeks of this, and he *looked forward to it.*

"Hey," Andino said.

Wordlessly, Haven leaned over the counter, and pressed a kiss to Andino's mouth. She gave him a grin, and a wink when she pulled away far too soon for his liking.

"Busy day?" she asked. "Because you're not even fully dressed, and I don't think I've ever seen you look disheveled."

Andino laughed under his breath.

He killed a man today.

"You could say it was busy," he replied.

Haven frowned. "Sorry."

"You?"

"Took the day off, actually."

She reached for her bag, and it was then that the bandage on her wrist caught Andino's eye. He quickly finished up getting Snaps' bowl of raw meat, steamed veggies, and gravy mixed up for the pup. He filled the second bowl with fresh water, set them on the floor, and washed his hands up for a second time as he'd been tearing apart raw meat.

"What's that?" he asked.

Haven looked up from the phone she'd pulled out of the bag. "What?"

"On your wrist."

"Oh." A sly smile curved her lips. "A new tattoo."

Andino chuckled. "You're going to run out of room, Haven."

"*Never.*"

Rounding the island, he reached for her wrist, and tugged her closer to him until her chest was pressed tightly to his. He flipped her wrist over at the same time he dropped a hard kiss to her mouth—fast, and not as fleeting as hers had been. No, he took the time to enjoy her kiss, and the way her tongue teased his in a way that made him wish her mouth was somewhere else on his body.

"Wanna see?" she asked when he pulled away.

"Is it something silly?"

She slapped his bare chest. "None of my tattoos are *silly.*"

"That's fair."

Haven glanced at the clock on the wall, and shrugged. "Yeah, I guess the bandage has been on long enough."

She let him peel back that small, three inch by three inch bandage to find the new ink on her skin. Andino stilled from head to toe at the black and white image staring back at him from her inner wrist. His grip on her arm tightened instinctively the longer he stared at the tattoo, silence in his mind, though his heart ...

Oh, there, it *raced*.

"Do you like it?" she asked.

Andino blinked. "It's a whale."

"Mmhmm."

"A *killer* whale."

Haven laughed softly. "Yeah."

"An orca."

He kept that firm hold on her, and refused to let go even as his gaze drifted between the small smile on her pink lips, and the tattoo on her wrist. There was no possible way she could know—no way she had any idea how he felt about something as silly and simple as killer whales.

No one knew.

No one but his mother and his father.

No one.

"I had a dream—I was on a boat, and I was whale watching," Haven said, shrugging. "That's never even been a thought in my head. I guess whales in dreams can mean different things. Something big in your life, or even something spiritual with your mind and heart."

Andino swallowed hard. "Or that everything is going to be okay."

Haven's brow dipped. "Or that, yeah. How did you know—"

His throat tightened.

She couldn't *know*.

There was no way ...

"When I was a kid," Andino said, "I watched a show about orcas, and according to my parents, I was obsessed after that. Nothing satisfied me unless it was whales. I did that sometimes; went from one thing to another in my interests, and they always just let me do whatever. The whales, though ..."

"Hmm, what?"

"They stayed with me for a long time," he admitted. "It was a couple of years before the child-like obsession waned, but even then ... just come here."

He turned fast, and pulled her along with him as he left the kitchen, and headed down the hallway. His office was downstairs, and although

Haven had spent a couple of nights in his house, she'd never gone in there as far as he knew.

"Andino!"

Her laughter was high, and sweet.

His chest just *ached*.

His mind was chaotic.

She couldn't *know*.

Was that supposed to be some kind of sign for him?

A whale?

Andino pushed the office door open, and flicked on the light. He glanced at Haven just in time to see her gaze land on the large painting behind his desk—a canvas that dominated the wall—of a killer whale in abstract form. He'd found it at a dealer once just shortly after he bought his house.

"Oh, wow," Haven said, grinning.

"An Inuit artist did it," Andino explained, walking further into his office with her trailing behind. He picked up a photo on the corner of his desk, and turned it around for her to see him and his father on a fishing boat, and in the water behind them, a small pod of orcas filled the picture. "And this trip with my dad … yeah."

Haven took the picture from him, and looked it over with a deepening smile. "This is a sweet picture."

"I was ecstatic."

"I bet."

Andino came closer as Haven set the photo back on the edge of his desk. "So, you saw a whale in a dream, did you?"

"It seemed important."

Maybe it was.

More for him, than for her.

Who was he to say?

It was *just* a whale.

And she was just a woman.

"I take it you like the tattoo, then?" Haven asked teasingly, reaching for him again and circling her arms tightly around his neck. "Since it's your favorite animal, and all."

"I didn't say whales were my favorite animal."

"Oh, they aren't?"

He cupped her face in his hands, and pressed a quick kiss to her grinning mouth. "No, they definitely are."

But … she hadn't known that. He was still trying to figure out what this was supposed to mean.

Andino didn't believe in coincidences.

This life had taught him not to.

TEN

"Watch me, Mama!"

"I am, baby. I see you." Valeria shook her head as Maria skipped across the monkey bars without ever missing a beat. "She's going to make me go gray, Haven. Look how far she could *fall*."

Yet, her friend stayed right there on the bench with Haven even when Maria spun around on the other side of the monkey bars, and then jumped to grab on and do it again. Valeria was good like that—despite her fears that her daughter might fall, she let Maria spread her wings and explore.

Like a child *should*.

"She's not going to fall," Haven said. "Don't worry."

"Easier said than done."

The two women fell into a comfortable, easy silence as they watched Maria make friends with another little girl before the two children skipped off to the slides. Haven sipped on a latte they'd grabbed on the way to the playground while Valeria worked on peeling an apple with a pocketknife.

"I was thinking of taking her to see that princess movie tonight," Valeria said. "You want to come?"

"Have plans, actually. Sorry."

Valeria fake pouted. "Your loss."

Haven laughed. "Is this the same princess movie she went and saw last week, too?"

Valeria shrugged. "Maybe it is, and maybe it isn't."

"Except it totally is."

"Someday, you'll have kids, and then you will understand the struggle of watching the same shit over and over again with no end in sight, simply because it makes them happy to do it. Today may not be that day, mind you, but someday, *chica*."

Haven smirked. "Doubt it."

"Oh, you will. We all learn."

She wasn't going to argue with her friend simply because Valeria wasn't entirely wrong. Haven wanted kids—just not right now. She wasn't ready to start thinking about all the things having a child would change in her life, really.

Maria was enough for her.

For now, at least.

Valeria leaned over a little on the bench to get closer to Haven as she whispered conspiratorially, "So, tell me about these plans of *yours*."

Haven had to laugh at how interested her friend sounded. "Girl, you need to find yourself a man, or something. Get out, date ... *whatever*."

"But *why*?"

"Because I swear you've been living vicariously through me since we've been friends, and that's just sad. Getting details from someone else isn't nearly as fun as going out and getting the real thing for yourself, if you know what I mean. She's old enough for you to leave her with me to babysit while you go out and have a fun night. No one is going to think less of you just because you want to have—"

"It's not that," Valeria interjected quickly. "I just ... don't have time, Haven."

"That's a lie. You've got a great boss who works around whatever schedule you need or ask for. She makes sure you get all kinds of time off, and whatever else you need. So ..."

Valeria grinned. "You are a great boss."

"See!"

"I really don't have time, though," her friend said. "And not because I can't make time, but because I would rather not."

Haven frowned, and looked over at her friend as Valeria sliced a piece off the apple in her hand. "I don't follow."

"I guess ... it's been just *me and her* for so long, you know what I mean? I try to be there to tuck her into bed every night, and at least wake her up in the morning to tell her to have a good day at school. And so what, just because I want to get laid, I should take time away from her, go out and find someone who *might* be able to give me a good time? And then what if I do find somebody, Haven, how do I tell her that it's not going to be just me and her anymore? I don't want her to resent me because—"

"She wouldn't," Haven said confidently. "Especially if you were happy, you know."

"She *might*. She's a kid, okay."

"But not a stupid kid, or a vindictive one, Val."

Valeria sighed. "No, I know. I just mean ... maybe it's not her at all, then. Maybe it's me. Yeah, that sounds about right."

"Again, I don't follow."

"Maybe it's me that's not ready for all of that mess, Haven. I've been worrying about taking care of her and making sure that she has all she needs for so long that I come second to the rest. It's okay, though. I like it this way."

Haven felt a pang in her chest, but she stayed quiet. She didn't want to make her friend feel badly—she didn't want to open her mouth, and say something that might hurt Valeria. Like the fact that being alone just because she was comfortable, or scared, was sad. Valeria deserved someone to make her happy the way she had worked so hard to make her daughter happy for so long.

And she did it alone.

"Also, her dad was the first and last man I was involved with," Valeria added under her breath, "and that is enough of a reminder for me as to why I don't want to get mixed up with the wrong kind of man again."

Haven cleared her throat. "You know, you never talk about him."

Valeria nodded. "Nope, I sure don't."

By the tone of her friend's voice, she wasn't going to start now. Haven did wonder if she asked a question, would she get an answer? She wouldn't know if she didn't ask—closed mouths didn't get fed, after all.

"Did he ever try to stop you from leaving Mexico?"

Valeria stiffened beside her. It took a few seconds before her friend finally answered with, "He didn't know until I was already gone, I imagine. It wasn't the country I was running from, Haven. That was kind of the point."

Oh.

Then, her friend glanced over at her, smiling softly. "Enough about this. What are your plans for tonight since you're lucky enough to get out of seeing that godawful movie again?"

Haven grinned. "I promised to go over and see Andino tonight at his place after I finish up the paperwork at the club."

All it took was a mention of Andino, and Valeria's amused expression was quick to flit away. Haven didn't know when that had started—around the time she told her friend Andino's last name, she supposed.

Valeria never outright said anything bad about Andino, or Haven's involvement with him. In fact, she didn't mind prying information out of Haven just for the hell of it, but she could tell something was off with her friend whenever he came up in their conversations. Something that made Valeria uncomfortable.

"You're being careful, right?" Valeria asked.

"With Andino?" Haven laughed. "What's to be *careful* about, Val? I would think if he meant to do me harm, it would have happened already."

"No, I just mean … you do know what people say about the Marcello family, right? Their name is pretty well-known in New York."

Haven's amusement was quick to fade away, then, too. She *did* know what people said about the Marcellos—she didn't have her head stuck in the sand, and she wasn't deaf. She heard the whispers whenever Andino showed up at the club to see her.

There were stories.

People said things.

Rumors.

The Marcello family was not *just* an elite, rich family owning half of New York and living in beautiful homes on tucked away estates just outside of the city limits. No, apparently they were a much bigger, and *darker*, legacy hiding in plain sight.

Organized crime.

Mafia, people said.

She heard all the rumors.

She ignored them, too.

Haven didn't know if they were true—did the mafia even exist anymore in their day and age?—but also, she wasn't sure that she wanted to know the truth, either. All it would take was a simple internet search, she was sure of it, and she would have her answers. Yet, she stayed far away from that.

She refused to indulge people who talked, or even asked her about Andino. She didn't really want to know if those were the kinds of secrets he was hiding from her. And if she didn't ask, then she didn't have to know. She wouldn't have to deal with it.

Simple.

"Andino's not like that," Haven said to her friend.

Valeria openly frowned. "Maybe not with you. Sometimes, that's the problem, Haven. You don't see the bad shit until it's too late, and you're already too deep. Then, how are you supposed to get the fuck out and save your own skin?"

"Is that what happened to you?"

Her friend glanced away. "Something like that, yeah."

"Sorry—I shouldn't have asked that."

"It's all right." Valeria blew out a steady stream of air, and searched for her daughter on the playground once more. Quickly, she found Maria, and relaxed again into the bench, but not by much. "Just … be careful, okay? We can't always see the monsters lurking. They never look like monsters, Haven."

"He's not like that."

Valeria glanced over at her. "But you know he's something. You've said that to me yourself. You've said that you know he's not all that he seems, and some of his business is a little sketchy. What kind of *something* is too much for you, Haven?"

That was a good question.

And not one she was ready to answer.

"Listen," Valeria murmured, "I don't mean to shit on your guy, okay. It's just that I was lucky—my *daughter* was lucky, too. And if something puts our safety in jeopardy—something like him, even if you don't think he's that kind of bad news—then, I'm going to have to make a choice."

"What kind of choice is that?"

"Well, that's the thing. I won't be able to tell you." Valeria shrugged, and smiled kindly. "Luck tends to run out, then."

Did it?

Haven wouldn't know.

• • •

"*Holy fuck, yeah.*"

Haven grinned, but she wasn't sure Andino could see it properly given her lips were wrapped around his *dick*. His fingers tightened in her hair just enough to make her release the hard suction she had on his length, so she could gasp in a sharp breath. His gaze darted down to find hers, and she swore she saw the promise of sin staring back at her.

"Get that mouth of yours back on my cock, Haven."

"So demanding," she whispered.

"You started this."

She had, too.

Damn near from the second she walked into his house.

Frankly, Haven blamed Andino for that. How did he expect to just go around wearing three-piece suits all the time and looking like every woman's walking wet dream? Did he think *nobody* wanted to fuck him when he looked like that?

She had news for him.

"Suck my dick," he uttered again, "and I'll give you something good, baby."

Oh.

She so wanted to know what that would be.

Andino always kept his promises.

The second Haven took Andino back in her mouth again, his hips flexed upward hard. Hard, and soft, and hot on her tongue—his cock pulsed with each beat of his heart through the vein on the underside of his shaft.

He liked it best when she teased him.

Licked his shaft.

Used her teeth.

Took him slow.

He made the sexiest sounds when Haven sucked him hard, and used her hands to work him faster while her mouth kept him hot and wet. It was those sounds that were her undoing—those fucking sounds that made her wet when he reached behind her to stuff two fingers into her pussy while she sucked him off.

"Christ, *just like that*," Andino groaned. "Fuck, you're soaked, girl. You like sucking my dick, huh? *Shit*, yeah."

She knew he was going to come as soon as his dick jerked in her mouth, and his balls became tight in her palm. His body tensed, and those hands in her hair pulled just a little bit harder before a thick moan fell from his lips.

Haven looked up just in time to watch the show.

And *good God*, what a beautiful show it was.

Andino's head fell back, his teeth cut into his bottom lip, and his handsome features contorted in a mix of bliss and satisfaction. Nothing looked better—nothing sounded better than her name on his mouth when he came.

He spilled onto her tongue, and she swallowed back every last drop. He was probably still leaking a bit of come when he yanked her off his cock, and pulled her up for a bruising kiss. It was his kiss that drove her the craziest—she was sure of it.

A dominating, wanting kiss that took away her breath, and made her heart race. His kiss was enough to make her wet all over again, and ready to get on her knees to please him however the fuck he wanted her to.

"Roll over," he grunted in her ear.

Haven was quick to comply with a breathless laugh. Those warm hands of his trailed down her spine, and over her ass before they grabbed onto the backs of her thighs roughly. She liked that bite of pain—it only added to the pleasure that was soon to come.

She waited for it.

Needed it.

Andino's hesitation made Haven perk her head up from the mound of pillows on his bed. "What's wrong?"

"Nothing, just—"

Ah, there it was.

She heard it.

In the background of their fun, someone was knocking on Andino's door. Snaps had been put into the fenced backyard to play because he was nosy as hell every time they went into Andino's bedroom, and nobody wanted a dog looking at them while they were rolling around naked in bed.

"Just ignore it," Andino muttered, bending over her to kiss the back of her neck. "They'll go away."

She was willing to agree.

Except the knocking continued.

"It's a little distracting," she said.

Andino groaned, but not the good kind like before. No, this one was filled with his annoyance. "Don't fucking *move*. Don't get dressed. Don't do anything but stay right where you are ready for me to crawl back between your thighs. Got it?"

Haven laughed. "Whatever you want, Andino."

She was fine to stay in the bed and wait for him even as he took a minute to pull on something to make his lower half suitable for guests—although he didn't bother with a shirt. She ogled him the entire time, even when he gave her a look for staring.

"What?" she asked innocently.

Andino laughed. "Nothing—remember what I said."

"Stay here and be ready for you to fuck me."

"I didn't say it like that."

"But?"

"Yes, do exactly that."

He gave her a wink, and then he was gone. Haven rolled over to her back in the bed, and stared up at the ceiling as she listened to Andino's quick footsteps pad down the stairs. With the house being as quiet as it was, she could hear practically everything.

Including the way he opened the front door with a nasty, "What the fuck, you can't call or something?"

Haven stiffened when a female voice replied, "You ... you fucking *asshole.*"

Yikes.

They had a deal—her and Andino. He wasn't to be fucking anyone else, but she didn't like the sound of a woman rushing into his home at night, and calling him names. That didn't bode well at all for their agreement.

"Hey, don't come here to my home calling me names, Catty," Andino snapped. And then, a second later, Andino asked, "You told her, then?"

A new, male voice answered this time. "Guess so."

"Don't even pay him any attention. It's me you need to be talking to, Andino," the female said, her tone thick with anger. "How dare *you*?"

Yeah, okay ...

Haven had been fine to wait in bed for Andino, but now not so much. She didn't like the way the conversation was going downstairs, and if this was another woman who he was involved with, Haven wasn't going to be quiet about it. Getting out the bed, she wrapped a sheet around her body to make herself less naked—nothing else, though. She headed into the hallway as the voices continued downstairs.

"I beg your pardon?" Andino asked.

"You know why I'm here. You know what you did ... what you've been doing!"

"Catherine, it's not even a big deal. So your parents know you've been hustling for me, whatever."

Wait.

Haven's footsteps hesitated at the top of the stairs.

Hustling?

Like … drugs?

Dealing *drugs?*

Andino continued on, and his voice brought her out of her thoughts again. "Who gives a shit? They clearly don't. They just kept quiet because they wanted you to tell them. I went along with it, all right. That's it."

"No, that's not it," the woman hissed. "That's not even close to being it, you prick."

Yeah, she sounded pissed.

Haven was just … concerned.

About what she heard.

What it might mean.

What it *did* mean.

It was sadly amusing to her—and incredibly ironic, as she wasn't so stupid that she couldn't see that, too—how she had been entirely willing to overlook the fact that she knew Andino was probably involved with some sort of shady business. So much so, that she actively refused to seek out any information about him lest she stumble on something that would make her drop him like a hot rock.

Instead, it found her.

She wasn't ready.

She didn't want to know.

And yet, she knew something now.

"You've listened to me say over and over again how anxious it made me to even think my parents would find out that I was hustling drugs," the woman—hadn't he called her Catty?—said as Haven started coming down the stairs with soft footsteps. "You played along with that, Andino, you joked with me about it, and fed those fears to get a rise out of me. Or, that's what I thought. Because we're family, right, so you didn't mean me any harm. You couldn't, but you did. You did that shit not because you knew how I felt, but because of what you wanted."

"I—"

"Money," the woman barked. Haven came just far enough down the staircase that she caught sight of the beautiful, dark-haired woman thrusting her finger into Andino's chest hard enough to make him back up a step or two. "That's what this was about for you. Not the fact that telling me could have saved me a lot of unnecessary worrying and work hiding what I was doing all these years. No, you didn't tell me because you liked the money I was making."

"Exactly that," Andino stated.

Haven, like the woman, stiffened and blinked.

He said it so coldly.

So … uncaringly.

That was not the Andino she knew.

The woman dropped her hand. "You're not even ashamed of it."

Andino shrugged. "Nope. You're fucking predictable, Catherine. All you would need was the slightest idea that your daddy didn't like what you were doing, and you would fuck off somewhere else. Or even better yet, you'd run to your mother and get in on her shit. Here's the thing, I wasn't letting that happen. So yeah, I played along. Yeah, I worked your fears a bit to make sure you kept your business with me separated far away from your parents. And fuck yeah, I would do it again in a heartbeat."

Andino smirked, adding, "This is my crew, Catherine, and my money we're talking about. It's *business*. I supply *you*. I keep you going. You make me *money*. That's how it works, and I want it to keep working. There's nothing else to be said about it."

Catherine nodded, and stepped back. "Well, fuck you, Andino. I've got news for you. I'll never deal for you again. Not after this. I promise you that."

"Catty, you don't get it. That's not how it works in this business. You don't get to just drop the person that's kept you above water and helped you make a name. You owe me for getting you where you are, sweetheart. You can be pissed off about it all you want. Still, when next month rolls around, make sure you've got my money, and you're picking up your next package to run."

"Hey," the man who had been mostly quiet said as he stepped in between the woman and Andino. "If she's done, man, then that's the fucking end of it. Let her be done if that's what she wants."

"That's not how it works, Cross, and you know it."

"It's going to work that way this time," Cross replied.

"No, I don't—"

Haven was done—she had enough. "Andino, is something wrong?"

At her quiet question, all eyes turned on her in an instant. Haven might have felt uncomfortable about it, but she was still reeling about the conversation and the things she just learned.

She was dating a drug dealer … at the least. She was fucking a man who handled drugs. Again, *at the least*, her mind taunted. Because it probably wasn't only drugs, Haven knew. Andino *was* a Marcello, and even while she didn't entertain the rumors and whispers, she still heard them.

She had been listening.

A little …

"Who are you?" Catherine asked, staring right at Haven.

Haven glanced at Andino, unsure if he wanted to take this one, or she should "Um …"

"None of your business," Andino snapped at the woman before glancing back at her on the stairs. "Haven, head upstairs, all right?"

Haven scowled openly at Andino, hoping to all hell he could see just how pissed off she was in those seconds. She didn't want to be dismissed— she also didn't want to stand there when she had other things to handle, either. Flicking a hand over her shoulder, she headed back up the stairs even as the conversation continued behind her. She could hear their talk even when she disappeared back into the bedroom.

"Who was that?" Catherine asked.

"I told you—"

"Yeah, yeah, mind my business. Who is she?"

"A woman," Andino snapped.

Haven dropped the sheet, and started gathering her clothes. She already had her shirt tossed over her head when she heard the next statement from downstairs.

"She just shows up to your place wearing a sheet or something? Since when did you start seeing someone?"

"My personal life is not up for discussion," Andino said sharply. "There's enough fucking people in this family who seem to think it is. Now, get the fuck out. The next time you come to my house, make sure you call first."

"Fuck you," Catherine spat.

"Remember what I said, too. This is business, Catherine. You don't get to walk away from business just because you want to."

"And you hear me—I won't ever deal for you again, cousin."

Cousin.

That should have made Haven feel better—in one way. At least, this … Catherine wasn't some woman Andino was fucking, too.

Instead, she was just lost.

Confused.

Concerned.

Haven heard the front door slam shut with a loud bang, but she was already dressed and slipping back down the stairs before Andino had even turned around. Yeah, she was fast like that when she just needed to *get the fuck out.*

"Haven," Andino murmured.

She shook her head, and passed him by as she moved down the last few steps. "I need to head out."

"Haven, *wait.*"

"I heard everything, by the way. Sounds travel when a house is silent."

She caught sight of his flinch out of the corner of her eye.

"Listen, it's not a big deal."

"It is kind of a big deal to me." Pulling her ballet flats away from the wall, she slipped her feet into the shoes. "But at the moment, there's nothing to talk about, Andino."

"Then, why are you running out of here like—"

"Because I don't *want* to talk about it right now." She stood straight, and spun around to face him. "Who are you?" Andino opened his mouth to speak, but she was quick to interject with, "And no, don't give me some garbage again. Give me the *truth*. Who are you, and what do you do, Andino?"

A tic worked its way through the strong line of his jaw, and he swallowed hard. Still, he said, "I never said I was a good man, Haven."

"You didn't say anything, actually."

"I didn't know *how*," he said, his tone sharp, yet aching. "And so fucking what, maybe I liked that you didn't know *everything* about me like everyone else does."

Haven blinked, stunned for a second. "Is that it? You liked that I was in the dark about the things you do, and who you really are?"

"Don't say it like that."

"Like *what*?"

"Like you don't know me—like you've never sat down to have dinner with me, or watched me with my dog, or woke up next to me in the morning. Don't act like you know *nothing* about me when you probably know the parts that matter the most, Haven."

Ouch.

"And yet," she told him, "you forgot other parts. You know, shit that might matter to me."

She turned to move for the door, but Andino followed. "Wait, please—"

"I need some time, okay? Just … give me some time, Andino."

Thankfully, he let her go.

And sadly, she still felt cold.

ELEVEN

November ...

• • •

December ...

• • •

The truth always came out eventually. That was thing about secrets and lies. No matter how strong a web of lies was woven, it only took one thread to unravel for the rest to come crashing down. And secrets? Well, one could only keep those hidden for so long before someone stumbled upon something they shouldn't.

Or in Andino's case ... his boss finding out who he'd been working with behind the man's back. Yeah, maybe he should have known better, but for now, he was going to blame it on life getting in the way, and making him fucking stupid.

"Cross Donati?"

Andino was a little busy staring at the bareness of the grand entry in the Marcello mansion to really care about how loudly his boss was yelling at him. Bare, he thought, because here it was the twenty-sixth of December, and not a decoration hung from the walls. No green garland twisting up the bannister of the grand staircase, and no Christmas tree in the middle of the hall tall enough to touch the ceiling.

Every year that he could remember, this mansion became a winter wonderland at Christmastime. It never failed. Sure, his grandmother, Cecelia, had stepped back over the years to allow her sons' wives to do the majority of the work and planning for their decorating and parties this time of year, but *still.*

It was never *not* done.

It was never bare of decorations.

Andino found it a little distracting.

"Cross *fucking* Donati," Dante snarled.

He glanced at his uncle, but he didn't know what Dante wanted him to say. Likely nothing, considering the way the man was staring at him. Sometimes, being silent was better, especially when all your shit finally caught up to you.

Or, that's what his father always told him.

116

Speaking of who …

"You were told not to work with Cross," Gio said.

Andino shrugged. "Dante needed his guns run, didn't he? What did you all want me to do?"

"Find someone else!"

Dante's shout echoed.

It all felt like vibrations bouncing off Andino's form. He was numb to this—to their anger, and disappointment. Unfeeling about their fucking *feelings*. It was business at the end of the day, and Andino only cared about making sure business was done.

Nothing more, and nothing less.

"And when were you going to tell us that you had Cross running our guns?" his other uncle, Lucian, asked.

Beside him, John shifted from foot to foot, clearly uncomfortable. He was finally back and settled after chasing his sister all across the fucking United States, but he was trying to lay low, and keep himself out of trouble. Not that Andino blamed his cousin, really. Still, where one of the two went in this family, the other one was sure to follow.

Or, it seemed that way.

"Andino made a choice," John said, "and given the circumstances, it wasn't the *wrong* choice, necessarily, but—"

"It *was* the wrong choice," Dante barked, "and nobody asked you, Johnathan."

John stiffened, but quieted.

Andino, on the other hand, was just about done with this whole fucking thing. "So, it didn't work out. The gun run was botched—it happens. Who the fuck thought the buyer was going to come back on us like he did? *No one.* It worked out, though. We all fixed it. And we got Catherine back, didn't we? *Alive.*"

Dante's jaw tensed, and his gaze hardened.

Like ice and fire.

Freezing cold, and burning.

"Yes," his uncle said, "and lucky for you that my daughter made it out of that mess alive. *You* would have been the one answering for that mess, Andino. *Family first*—it's our rule. Did you forget about it?"

Not really.

It just got lost in the mess that was everything else in his life at the moment. He figured his uncle was a fucking hypocrite in that way, anyway. Dante barked that family first bullshit like he meant it—but mark Andino's words, had he slipped in business, his uncle would have let him know it; family or not.

Because yeah, the Marcellos looked out for one another.

They also liked *money*.

"And you didn't answer the question," Dante added, his tone dropping to that dark, angry timber again. "*When* were you planning on telling me that you deliberately disobeyed me by having Cross Donati run our guns down the Gulf because our usual man got picked up on charges? Go ahead and figure out *another* lie, Andino. I'll wait."

"Hey," Giovanni said, his gaze narrowing. "Watch it, Dante."

The boss didn't even pass Andino's father a look, but he did hold up a hand as to ask his brother for silence.

"*Well?*" Dante asked when Andino stayed quiet. "I'm waiting."

Andino sighed, and shook his head. His uncle was not going to drop this until he got what he wanted—or at least, something suitable to his pissed off mood. "Maybe after it was successful, and the rest of the money was in your bank. Or ... never?"

Dante scowled.

Did he want the truth, or not?

"Do you have anything to say for yourself?" his uncle asked.

"I did my job," Andino said, shrugging his broad shoulders. "Shit didn't work out, but the fact will remain the same in that *I did my job*, boss. The guns needed to be run, and you didn't have to like who was running them as long as they got to where they needed to go. That's the thing about this business, right, or so the three of you have been preaching to the rest of us for our whole life. As long as the fucking job gets done, and money goes in the bank, then the rest doesn't matter. *Unless,*" he added with a bitter laugh, "Dante decides to get stuck up in his feelings about a certain person because then everybody's going to have a fucking problem." Andino scoffed. "Isn't that how it seems lately?"

Silence answered him back.

His uncles were stunned.

His father was wide-eyed.

Beside him, John stared at the floor, silent but with a ghost of a smile on his lips.

Because *yeah*, where was the fucking lie?

"Leave," Dante murmured.

Andino didn't need to be told again. He turned fast on his heel to get the hell out of that house—it seemed like his best bet considering how much he managed to piss off his uncle tonight, and he really didn't need to be going for a second round.

"*Not you, Andino.*"

Ah, shit.

"Everybody else, move your asses somewhere else," Dante said. "Upstairs, outside ... I don't give a fuck. Get out of my sight until the rest of the men get here. *Go.*"

Andino turned back around to face his uncle. Dante looked like he was hanging onto his last rope of patience, and it was getting thinner by the fucking minute. This was life as a Cosa Nostra boss, though, no way around it. Stress was constant—from the business to the family, and more importantly, the men working under the boss.

This was what it was.

This was the duty Dante handed to Andino.

Like he should be grateful for it.

Dante only spoke again once the rest of the men of their family had scattered elsewhere—Giovanni outside with a mutter about needing a smoke, and Lucian and John upstairs to the large office that Dante liked to use whenever he visited the mansion, likely.

"What is *wrong* with you?" Dante asked.

Andino blinked.

That was not the question he expected.

"I beg your pardon?"

"You, Andi," his uncle murmured, gesturing at him. "What is wrong with you? This—all this insolence and disobedience—this is not the made man your father raised. You know your place, and you're quite comfortable in it. You don't cause problems, and you do *good* work. Stop behaving like a man who doesn't know how to act in this family and life, Andino. What's changed?"

Andino laughed.

Instinctual, maybe.

Nerves and anger, most definitely.

"What *changed*?" he asked.

Dante nodded. "That's what I said."

"Everything fucking changed!"

Andino couldn't believe the gall of his uncle to ask something like that as if he didn't know exactly *how* he'd upended his nephew's entire fucking life by shoving something onto his shoulders that he'd never asked for, and without any kind of proper warning. Like it wasn't a big deal.

It was a big deal!

And *now* … now he wanted to tell Andino how he could or could not *be* as Dante's little *boss in waiting*?

Fuck all of that.

Fuck that noise.

"What changed," Andino said, taking a step toward his uncle although Dante stayed firm in his position, "was that somewhere along the lines, you decided you get some kind of say in what kind of boss you want me to be. Somewhere in this bright fucking idea of yours to make me the next boss of the Marcellos, you figured you could turn me into *you*. I am not you, Dante. I am me. And that means you don't have to like the way I do business, or who the fuck I do it with, or how I decide to sit down in your seat once you're done with it."

His uncle's stance softened a bit. "Andino—"

"The *only* thing you get to decide—you already did. You put me here. You decided this for me. You chose my future, and what you and everybody else wanted for it. And you didn't give one good goddamn about what I might have wanted. So, *fine*. Fuck you, too. You got your one choice about me, but the rest?"

Andino laughed, and sneered. "The rest, boss, is up to me. Don't forget it."

He could be a good boss—he knew it because of who he was, his bloodline, and the way he'd been raised in this family. He could be a good boss because this was who he was, and this was all he'd ever known.

He could be a good boss.

Except he'd never asked for it.

And here he was.

So, fine.

Fine.

Andino would be their next boss—like *fuck* was anybody going to step in his way, and tell him how to *be* it, though.

No one was going to do that.

Dante cleared his throat, and fixed the cufflink on his dress shirt. His tone lost a lot of that heat and anger with his next words. "I don't expect you to be me, Andino."

"It sure seems like it."

"I don't need you to be like me." Dante shrugged, dropped his arms to his side, and stared long and hard at Andino before he spoke again. "What I need, Andi, is to know that I made the right choice. That when push comes to shove, you're going to put your duty ahead of your own wants, and do what is right and best for this family and organization. That's all, *nipote*."

Andino clenched his jaw, and muttered, "Stop trying to put me in your seat the way you want me to go there."

"All right."

"All right?"

Dante nodded. "That's what I said. We'll start tonight, even."

"Tonight," Andino echoed.

"Why do you think I have the men coming here? It's the night after Christmas, Andino. I am sure they want to be with their family, but instead, they're coming to this mansion to have their vote and voice when I officially put you into the underboss position. See, even though you disappointed me, lied, and more … I was not so pissed off that I couldn't see what you were *trying* to do. I don't need you to be like me to know that I made the right choice, Andino, but I don't know how to be any other boss than the one I am."

Yeah, he got it.

He *knew*.

"I'd do the right thing, for the record," Andino said.

Dante sucked in a long inhale. "Would you?"

"For this family—I'll always make the right choice."

Him, too, though.

Andino would always make the right choice for himself because nobody else was taking care of him at the end of the day. And what good was a family like the Marcellos if the man heading them was simply nothing more than a shell molded by someone else?

Andino couldn't be Dante.

He could only be himself.

"Hey," came a voice from behind Andino. He glanced over his shoulder to find his father leaning in the entrance, and staring at Dante. "The men are starting to arrive."

Dante nodded. "Thanks, Gio."

"No problem."

Andino's father was gone a second later.

"Andino," Dante murmured.

He looked back to his uncle. "What?"

"You're not going to have any problems tonight with the men of this family, for the record," his uncle said. "I hope you know that—you've been handling them and their business or issues for months now with no problems. You've been acting as the underboss for me and them long before it was ever official. They *like* you. They respect you. There will be no issue when I put it to a vote on whether or not to move you up in an official capacity."

Andino sighed. "Yeah, I know."

Nothing his uncle said was a lie.

This whole night would be nothing more than the theatrics of the mafia—they could have just as easily made a few phone calls, and let the men have their voice that way. Unfortunately, that just wasn't how Cosa Nostra worked.

And without their traditions—without their *rules*—what would they be? Andino wasn't sure he cared to find out, honestly.

"Just ... tell me this," Dante said quietly. "If I gave you the choice right here and now before we begin tonight to go back to how you were before I put the duty and the legacy of this family in your hands, would you take that option? Would you go back to being who you were before with no expectations for anything different?"

Andino didn't even have to think about it. Oh, sure, he still had his fucking feelings about this whole thing, but it wasn't so much being the boss as it was … not being able to be himself when too many voices were shouting around him to be someone different. It was everyone else trying to control his life like they had any business doing so—it was not being the boss that really bothered him, necessarily.

"No," Andino said.

"No." Dante nodded like that was the answer he was expecting, and then asked, "Why not?"

"Because I would make the right choice for this family."

Dante smiled. "And what does that mean?"

Wasn't it obvious?

"I'm the right choice," Andino said.

• • •

Snaps whined as Andino climbed the front steps leading to his home. "Come on, buddy, can't the walk wait?"

It was cold as hell for the end of December.

Too cold, maybe.

Snaps didn't care.

Glancing back over his shoulder, Andino found his dog sitting firmly on the cold sidewalk, unmoved. Snaps was making his position clear even if he couldn't speak. He wanted his fucking walk, and he wanted it *now*.

It didn't matter that Andino had been on his feet all damn day chasing after Capos, and being the go-between for his uncle, and the rest of the men. Snaps didn't have any understanding that life for Andino didn't stop just because his spoiled pup wanted a walk or two around the cold block.

Who cared that it was winter?

And *snowing*?

Not Snaps.

"Fine," Andino grumbled. "We'll go for a walk."

Snaps was quick to get up on all four paws again, and shake his stubby tail. He was happy again, but all Andino could think about was how quickly it was going to take for frost bite to set in on his fingertips.

Fuck, it's cold.

"At least let me grab gloves," he told the dog.

Snaps chuffed, but at least he didn't have those big, sad eyes and the pouty face going on anymore. That was something, anyway.

He was pretty sure his neighbors, and anyone who saw him with Snaps, probably thought he was crazy. He talked to his dog like the animal could understand and converse right back on a regular basis. Snaps *could*

122

understand, he just didn't talk back. At least, not in a human way. No, the dog had his own attitude and spin to put on a conversation.

If anything, lately, Snaps was the only thing making Andino's days a little bit better. The dog made him smile, and got him out of the house more often than he would willing choose to leave himself. It had been this way ever since Haven left his house two months ago without as much as a look back.

Fuck.

He'd thought ...

Maybe she'd call.

Maybe she'd come back around.

Maybe, maybe ... *maybe.*

It killed him to let her walk out of his place like that with her head full of assumptions—not all of them wrong—and leaving them hanging in the fucking wind like she did. But what could he really do?

She was her own person. She could make her choices. He had to respect them even if all he had wanted to do was everything and anything *but* let her go.

So, here he was two months later, and he still hadn't figured out how to let go of the blonde, tattooed woman he wasn't allowed to have. Kind of fucked up in a way, but it was just one more thing on the pile of shit that had become Andino's life.

He reached his front door, and hesitated to grab the knob because of the flyer stuck in between the crack in the doorjamb. He pulled it out, and his gaze drifted over the New Year's Eve party announcement for a familiar business.

Safe Haven.

Yeah.

The world was having a good laugh at him.

Or God.

Someone.

It wasn't unusual for clubs to print out thousands of flyers, and pay someone a set fee to go and tape the promotion to every door they could find within ten miles. It just so happened to be Andino's fucking luck that his house was about ten blocks away from Haven's club.

He looked over the details again, and considered ...

Should leave her be.

She's not like you.

Don't let this life touch her, Andino.

His mind—as punishing as it was—happened to be right in a lot of ways. Haven was untouched by his life, and the mafia. She wasn't like him in a lot of ways, but he found comfort in the fact that she was familiar enough that he wanted her.

God.

He wanted her.

Crumpling the flyer in his hand, Andino glanced down the street and watched the falling snowflakes fill the air in heavy, white sheets. His mind was the smart part of him—logical, in control, and always pushing to do the right thing even when it felt wrong to him. His heart, though, that was a whole other matter.

Thing was—Andino hadn't even realized his heart had a fucking voice until Haven showed up in his life.

His heart wanted something different than his mind, of course.

It'd been two months.

He *should* leave her be.

Hadn't she made her choice?

It was just too damn bad that Haven hadn't allowed Andino a choice, too. That was the thing—there had been two of them involved in whatever they were, and only one of them made the decision to walk away.

That hadn't been him.

TWELVE

New Year's Eve was always busy, but when Safe Haven decided to put on a special with a burlesque show, a promised dance from a favorite— *Valeria*—who didn't dance often, and also cut prices on drinks amongst their regular acts?

The place became a circus.

Jackson slid behind the bar looking entirely out of his element as he shoved three bottles of the club's most requested vodka onto the shelves. *Poor guy*, Haven mused. He was far more accustomed to handling the employees, and doing paperwork when the need called for it. Working behind the bar and dealing with patrons was beyond his paygrade, really.

"Is that all you need, or—"

"Take a break," Haven called to the manager.

Hell, he might have a fucking aneurism if he didn't, what with the way that vein in his forehead was bulging out. She really couldn't afford for one of her employees to drop tonight when the place was just getting started.

Also, ambulances *really* dampened a party.

"Are you sure?" Jackson asked. "I don't mind helping."

Haven rolled her eyes. "You mind—this isn't your job, I get it. Go take a break, and then check in with Val for me, okay? She's on in forty minutes or so."

Jackson saluted Haven with two fingers. "You got it, boss."

He was quick to leave, then.

Fine by her.

Shouts and cheers lit up the crowd, taking Haven's attention away from the line of shots she was pouring for a group of smartly-dressed men at the bar. They were polite, and gracious, and didn't fucking leer. All things Haven appreciated in her customers, but especially when she was one of the women stuck behind the bar for the majority of the night. Compared to some of the patrons who came through on any given night, these men were *saints*.

Across the floor, Haven watched the main stage as the line of burlesque dancers dropped off behind the curtain one by one. Eventually, they were all gone from the stage except for the main girl with the biggest head piece who was almost entirely naked but for a few well-placed pieces of her costume.

Those girls put on a damn good show.

Well worth their price.

Haven was all the way down the bar ten minutes later, and mixing a margarita for a chatty redheaded woman with another girl hanging off her arm when Valeria slipped in behind the bar. Her friend shot her a wide smile as she automatically started taking orders from whoever hadn't been served, and was still standing there waiting.

"What are you doing?" Haven called down. "You're supposed to be on the stage in thirty minutes!"

Valeria shrugged as she reached for a bottle of schnapps. "You need an extra pair of hands—here they are."

"Yeah, but—"

"It's fine, Haven. I'm ready."

She didn't look like it.

No outfit.

No heels.

At least, Val's hair and makeup was done.

That was something.

"Fifteen minutes," Haven told her friend. "That's it, and then you have to go back and finish getting ready. Got it?"

"Someone's bossy tonight, huh?"

Valeria winked.

Haven only laughed.

She was grateful for the extra help, though, no matter what she said to Valeria. Between her, the girl working at the other side of the bar, and Valeria handling the middle, the patrons were covered, drinks were flowing, and Haven ended up needing to call Jackson in early from his break, so he could empty the register of larger bills.

It was a good night.

A *great* night, really.

A lot like every other night lately.

Haven *was* grateful for it—to be busy, and to be successful. But mostly, work gave her an escape. Something to keep her mind distracted, and her hands busy. She'd put in more hours at this club over the last couple of months than she had even when she first took it over from her father after buying him out.

Why?

She needed the distraction.

She needed *something* ...

Anything to keep her mind from drifting back to the way Andino Marcello looked the night she left his place. Something to keep her from picking up the phone, and shooting him a text just to see how he was.

The guy had proven he was bad news.

He *purposely* hid things from her about himself that might have made Haven reconsider her involvement with him.

And yet, she still missed him.

Still thought about him.

Still *wondered.*

"You okay?" Valeria asked.

Haven glanced up from the bar, and realized she'd been wiping the same spot with a rag for the last two minutes. She found a patron waiting on the other side to be served, and Valeria to her left looking at her like she had suddenly grown a second head.

"Sorry," Haven said. "Went somewhere else for a second."

"Okay."

Haven looked at the patron with a wide smile. "What can I get for you, sir?"

"Long Island Iced Tea."

Really?

Well, it was his drink.

Not hers.

"You got it," Haven said.

Valeria slipped past Haven to head for the small waiter's door behind the bar. "My dance is twenty minutes *at most.* If the bar is still crazy by the time I am done, I will be back here to help you. No arguments—got it?"

Haven laughed. "Now who is the bossy one?"

Her friend winked, but said nothing as she disappeared into the crowd. Without that extra pair of hands helping behind the bar, it wasn't long before people were backed up again waiting for drinks between the patrons coming to the bar themselves, and the servers on the floor bringing drink orders to Haven and the other bartender.

She was grateful for this night.

For the work.

The *money.*

This distraction ...

She just wished—

Haven's thought process dropped off midstream as a buzzing sensation skimmed over her body. It was like static crawled over her skin while butterflies beat in her stomach. She knew exactly what caused that strange reaction damn near instantly.

The crowd swelled, and moved closer to the stage while the DJ announced the next act—Valeria. Still, Haven couldn't find him. She looked, but she found nothing.

A sea of faceless people.

It had to be him, though.

Andino.

He was the only fucking thing that made her feel alive just by walking into a room. She didn't have to see him for that reaction to be the same. Two months later, and he still managed to do that to her.

So, where was he?

• • •

"Haven," one of the three servers said as she came up to the bar, "drink order for table fifteen."

"Thanks, I'll have it for you—"

"No, they requested you serve it."

Haven hesitated on taking the slip from the girl's hand. "Me?"

Talia nodded. "That's what they want."

Ugh.

It wasn't uncommon for a regular—or even someone Haven knew personally outside of the club—to request she be the one to serve their drinks when they were sitting at a table. Mostly, they just wanted to say hello, or have her sit down with them to have a drink.

Nothing big.

Except tonight was *busy*.

She really couldn't afford to be away from the bar for too long, but she also didn't want to offend a regular or a friend, either. What could she do?

Oh, yes.

Learn to tell people *no*.

Tonight was not the night when she learned how to do that, though. Lucky for whoever it was that wanted their drink served by her personally.

Haven pointed at the server before the girl could turn away, and go back to taking orders from the floor. "You can pour a shot, and figure out which beer is which, right?"

Talia shrugged. "Yeah, but that's about all I can do."

"That's all you need to do for ten minutes. Any special drinks, and you direct them down the bar. Cover my spot, thanks."

Haven quickly poured the three fingers of scotch that Talia had scratched on the drink order, grabbed two napkins from under the bar, and headed out on the floor to find table fifteen. She knew which table was which—fifteen was the table closest to the furthest stage at the far end of the club. A single person table meant for one, and not for more.

A group of guys got up from a table Haven was passing, causing her to step wide to the side in order to keep out of their way and save the drink in her hand at the same time. They hadn't even seen her coming—no wonder, considering how full the club was at the moment—and she hadn't seen them getting up until it was too late.

One gave her a smile. "Sorry."

"No worries."

Spinning back around to face whoever was waiting for her at table fifteen, Haven froze on the spot at the man sitting there. She should have *known.*

Goddammit.

That strange feeling from earlier that made her think Andino had been watching her from somewhere in the crowd had left after a while. She'd gotten lost in work, and stopped looking to see if he was actually there or not. She wouldn't say she had *forgotten*—her mind simply put him and his *possible* presence on the backburner while she went back to doing her fucking job. Clearly, that had been a mistake on her part.

Here he is.

"Andino," Haven greeted, sliding in beside his table and ignoring the patrons at the booth next to his. "I'd like to say I'm surprised to see you here, but I can't say that I am."

He glanced sideways at her, all striking green eyes, a strong jaw relaxed in his smile, and an aloof attitude that made her think *cool, calm, and always collected.* Wasn't that Andino in a nutshell? She didn't think this man knew how to be fucking emotional.

Goddamn him, too.

He looked *good.*

He'd ditched the usual three-piece suit for dark wash jeans, a plain white T-shirt, and a black leather jacket with the sleeves pushed up his forearms. *And those arms.* God, she loved his arms—next to his face and his cock, she swore they were his best fucking feature.

"You were expecting me?" he asked smoothly, arching a brow.

Haven saw that trap for what it was, and refused to walk into it. There was no way in hell she was about to explain to this man that, *yes*, she absolutely had felt his presence from the moment he walked into her business. Frankly, she didn't know how to deal with that. She wasn't at all sure that *he* would know what to do with it.

And did he really need that information?

Haven didn't think so.

"What are you doing here?" she asked.

Andino's attention went back to the stage, and she felt the loss of his gaze instantly. The buzzing through her nerves, the humming on her skin, and the tightness in her chest was gone the moment he looked away from her. The heat traveling through her body was quick to leave, too—a coldness remained in its wake.

Look at me again, she wanted to say.

Make me feel like that again.

Only you do that to me.

Haven kept quiet.

She was a damn *mess*. It had been her who chose to walk away from Andino, and not the other way around. She did that for good reasons—all good reasons! Him showing up, and looking at her should not make a difference to why she had chosen to walk away.

And yet …

Here she was.

Entirely fucked.

All because of *him*.

Andino nodded at the stage subtly, saying, "Watching the show."

Haven stiffened, but didn't bother to look at what he was talking about. She didn't need to look at the stage to know it was one of her girls dancing—Marney, actually, who specialized in erotic dancing with little tricks, but more sensual moves and things of that nature. She was a favorite of the patrons, and—

"She's new, isn't she?" he asked quietly, passing Haven another glance.

She couldn't tell if he was actually interested in watching Marney, or just trying to see if he could piss Haven off. He was *succeeding*. She'd never really felt jealousy before—didn't have time for nonsense like that.

And yet, there she was.

Green all over.

It burned like bile in her throat, and made her fist clench into a tight ball at her side. She was sure she was scowling because she sure as fuck wasn't smiling in those moments. Heat shot through her body the longer Andino watched the stage instead of staring at her. She was holding his drink of scotch so firmly that she very well might break the damn glass.

"She is new," Haven managed to say. "Started last month."

"Very beautiful."

Jesus Christ.

She had all she could do not to pour that goddamn drink over his head. Unfortunately, that wouldn't look good for her, or her business. She didn't need to be making a show over a *man*. And besides, watching the girls strip was kind of what this place was about, anyway.

Haven set the drink down in front of Andino—maybe a little harder than was necessary—but his gaze never drifted away from the stage. "Since when do you drink scotch?"

His lips curved upward at the edge.

Just the *hint* of a smirk.

Sexy in a blink.

Dark.

A promise of sin.

His gaze finally drifted away from the dancing woman, and lingered on Haven's face in a way that made her think she was the only thing he was actually seeing. He made her feel like all the noise in the club silenced, that every person faded into the background, and it was just him and her right then, and there.

You walked away for a reason.

It was a good reason.

Except … when he looked at her like that, and she was reminded of all the other things she did know about Andino that had nothing to do with the stuff she didn't like … well, it was easy to forget, and wish she could turn back the clock.

"I don't drink scotch," he said.

Haven lifted a brow. "Then, why—"

"I thought you might know it was me if I asked for whiskey." His intense gaze traveled down the flimsy crop top she'd pulled on to wear to work, and then lingered on her jean-covered legs for a while. "You're looking good."

"Thank you."

Andino's tongue peeked out to wet his bottom lip—an action that made Haven wet between her thighs considering she knew just how good he was at putting that tongue to use between her thighs.

Yeah, you went there fast, girl.

Of course.

"Did you really come to watch the show, or did you come to see me?" she asked.

"Maybe both."

"I could just have a bouncer escort you out, you know."

Andino shrugged his wide shoulders, and went back to staring at the stage. "I mean, you could try, baby. We'll see how it works out for you."

Asshole.

Haven huffed, and spun on her heel to leave.

"I will take that whiskey, though," he called behind her. "Have someone else serve it, if you want. You seem a little pissed off."

You think?

• • •

"Last call!"

Haven's shout echoed over the bar, and throughout the crowd. Hands flew up from those close to the bar to grab their final drinks before the night was over, and Safe Haven officially closed their doors.

Valeria was back behind the bar helping, but things had slowed down quite a bit. The main acts were over, but there was still one girl left to finish her dance before the security would begin helping people out.

And calling cabs for those who clearly needed one.

"Take five," Haven called down to the other bartender. Even if it was last call ... "Me and Val can handle this final rush."

The girl nodded, and gave a little wave as she left the bar. It was only her second break of the evening, and Haven was sure her feet and hands were tired as hell. She'd more than earned every dollar tonight, though.

Girl needed a bonus.

"Is he still here?" Valeria asked.

Haven looked up from the cups she was wiping out. "Who?"

"*You know who.*"

Oh, yeah.

Andino.

Haven's gaze drifted over the crowd to where Andino had settled himself into table fifteen for a good portion of the night. Now, the table was empty—it had been empty for quite a while. She had sent someone else to deliver his whiskey, and according to the girls on the floor, he'd not asked for another drink after that one.

"Gone from the table, anyway," Haven said.

"Think he's waiting outside for you?"

"Maybe, and maybe not. It's hard to say with Andino."

Valeria slipped down the bar, and grabbed one of the clean glasses from Haven with a soft smile. "Okay, *better question.*"

"Shoot."

"Do you want him to be waiting out there for you?"

That made Haven stop.

She hesitated to answer.

Considered ...

Her answer should have been the easiest thing she ever said—*no, I don't want him to be waiting out there for me after I left him hanging two months ago while I was still wet between my thighs.*

Instead, she found herself saying, "I don't know, Val."

Valeria nodded, and started mixing the drink for a waiting patron. "It's okay to be confused, you know."

"Weren't you the one who told me to be careful about him?"

"And I still think you should. I also think if you go into something knowing what you're doing, then that's a different story, Haven."

Fair enough.

"I don't know what I want," Haven admitted.

"Yeah, I get that." Valeria stood up on her tiptoes, and scanned the crowd before shouting out, "Hey, Lachy!"

The head of the club's security was quick to cut through the crowd at the sound of his name being called by a bartender. He was good like that—always looking out for any employee regardless if they poured drinks, served them, or worked on a pole. He didn't care what someone did as long as they were happy doing it, and safe all the while.

The large man shouldered his way through the people trying to get their last drinks at the bar, and rested his beefy arms on the top. "What can I do for you, Val?"

She gestured at the entrance. "Could you check outside for me—big guy, but not as big as you, dark, short hair, green eyes, and goes by Andi—"

"Val," Haven snapped.

"Andino," her friend finished. "We don't want him gone. We just want to know if he's out there waiting for Haven. He's a friend."

"Val!"

Valeria continued ignoring her. "If you wouldn't mind, Lachy."

"Is he trouble?"

"Define *trouble*," Haven muttered under her breath.

"Harmless to *us*," Valeria said, giving Haven a look. "Right?"

Lachy looked to her as well for an answer. "Well, boss?"

Haven sighed. "Yeah, he's harmless. Just a friend."

"I'll check."

Once the security was gone, Haven gave Valeria a side-eye that could rival the Devil's. Her friend only smiled in response.

"Listen, I have watched you sulk for two months—"

"I have not been *sulking*."

"When you're not working, yeah, a little," her friend returned. "I do just want you to be happy, Haven. And *safe*."

"I'm not sure Andino is safe."

Valeria made a noise under her breath. "But is he safe for *you?* That's where it counts. That's where I went wrong way back when."

That was a good question.

Wasn't it?

It didn't take long before Lachy was approaching the bar again, but Haven could tell his answer about whether or not Andino was outside waiting before the man even opened his mouth to speak. He shook his head—*nope*. Not there at all.

"Damn," Valeria murmured. "Sorry, Haven."

"It's fine."

Haven just felt … sad.

And confused.

It wasn't fine at all.

THIRTEEN

Andino popped a hand down, and let Snaps take the scrap piece of shredded chicken from his fingertips. Just as quickly, the dog went back to his own bowl of food, and worked on the mess in there. Washing his hands again, Andino was just about to set the skillet of shredded chicken on the stove when a familiar tune rang through his house.

Snaps' head popped up, he sniffed, looked back at Andino, and then started eating again.

"Really?" Andino asked. "You're getting lazy."

Some guard dog.

Andino corrected his inner thoughts as he headed for the entryway—Snaps *was* a good guard dog, and he was the best protection Andino had considering no one ever saw Snaps coming for their throat until it was too late.

But inside his house?

Snaps just wanted to be a dog.

Usually.

Andino didn't even bother to check the window behind the sheer curtains to see who was waiting outside on the front step before he yanked open the door—probably a mistake, all things considered. He might have appreciated the extra two or three seconds to prepare himself for the tornado standing there with blazing blue eyes, and blonde hair streaked with purple and teal.

Andino hadn't lied the night before.

This woman looked *good.*

Damn good.

Skinny jeans that molded to her legs. A trench coat tied tight at her middle to show off that trim, sexy waist of hers. Suede boots with a couple of inches on the heels to add to those long legs she had going on. Her face was mostly clear of makeup, and she'd thrown her hair up into a messy bun. Yet, it all looked effortless, and beautiful.

Christ, yeah, she looked good.

"Was there some point to that last night?" Haven asked the second Andino opened the door. "Were you just trying to *prove* something—was that it?"

He glanced up at her face—entirely unashamed that she probably watched him check her out—to find she was glaring at him. "I'm sorry?"

"Don't *act* like you don't know, Andino."

"I don't know—"

Haven's hand came up to land against Andino's chest, and then she pushed hard enough to make him take a wide step back inside his house. She was quick to follow behind, and slam the door closed. Once they were inside, she rounded on him again with those blazing eyes intent on burning him to the ground right where he stood.

Fuck.

She looked better when she was pissed off.

He should get her that way more often.

Snaps came around the corner, and down the hall with his tail wagging damn near to the second he heard Haven's voice echoing in the house. Had it been *anyone else* who raised their voice and put their hand on Andino, that dog would have ripped them to shreds.

But this was Haven.

Snaps never even growled at her before.

From the jump, too.

Like the dog just ... knew.

This woman was something—something amazing, and something important to Andino. They just hadn't figured out the details yet.

"Hey, buddy," Haven greeted the dog, running her hand over the top of his head.

"He misses you," Andino said.

Haven's gaze narrowed as it landed on him again. "Oh, does he?"

Ouch.

Yeah, he heard the heat there.

"I miss you, too," Andino admitted.

Haven's posture didn't soften even a little bit. "Why did you show up at my club last night, and then just disappear after like I wouldn't have questions for you?"

"Figured I pushed my luck enough just by being there, actually."

"That so?"

Andino shrugged. "Yeah, and probably your good graces, too."

Haven's lips flattened into a grim line. "You didn't think that after two months of no contact, that should have been a clue for you that there was nothing ..." She waved a hand between the two of them, adding, "Here."

"A lack of contact doesn't equal *nothing*, Haven. All that means was that you got stuck in your feelings about something you didn't know how to handle, so instead of doing something about it, you chose to do nothing. Well, here we are, and I decided to do something."

She stood a little straighter.

Andino cocked a brow at the challenge he saw reflecting back in her eyes. She was going to deny it, and tell him he didn't know what he was talking about. He could see it coming before she even let the words slip out of her mouth. Still, he gave her the benefit of being able to say it.

And then he tore that apart, too.

"There is *nothing*, Andino," Haven snapped.

He stepped forward—close enough to her that the suede of her trench coat brushed against his bare arms. Those pretty, blazing eyes of hers were all he could see. That, and the camber of her frown. He hated when she frowned.

"Then why were you so pissed off when I wasn't there at the end of the night, Haven?"

"I wasn't—"

"Weren't you?"

Haven snapped her mouth closed, and her gaze darted down to stare at Snaps who was now looking up at them. Deflection, he knew. She didn't want to look at him because he would find her lies there. This was just easier—easier for her to do if she didn't have to look at him while she lied to herself.

Andino inched closer still. "That doesn't sound like *nothing* to me."

"You need to—"

"What, stop? Back up? Give you space? You've had two fucking months, woman. It's time to figure it out."

Haven's head snapped up again, and her gaze practically nailed him to the wall. "That's the thing, isn't it? I can't figure any of this out because you didn't give me the benefit of at least *telling* me first, so I wouldn't have to find out what you did, and who you are."

Andino grinned. "And what am I?"

"A drug—"

"Wrong," Andino said. "Well, kind of. That's one of many things, and it falls under an entirely different category."

"Stop interrupting me."

He waved a hand. "By all means."

"And don't be snarky, either."

"You're making this less fun by the second, Haven."

"I just ..." Haven squeezed her eyes shut, and let out a hard sigh. "I don't even know."

"Yeah, I got that."

"*Stop, Andino.*"

He chuckled. "No, I mean ... I get not knowing, or being messed up over shit that isn't clear between us. Listen, my fucking life is crazy right now. This—whatever this is with us—is complicated for more reasons than you even know. That doesn't mean I don't want to figure it out, you know?"

Because he did.

God, he *did.*

Haven didn't reply, and she looked away again. Andino couldn't have that. He wanted her looking at him—only at him. At least, when she was doing that, he knew what to expect. He could prepare for her next move, and work accordingly.

All he wanted was to keep this woman.

For now, anyway.

"Haven," he murmured.

She still didn't move.

Didn't look at him.

"*Haven.*"

No, even that time didn't do it.

Andino's patience for keeping his distance—as little as there was between them—was gone entirely. He closed that last bit of space, slipped his hands up under Haven's chin, and dragged her to his body to fit her form tightly against his. A shaky breath left her lips as he tipped her head back, took a single second to stare down into her eyes, and then he was kissing her.

A hard, bruising kiss.

The world disappeared.

It was just him and her.

She responded back instantly—those lips of hers moving against his in a rhythm they both knew all too well between one another now. She wasted no time fisting her hands into his T-shirt, and holding tight to keep him close. Those lips of hers parted, giving him access to the heaven that was her mouth, and Andino took it.

God.

He took it.

There was something about her mouth that drove him *crazy.* Something about the way she let him devour and conquer her with every single kiss, and yet, never actually gave up the fight to dominate. There was something in the way her tongue danced with his that spoke more truths about them and whatever this was than she ever did.

And he didn't mind.

Not a bit.

Her kiss held secrets.

It hid truths.

Her kiss woke him up.

He *needed* it.

"Fuck," Andino groaned, threading his fingers through Haven's messy bun to let her hair down. "I missed doing that."

Her tongue peeked out to sweep her bottom lip, and she watched him through thick lashes. "Did you?"

"Too much, maybe."

"Then, maybe you should do it again."

"I fucking plan to—" It was Snaps nudging Andino in the back of his leg that reminded him—yeah, some*thing* else was there with them. "*Snaps, go to your bed.*"

Haven's eyes twinkled with mirth even as she pressed her lips to keep from laughing even as the poor dog whined, but did as he was told, anyway. Andino waited until Snaps paws could be heard climbing the stairs before he turned back to Haven.

"Where was I again?"

She grinned. "Kissing me."

"Yeah, kissing you."

"You should do it—*now*."

Andino was still staring at her mouth, and barely holding himself back from doing just that. "As long as you'll stay when I'm done."

Haven's gaze jumped to his. "Stay."

"I'll even cook for you—that's what I was doing before you came. Cooking."

"You cook?"

"Quite well," he murmured.

Haven nodded. "Okay, I'll stay after, and you'll cook for me."

That was all he needed to hear.

Andino closed the distance between them by kissing her harder than before. The force of his action sent Haven moving backwards until her back hit the door. She pressed against the glass as he devoured her mouth, and thrusted his hands into her now-loose hair. Where had the hair tie fallen that she'd used to keep it up? He didn't even *know*.

All Andino cared to think about was her.

Her, and the way she pressed her lower half into his groin.

Her, and the smell of her skin.

Her, and that sweet little gasp she made when he sucked on her neck.

Her, her, her.

It was all about her.

Only a little about him.

Haven's breathless laugh lit up the hallway as Andino yanked that trench coat of hers open, and tugged it down her arms roughly. "You're so fucking *impatient*."

He pulled back to stare at her.

She was all pink skin, and heaving shoulders.

Beautiful, really.

"Do you want me to go *slow*?" he growled.

Haven was quick to snap her mouth shut. "Nope."

"Didn't think so."

Andino's mouth was back on hers in a blink—tasting her and fighting with her. That's kind of what kissing Haven felt like to him. As though he were warring and loving all at the same time. A dichotomy if there ever was one, but it was one he enjoyed *greatly*.

Her fingernails dragged stinging lines down his railroad path of abs when her hand snaked under his T-shirt. *Fuck*. She was not playing around tonight.

He liked that.

"Jesus," he grunted against her lips.

Haven smiled in that sexy way of hers. "Pretty sure that's not my name, Andino."

"No, but I am a praying kind of man."

Even if God didn't answer.

Haven was the one to kiss him that time—things moved a hell of a lot faster at that point because Andino couldn't wait any fucking longer. He'd been without this woman for two months. Two months too goddamn long, and he didn't want to hold off for one more second before burying his cock as deep as he could into her cunt.

Andino kept Haven locked in their kiss even as he pulled her away from the door. Her talented fingers worked at the buttons and zipper on his pants while he yanked and pulled on hers. They only broke apart long enough to shed the clothing between them, but his mouth was on hers again before he even fell back to the couch.

Haven climbed on him without hesitation—straddling his thighs and swaying her body over top of him in the most mesmerizing way. She ran her fingers through her loose waves of hair, and stared down at him with that knowing grin firmly in place.

"You want me to ride you?" she asked.

"For now. Later, we'll see what flat surface I can bend you over, and how loud I can make you scream."

Haven winked, and her fingers circled around his already hard-as-steel dick. Just the pressure of her hand tightening on his cock was enough to make Andino grunt under his breath, and flex his hips upward to get more of that friction on his length. His hands landed on her hips, and his fingertips pressed hard enough to leave bruises behind.

"Easy there," she whispered.

"You don't like *easy*."

Haven laughed. "I really don't."

She stroked his cock once more, and then she was lifting just high enough so that she could rub the head of him along her slit. She gave him no warning before she dropped down on his length—no second to adjust before he was balls-deep into her, and entirely out of fucking breath.

Like a punch to his chest.

A kick to his gut.

He was in her—covered and wrapped with her—and the world tilted sideways once more. But fuck him because he liked this way better.

"Oh, God," Haven whined, circling her hips while staying firmly seated on him. "Right *there*, yeah."

Andino let her have her moment—he let her tease, and play, and feel. After all, he liked the sight of it just fine, and there was something addictive about watching Haven move when she was on top of him. From the way she flicked her hair back, to the tilt of her head. Even how she watched him was something sinful to be appreciated. He memorized the curves of her body as she moved, and the way her shapely ass fit into the palms of his hands when he grabbed and squeezed her backside.

All of her was perfect.

From her wet cunt.

To her trembling lips.

All. Of. Her.

Andino let go of Haven's ass and tangled his hand into her hair. Tugging just enough to get her attention all on him again, he murmured, "Enough playing. Time to *fuck*."

A smooth, slow smile spread over her lips.

"Can't say no to that, can I?"

Andino barely had to do a thing except keep his hands on Haven, and watch her move. She kept herself steady on him with one hand on his throat, and another planted firmly on his chest. Those fingernails of hers dug in deep, and kept his nerves awake with the sting of pain while she rode him hard and fast.

Wild.

Raw.

And oh, so good.

And when he couldn't take it anymore—when he was lost in the sounds of her noises and the way she looked and how she felt around him—he yanked her down for a kiss that shattered his mind.

Yeah, he'd definitely missed this.

• • •

Andino laughed at the sight of Haven tossing Snaps' latest teddy bear high into the air. She practically squealed, and she *might* have jumped up and down on the spot, when Snaps darted across the kitchen, spun sideways, and did a back flip to catch the teddy bear in his mouth.

"*Did you see that?*"

Andino nodded. "I taught him that."

"What else can he do?"

"Pretty much anything—as long as it doesn't require thumbs. He likes to learn, and he enjoys pleasing people."

Also biting people when he doesn't like them.

Andino didn't add that little fact out loud. He didn't think Haven would appreciate it, really. She liked Snaps. No need to go scaring her, too.

Haven smiled. "Does he bring in the newspaper, too?"

"No, he ruins those."

Haven cocked a brow. "Really?"

"Newspapers hinder his walking time. You know, because then I'm sitting, and not walking him."

At that statement, Andino gave his dog a look from the side. Snaps simply stared back with his purple teddy bear that Andino had picked up from a street vendor hanging from his mouth by a skinny arm. The dog regularly went through toys like it was going out of style. Nothing was safe from the wrath that was Snaps when he wanted to ruin something. Even those indestructible dog toys—those were fucking child's play to Snaps, frankly.

Snaps dropped the teddy bear to the floor, and let out one loud bark. Andino gave him another one of his looks, saying, "We know you want to play."

The dog just barked again.

And then again.

Andino quickly figured out Snaps wasn't trying to get someone to play—he was alerting him to someone coming in the house, but Andino's attention was otherwise distracted what with Haven being there and all.

"Andi?"

Shit.

At the sound of a woman's voice calling his name, Haven's gaze narrowed in on him instantly. Andino was stuck between cursing the heavens, and wanting to laugh because of how pissed off Haven looked in that moment.

"Relax," he told her, slipping around the island, "it's my mother."

Haven softened her posture. "Oh. Kim, right?"

"Kim, yep."

"Andino?"

He could have tried to get his mother out of the house before she even knew Haven was there—no doubt, she was going to go back to his father, let Giovanni know there was a woman at their son's home, and then his dad would take that info to Dante. It was only going to take his mother *describing* Haven—she didn't exactly blend in—and they were going to know exactly who his mother had found at his place.

Sure, he *could* have tried to stop that from happening.

What was the point?

"In the kitchen, Ma," Andino called back.

Haven gave him a look he couldn't decipher as she slid around the island to stand next to him, and help build the fajitas he'd been working on. He didn't even get the chance to ask Haven about her look, or what it meant, because his mother walked into the kitchen a second later.

And promptly froze right where she stood.

"Oh … hello," his mother said quietly.

Andino smiled at the way confusion lit up his mother's tone. He didn't miss the way she checked Haven out—like all good Italian mothers would do when they caught a woman with their son. Kim was soft-hearted, and sweet-natured, sure, but when it came to her son? Her *only* son? This woman turned into someone else entirely.

"Hey, Ma. I didn't know you were coming over tonight."

She usually called.

Kim laughed nervously, and waved a hand. "I was in the neighborhood. That's not important—who is this?"

"I'm Haven," the woman next to him said, smiling softly.

"Haven," Kim echoed. "Pretty name."

"Thank you."

"Not Italian, though."

The look his mother gave him spoke a thousand words without her even needing to say a thing. Andino was quick to drop her stare and go back to work on finishing his meal, so he could finally fucking eat.

"Definitely not Italian," Haven replied, although some of the softness was drifting from her tone. "Born and raised in Brooklyn, though."

Kim nodded, but her attention was still on Andino. "You didn't mention seeing anyone to me."

"Because I didn't feel the need to, Ma."

"Didn't feel the—"

"No," Andino interjected, glancing at his mother. "It wouldn't matter if I did, right?"

He felt Haven's eyes turn on him, but it was the buzzing of her phone on the counter that stopped anyone from saying anything else.

Shitty luck, maybe.

Or *karma* stepping in.

Who fucking knew?

"Sorry," Haven said, grabbing the phone. She did a quick check of whatever was rolling across the screen, and then frowned before setting it down. Her attention was back on Andino, then, and he gave her a small smile—one he hoped was supportive, but he could see there were questions in her eyes. More things for him to have to answer at a later date, likely. "Problem at the club—I have to go."

"You'll be back, won't you?"

She shrugged. "Maybe. I guess I owe Snaps a treat, too."

Andino nodded. "Yes, for *Snaps*."

She winked, and then gave him a quick kiss on the underside of his jaw before moving around the island. As she passed his mother by, Haven was quick to say, "It was very nice to meet you, Kim. Andino only has wonderful things to say about you."

His mother smiled faintly. "That's a shame, sweetheart."

Haven's brow furrowed. "I'm sorry?"

"It's a shame that he tells you wonderful things about me, but he's never said a word to me about you."

"*Ma*," Andino snapped.

It was too late.

The words were out there.

Haven gave Kim a tight nod, and a look over her shoulder to him that burned, and then she was gone. Andino stopped working on his food, and placed his hands to the edge of the counter until he heard the front door close.

Only then did he ask, "What the *hell*, Ma?"

That hadn't been like Kim at all.

Kim glanced over her shoulder to where Haven had gone as she said, "I actually meant to say it was a shame, Andino. She seems lovely. Not appropriate—as your father and uncles will tell you—for a boss, but still quite *lovely*. Why didn't you tell me you were seeing someone?"

"You just answered your own fucking question."

"Language." Kim sighed, and brought her gaze back to him. "Because of *la famiglia*, then?"

"She's not Italian. Not Catholic. She's not … reputable, or respectable by *their* standards. She's great, but she's not—"

"What they would want," his mother interjected. "Do they know?"

"They did before for a hot minute."

"Not now?"

Andino shook his head. "No."

"You have to tell them."

"It's none of their fucking business, Ma."

Kim's lips flattened into a grim line—not a frown, but most definitely not a smile, either. "It is their business. It is the family's business. That's how it works for the boss, Andino."

"Yeah, I know."

And he did.

He wouldn't blame his mother, either, when she told his father about the woman she found at their son's home. She, like his father, loved him. They also loved their family—that meant protecting it, no matter what.

A newcomer?

An *outsider?*

The unknown?

All of which, Haven most definitely was ... those were dangerous things to people like them. So no, he wouldn't blame his mother at all.

FOURTEEN

"Are you going to be busy later, or are you closing tonight?"

Haven chewed on her inner cheek to consider her answer instead of speaking right away. "Maybe, but I don't know. You know how things come up at this damn club."

Andino's dark chuckles echoed over the phone. "Yeah, I know."

"Where are you going to be?"

"The restaurant for most of the evening."

"What time are you leaving there?"

"Likely midnight," he replied.

Which meant, he had a lot of work going on. Andino never *said* that was the case, other than alluding to it, but he only stayed late at the restaurant when he had work to do.

"And about the other day," he added.

"What do you mean?"

"A few days ago—when my mother showed up at my place."

Haven frowned.

Yeah, *that*.

How could she forget that?

"What about it?"

Andino cleared his throat. "I apologize for what she said right before you left. I know it made you uncomfortable, but I also don't think she meant it the way it come out. That's not my mom to be purposefully mean, or to hurt someone else. She's not like that. I think she was genuinely caught off guard just because—"

"You've literally never told her about me."

"Kind of, yeah."

And that's what bothered Haven the most.

Hurt the most, really.

Maybe she shouldn't have automatically expected Andino to open his mouth, and spill the fact he had been seeing Haven to his family. She didn't know his people, or the dynamics of their family, for that matter. And they were only *just* starting back into this thing together after taking that break away from one another.

A break *she* chose.

Haven had to keep reminding herself of that fact.

"I don't expect them to *know*," she said quietly. "But I just … I guess it took me off guard, too. Not once in the entire time we were seeing each other, you didn't think to mention me to any of them? I mean, we never visited anyone, and you didn't bring me around but ... I don't know."

"I wanted to," he said.

"Then why didn't you?"

"Maybe I don't share well when it comes to things that are mine," Andino muttered. "Who knows?"

Haven rolled her eyes. "That's not a good answer."

"I know." Andino sighed, and said, "Listen, I have a guy coming in for a meeting in five minutes—we'll finish this later, yeah?"

"If I can get out of here early enough."

"All right, baby. Bye."

"Bye, Andino."

Haven hung up the phone, and although she was smiling, there was still a heaviness settling deeper into her heart. It had been growing heavier by the day, and started right about the time when she left Andino's home.

She didn't know how to shake it.

Didn't know if she *could*.

"You're messing around with the Marcello again?"

Haven glanced up at the voice coming from her doorway. There, Jackson leaned in with a curious expression, and guarded eyes. She had the strangest urge to snap at him for—*yet again*—listening in on one of her private conversations. Really, she just figured she needed to remember to close her fucking door. Unless the idiot just pressed his ear against the wood, or something.

Who knew?

"I thought that was over a while back?" Jackson asked, folding his arms over his chest.

"Remind me again," Haven said, "when my personal life became any of your business. Or anyone else's business in this club, for that matter. Don't *I* sign your paychecks, not the other way around? Not sure that entitles you to know anything about me, actually."

Jackson put his hands up in surrender, and took a step back. "Ouch, Haven. I'm just looking out for you, that's all. This isn't me trying to get closer to you in that kind of way."

Probably not.

He *had* been good ever since that day *months* ago when she told him plain and simple that no, he was not her type. And no, that was not going to change. He'd been respectful and appropriate from that point forward—Haven had to give him credit there.

Not much else.

"You don't need to look after me," she said, standing from her desk. "But thank you for caring. I am a big girl, though. I can handle myself."

"Just didn't take you for the type, I guess."

Haven's gaze narrowed on her club manager. "*What* type?"

"I mean," Jackson said, shrugging, "every woman likes a bad boy, right? That's kind of par for the course—but *Marcello* bad?" He made a noise under his breath, adding, "That's a whole different ball game. Just didn't take you to be the type to date a mobster, that's all."

She stiffened all over.

It was not the first time someone used that title alongside Andino's name, or even his surname. It was like those who knew the family or knew enough about them to talk didn't have a problem with labeling them as *mobsters, mafia,* or something similar.

Haven had heard the whispers.

She knew the rumors.

She'd never listened.

Until right now.

"Is that what it is—the mob?" she asked.

Jackson cocked a brow. "You don't *know*?"

"I didn't ask a question to get a question, Jackson."

"Relax, woman. I just meant … yeah, that's what it is. Kind of widely known, especially where they do business. You know that bookie that comes in three or four nights a—"

"The illegal bookie. Nathaniel. Yeah, I know he works for Andino."

Jackson nodded. "You're right—*kind of.* I only know a little because Nate is my friend, and you know, when he's drunk, he talks a bit. Andino is more like his umbrella. Protection, if you will. Working under Andino and his crew gives Nate a bit of leg room, and respect. He doesn't have to worry about someone coming after him in his business because he's got a mafia capo watching his back, and lending him credence in his work. You get what I mean? All he has to do is *use* Andino's name, and people know, Haven. That's the kind of family you're messing with."

She heard a lot of things.

Only a couple felt important.

Mafia.

Capo.

They felt important because mostly, she didn't know what they meant. Oh, sure, she got the mafia—she understood that well enough just from being alive. Hadn't everyone heard the mafia mentioned at least once in their lifetime?

She didn't think this was the same.

And she should probably know …

Haven wasn't stupid. There were some people who believed the mafia to be dead, especially in New York where it had once been a hub for organized crime. She didn't think it was dead, but maybe over the years, the mafia had simply quieted in its business to keep from getting negative attention.

After all, how could a criminal empire continue to thrive when the police were constantly hounding at its doors?

It didn't make sense.

Then again, very little about Andino made sense to Haven at times. Especially the way he kept her in the dark, or so it seemed. She was ready to turn the lights on. She didn't want to be in the dark anymore.

"Close my door, please," Haven said. "I'll be out in twenty to start the pre-meetings before opening."

Jackson gave her a two-finger salute. "You got it, boss."

The second her office door clicked shut, Haven sat back down at her desk, and reached for the laptop she had shoved to the corner. Pulling it closer, she opened it up, and brought up a search browser.

Surely, if *that's* who Andino—and his family—were, then wouldn't she find something? If she actually looked, wouldn't she find *something*?

Haven decided to look.

• • •

Haven wiped down the bottles she'd pulled from the shelves, and watched the two men at the end of the bar chat away quietly. They looked unassuming, for the most part. They could pass for any well-dressed New Yorkers in their three-piece suits. Minus the Rolex watches on their wrists. Oh, and the very expensive Italian leather loafers she had gotten a peek of when she moved around the bar to help one of the servers when needed.

All it took was someone staring at the two for longer than a few seconds to see the similarities between them—the same jaw shapes, mouths, and eyes.

Green eyes.

God, she knew that green.

Andino had those same eyes.

And the one man?

Even if Haven hadn't spent a good two hours of her afternoon dropping down the rabbit hole that was the internet to search the New York mob, she would have recognized something familiar in the one man.

Maybe the dimple in his cheek when he smiled—just like Andino—or the cleft in his chin. It could have been his size with those wide, expansive shoulders, or the way he grinned that brought on a sense of déjà vu for her.

Who knows what might have done it?

She wouldn't have needed to know his name—she *did* but only because she had found his picture on one of the many sites she scoured for information—to know the one man just had to be Andino's father. They looked like father and son, although the man sitting at her bar had a bit of salt peppering his dark hair.

The men thought they were being sly.

They thought she didn't notice them.

Not once had she engaged either of the two other than to call a server down to fill their drinks when they first arrived an hour ago. She hadn't even bothered to go down and engage them for that, either.

What would be the point?

"Quite a place," she heard the one man say.

Dante, she now knew.

According to what she had found, he would be Andino's uncle … and the boss of the family. Or … organization. Depending on where you looked, someone called the Marcellos something different. It varied.

"I like it," Giovanni—Andino's father—said. "Reminds me of that club my mentor used to run—remember that?"

Dante laughed, and nodded. "I do, actually. *That* was quite a place."

Haven wondered … did these men *know* that their entire lives were on display in the recesses of the internet? That with the right keywords, and a deep enough search, there were forums dedicated to these men, and the organization they were running in New York. Did they know that even their wives had been profiled—their *children*?

Oh, sure, a lot of it was speculation—some of it was pulled from public record when a Marcello associate was taken into custody, or whatever else. But a lot of it was just people *watching* them, and keeping track because who else was doing it?

No one, apparently.

Andino's family was a whole empire—a criminal *empire*—and yet, from the surface, they looked like law-abiding, God-fearing, charity-donating people.

They looked like *good* people.

"All right, enough of this, I suppose," she heard Dante say.

"Just … she doesn't know, Dante."

"Shouldn't she, then?"

Oh, good.

Now they were talking about her.

Haven wasn't the type to shy away, and she'd long since figured out what these two men were doing in her business, and exactly why they had come. Her research—if one could even call it that—had allowed her another realization as she looked over every mob wife profiled that stood next to these men.

Common things bonded them together.

Lineage.

Ethnicity.

Standing.

Respect.

Religion.

More.

Things that Haven wasn't—not Italian, Catholic, or affiliated to their life and business. She was nothing that these men's wives were. Not in the slightest. And maybe things were starting to add up.

Haven moved down the bar, grabbing two beers—one for Dante, and one for Andino's father. She figured they had come in here to scope her out because of her involvement with Andino.

And if they wanted a conversation … well, she could give them one. On her terms.

Both men glanced her way as Haven popped the tops off the beers, and slid them across the bar. Dante didn't touch his—Giovanni was quick to reach for the bottle, and tip it in her direction with a kind smile.

"*Grazie,* Haven," Andino's father said.

"Thanks for using my name, I guess."

The man smirked.

Dante beside him, however, kept his face passive and unreadable. "You act like you know us."

She shrugged. "He used my name—you act like you know me."

"That could be explained—"

"Except let's cut the shit, and get down to what you came here for, Dante Marcello."

The man stiffened on the stool even as his brother beside him grinned, and stared down into his bottle of beer.

"I suppose I can see why my nephew took an interest in you, Haven Murphy. You certainly don't seem like the … average woman."

"Neither does your wife," Haven returned. "Suspected Queen Pin that built her business from the ground up starting in Italy, right?"

If her question surprised Dante, he didn't show it. In fact, he didn't even blink.

She turned on Giovanni with a pointed finger, saying, "And your wife …"

"Kim," Giovanni said. "Don't call her Kimberlynn, she hates it. It's stuffy."

Haven nodded. "Kim, then. Vegas affiliated, right? That's where she came from."

"She did."

"Gio," Dante murmured.

"What, she knows anyway?"

"Yes, but *how.*"

The two men looked at her.

Haven smiled. "Do you know that some of the men in your family actually have *fan clubs* on the internet? There are forums dedicated to following you, and tracking your life. Your daughter's birth, Dante, was announced in a dark web forum before even the New York Times announced it in the paper."

That made them blink.

Haven laughed.

"But don't get a fucking complex over the whole fan club thing," Haven said, "because as I have come to learn, you are just one family—one *organization*—of many. And those who follow you seem to know it, too."

"We did know about the forums," Giovanni said after a second or two had passed. "They're harmless, and a lot of what they post is harmless."

"Fascinating," Haven deadpanned. "What do you want to know about me?"

Dante smiled—slow and cold. "Nothing, sweetheart."

Her gaze cut to him. "I beg your pardon? You clearly came here because you wanted something from me, likely because you know I'm involved with Andino. I take it that's a problem for a few reasons, and none that I care to get in to at the moment. So, please don't treat me like I'm stupid, or—"

"Haven Murphy," Dante murmured. "Twenty-six, born on September eighth born to Neil and Mae Murphy. Do you want the time of your birth, too?"

Haven blinked. "Four in the morning."

"Four-oh-two, actually."

"My parents always just told me four."

Dante shrugged. "That's what the records say. They also tell me you were quite a student—top of your class, and accepted into every university you applied to. I know you took over this business here two years ago for your father when your mother's health failed. I know you took out a loan to pay off his debts, but never told him. Was that why you turned it into a strip club—for the money?"

"Sex sells," Haven replied, trying to keep her tone level.

"It does." Dante sighed, and folded his arms over his chest. "I also know their street address and zip code in Florida—I know the name of the doctor your mother goes to see every six months to make sure her cancer hasn't come back. I know the name of the kindergarten teacher who sings Maria's ABC's to her every day. So, no, *donna*, there is very little I don't know about you, and there is nothing you can tell me that I want to know, anyway."

Giovanni cleared his throat beside Dante.

Haven, however, never broke her gaze. "How long have I been seeing Andino?"

Dante chuckled. "Are you testing me? Since August. It's January now. You do the math."

"I don't need to. Did you come here to say something to me, then? If so, do it and get the fuck out."

Dante glanced at Giovanni. "She is interesting, though."

Giovanni ignored his brother, and gave his attention to Haven. "My apologies. We meant no harm; we were just—"

"Curious?" she asked.

"Our family is … well, you know, don't you?"

"Not because he told me, though."

Christ.

She couldn't hide the heat in her voice even if she tried. And she had been doing so damn well at seeming calm and in control, too.

Damn.

Giovanni nodded. "I see."

"Andino is part of a legacy that I don't expect you to understand," Dante said, standing from the stool and fixing his jacket. "He may think he can do whatever he pleases as long as the rest of us are unaware as to his activities, but that isn't the case. It *was* nice to meet you, Haven. You likely won't see me again."

"I can't say that would be a bad thing," she returned. "And I won't apologize for letting you know it, either."

Dante smiled, and then he just … walked away.

Just like that.

Giovanni was quick to stand from his stool, too, but he didn't immediately leave. "I *am* sorry for this. My wife mentioned seeing you at our son's home, and I passed the message along. I didn't think this would cause any trouble."

Haven arched a brow. "Do I look troubled to you?"

"You look pissed, actually. Sad, too."

"One is for your show here with your brother. The other one isn't. Don't worry about me. I get along just fine. As I am sure you know considering how much you already know about me."

Giovanni glanced away. "Can I assume, based on the what you said about Andino keeping his business and this family private from you, that you're not aware of the duty and responsibility my son is facing?"

No, she didn't have a clue.

"That would be a fair assumption," Haven replied, not unkindly.

"You should ask him, then," he told her. "And when you do, let him know that his father said the things we find worth keeping are rarely easy. That doesn't mean he should bend to the same expectations every other man has for this—he is not every other man."

Haven blinked. "I don't—"

"Understand, yeah, I know. *You* don't have to. He does."

• • •

"I'm sorry."

It was the first thing Andino said as he joined Haven on a park bench just a few steps away from where they had randomly encountered each other the first time all those many months ago. He spoke his apology softly—with genuine remorse—even as he handed over a vanilla latte. Her favorite kind; he just remembered.

"Is that apology an *in general* kind of thing, or are you apologizing for something specific?" Haven asked.

Andino sighed, and rested back on the bench to watch Snaps sniff the walkway. "Both, I guess. I have a lot to apologize for, and something happened yesterday that needs its own apology. Which do you want to start with?"

"Everything," she said.

"All right."

"And nothing at all," she added.

Andino chuckled. "Yeah, I know that feeling. I have to say, though, had that been me yesterday and people cornered me, I would not have been as calm as you were when you called me afterward."

Haven shrugged. "You didn't know they were going to do it, so."

"Knowing *when* they would do it is a no on my end. Knowing that at some eventual point, what happened was likely—yeah, I probably should have known that."

"You didn't think to warn me?"

"If I warned you, then I would have needed to tell you the rest, too."

Yes, speaking of that …

Haven glanced over at him. "I changed my mind. I don't want an apology yet—start with the other stuff."

Andino smirked. "Should have expected that, huh?"

"What else did you expect?"

"I don't know, Haven."

"Why didn't you tell me the truth?" she asked. "About … your family, and the rest, I mean. Didn't you think I deserved to know who I was sleeping with—that you come from a *long* line of criminals?"

"Is that all you see me—or even them—as? Just a criminal?"

Haven glanced down at her clenched hands resting around the latte in her lap. "You know I don't."

How could she?

153

She was well aware that there was far more to Andino than his last name, and the legacy his family carried with them. She knew that part of him far better than she knew the man who was apparently a mafia capo.

Andino's gaze drifted to Snaps again, but he didn't stay quiet for long. "You don't know this, but you came into my life at a point when everything around me had just been entirely upended. The future *I* wanted was no longer mine—a different path was chosen for me. So, maybe when I was with you, I didn't need to worry about being a Marcello, or all the changes happening in my life. I only had to worry about you and me, and this thing we were doing. You didn't know about the rest."

"And you liked that."

"You could say that, yeah."

"You liked me being naive to—"

"You're anything but naive, Haven."

"To *you*, I was."

Andino shook his head. "You knew something was up, regardless of what you want to say right now. You knew, but you chose to ignore it, or excuse it. That was your choice, and I don't have anything to say about it either way."

Fuck him.

Fuck him for being right.

"Will you tell me what you mean—about the future thing?" she asked.

She swore Andino clenched his jaw so hard that she heard his teeth crunch. And yet, he never changed from his aloof, calm demeanor, and he didn't look away from his wandering dog. Not that Snaps was going to go anywhere. The dog never misbehaved. She figured that was probably just easier for Andino.

"What did you learn?" he asked instead of answering. "About my family, I mean."

"What you are—who *they* are."

"Dante?" he asked.

"Your uncle."

Andino nodded. "Him, yep."

"He heads the organization, doesn't he?"

"The family, Cosa Nostra … who calls it what depends on who you ask, but yes. He's the boss."

"Okay," Haven said, confused at where he was going with this.

Andino cleared his throat, saying quieter, "He's ready to retire—most bosses don't even live to his age, let alone keep their seat for as long as he has in this business. Our family, though …" He trailed off with a dark laugh. "Our family reigns strong. Call it fucking luck, or say it like it is, in that we've got the stronghold. We're the force to be reckoned with in this city. We *control* everything. But all bosses step down, and someone else has to step up, you know. That's what I mean."

Haven stiffened. "*You?*"

"Me, yeah."

"You."

Her voice was an echo that time.

Andino smiled over at her. "That's how I felt, too. A little angrier at first. Mostly because nothing is ever easy in this life—every choice I make has to reflect the family and business in a good way. There are rules and customs we follow, so what I was expecting for my life was suddenly entirely different."

"Oh."

"You're one of those things," he added.

"I'm sorry?"

"Men in my position have a few expectations we need to meet before we can be considered ... unchallenged in our place," Andino murmured. "One of those things is to be married to an appropriate, respectable woman. Italian; Catholic; preferably affiliated in some way, although that's not always a requirement. It's a long-standing tradition."

"Marriage?"

Her voice was fainter than she wanted it to be.

Unsure, and wary.

Confused, more than anything.

"We're not ... getting married," Haven said. "I don't understand why that even matters."

"To my family, involvement with a woman that goes beyond a single event, is cause for someone to look into the relationship," Andino explained. "And this is my fault—what happened yesterday evening, I mean. That was my fault because while *you* don't understand, I do. I know you didn't ask for this by getting involved with me, Haven."

"I just ..."

"What?"

"I wish you would have told me," she whispered.

"I'm a selfish fucker, I guess. I always look out for everybody else first, and myself second. I started looking out for me a little bit, and here we are."

"So, I'm not, then."

"Hmm?" Andino looked over at her, and those green eyes of his pinned her in place. Intense, dark, stormy. His gaze was all of those things and more. "I don't follow."

"Not appropriate, or respectable for you. That's why they're concerned. I would challenge your ... standing, right?"

"That doesn't matter."

"They seem to think it does. So much so, that they cornered me at my place of business. So much so, Andino, that your uncle pulled any and all information he could about me and my life. Some of it, I didn't even know. And your father—"

"What about my dad?"

"He wasn't so bad, actually," Haven admitted. "He apologized, and was kind."

Andino smiled. "My dad is … pretty easy-going. And he probably relates to being the black sheep, considering all the shit he pulled when he was my age. Not that it matters now, I guess."

"He said something to me."

"What was that?"

"Well," Haven said, "he told me to tell you something."

Andino arched a brow, silently waiting.

"He said to tell you that the things you find that are worth keeping are rarely easy. That, you're you, and not every other man, so you shouldn't bend to them. Or … something like that. Please apologize to him for me being snappy; he was kind."

Andino was quiet for a long while.

Haven let the silence fill the space between them.

It only felt like it was growing.

She had a lot to think about now.

"I should go," Haven whispered.

Andino sighed, but before she could even get up from the bench, he'd reached over, grabbed her face in his hands, and pulled her in for a burning kiss that scorched her alive. And *God*, did his kiss make her feel so fucking alive.

Why did it have to feel like that?

Why couldn't this be easy?

By the time Andino finally pulled away from the kiss, Haven's lungs ached and her lips tingled. He still kept her close enough that his lips brushed against hers as he spoke.

"I am sorry," he murmured.

Haven nodded. "I know—I just need some time to figure some things out."

"As long as you come back."

"Should I?"

"I want you to."

Weren't they doomed, though? Wasn't that what she knew, now? Nothing was ever going to come from the two of them being together—he was who he was, and he couldn't change it. She didn't think he wanted to. He was so unapologetic about being what and who he was that she didn't even consider the idea that he might not want to be this person.

And even if she didn't know *this* part of him well, it was still a part of who he was. So, didn't she know him either way?

Didn't she know the parts that mattered?

It didn't change what she also knew.

It didn't change what they were because of it, either.

Entirely, utterly *doomed*.

"Come back," he said again. "Take your time, figure it out, and then come back."

She didn't know how to say no to him. Not when he looked at her like he was right then.

"I'll come back," she promised.

She simply didn't know what she would be coming back to. That was the part that scared her the most.

FIFTEEN

"Is Antony finally tired of you using his home and office as a meeting place, or what?" Andino asked when he strolled into his uncle's office.

He didn't miss the flash of warning in his uncle's eyes from where the man sat behind his large desk. "A bit early for him, that's all. Thank you for *finally* answering my calls and deciding to show up here to see me."

Andino shrugged. "You're welcome."

Dante scowled. "That wasn't meant to be my gratefulness, Andino."

"Yeah, I know."

And his response remained the same.

Dante glanced at his brothers who had each taken a seat on the couch against the far wall. Specifically, he looked to Andino's father. "Is there anything *you* want to say to your son before I get started here?"

Gio looked up from the watch on his wrist, and passed Andino a glance. To someone else, it may have seemed dismissive, but to Andino, he saw the struggle warring in his father's eyes. It probably had something to do with the words Gio had told Haven when they approached her at the club, but Andino couldn't know for sure.

"Not at the moment," his father settled on saying.

Dante nodded. "Fine."

Andino shoved his hands into his pockets, and rocked on his heels. "How about we just get right to the yelling portion of this meeting, and get it over with first?"

A dry, dark chuckle echoed from his uncle. "That's amusing. You have jokes today, Andi."

"Gotta keep the humor alive."

"And yet, I find absolutely nothing about this situation funny."

"That's a shame," Andino returned. "Humor helps me get through life."

"What's humorous about a man disobeying his boss, and forgetting his duties time and time again? Go on, *tell me*."

Ah, there it was.

That heat and anger.

That barely contained *fury*.

Dante was just spectacular at hiding it. That was, until he no longer wanted to hide it. Then, it came rushing out of the man like flaming lava ready to destroy anything in its path. It was kind of predictable in that way, really.

"You had no right to approach Haven—"

158

"Ah, wrong," Dante said, lifting a single finger in the air. "I had *every* right to do whatever I wanted to do as you can't seem to follow the simple directions I *give* you, Andino. You know what you were told about your personal affairs, and that woman specifically. Do not act like that was left for you to decide when it was not."

Andino tightened his jaw in an effort to keep his cool. "And I told you that you had your one choice about this whole boss business, and you made it already. The rest is up to me. You don't get a say."

"This is not the same."

"It is exactly the same."

"It's *not!*" Dante straightened a bit in his seat after his outburst, but his next words came out a hell of a lot calmer. Maybe that should have been a sign to Andino that he was seriously pushing his luck when it came to his uncle. But he figured—shit, he'd already gotten the man to this point, how much further could he push? "It is not the same and you know it. It's not the same because it is not just *me* who will decide if that woman is appropriate enough to stand alongside you, and represent *this* family. There is a Commission of men who make that decision, Andino. Bosses from organizations all over this continent who sit down at a table with you, and get a voice about what you seem to think is no one else's business. So, please, tell me how you're going to avoid that when none of us ever have."

Yes, that was a problem.

Andino wasn't stupid.

"*If* they object," Andino countered.

His uncle stilled. "Yes, if they object."

So, what if those who sat at the Commission *didn't* object?

That was the question.

Could that be possible?

It was a very faint hope dangling from a line in front of Andino, but still a hope nonetheless. And it was not one he was willing to let get away just because someone else might think it was an impossibility.

"But frankly, we have other problems," Dante muttered.

At that statement, the other two men in the room became visibly uncomfortable. Andino had missing something—he knew it right then and there.

He missed something *big*.

"What?" Andino asked.

Maybe a little too sharply.

Dante nodded, and pointed at Andino with a wagging finger. "See, that right there. *That* is a problem, Andi. This is an issue you should already know, and you have no fucking clue. I can see it in your face. You don't know anything about what I'm going to say—at least, not the things you should know."

"Stop fucking around with me."

"John."

Andino blinked. "What about my cousin?"

"And the Calabrese woman."

Oh, for fuck's sake.

"That again?" Andino asked. "She's just a woman—she's harmless."

"Do you know where John was last night?"

Andino's jaw worked to ease some of his tension, but it wasn't helping. As much as he wanted to lie and say, yes, he knew where his cousin was the evening before, Andino let the truth slip out. "No."

"Take a guess?"

"Somewhere you probably don't approve of, but shit, that's a lot of places, Dante."

"Andino," he heard his father warn from the side of the room.

The first time Gio had spoken up at all.

"Dinner," Dante said, ignoring Gio altogether. "He was at dinner with the Calabrese family."

"All of them?"

Because *damn*, John.

"Did you know John was still involved with Siena Calabrese?" his uncle asked.

Andino cleared his throat. "Not in a direct sense, but—"

"You knew."

"You could say that."

"How much do you know?"

Andino sighed, frustrated. "Only a bit."

Dante waved at him. "By all means, share what you know."

"I don't think—"

"I didn't ask for you to think. I asked for you to talk. And you're going to do that, Andi."

Jesus Christ.

"As far as I know," Andino said, "John started messing around with her again after he took over handling my business with the Calabrese. *You* wanted to lighten my work load, Dante, and that was one of the duties you moved to someone else. Point is—she works in their business, and that's how they met back up again."

"And you didn't think to tell us—although mind you, we don't actually need you to tell us anything, Andino. It's a good lesson to learn. Even when you think we don't know anything, chances are, we know everything."

"You're still following him, then?" Andino asked.

Dante arched a brow. "Clearly we have good reason."

Yeah, that was a bad idea.

A *really* bad idea.

"Boss?" Andino turned on his heel to find a Marcello enforcer leaning in the doorway, and looking right at Dante. "John has just arrived."

"Thank you."

Andino's attention went back to his uncle once the man was gone. "You called John in?"

"He needs a meeting, too." Dante gestured at his desk, adding, "Come and make yourself comfortable—*behave* like my underboss, and not John's best friend. Keep your fucking mouth shut unless it is to defuse a situation, and then maybe you can see what you've been missing in your selfishness, Andino."

He had no idea what his uncle was talking about, but at the moment, he didn't have much of a choice but to listen. Dante probably meant for Andino to stand beside the desk, but instead, he perched himself on the corner, and waited for his cousin to walk through the office doors. It didn't take long, and there John was.

It took Andino *one look*.

One glance at his cousin to know …

One second in his presence.

Just the one.

And then, Andino knew.

He saw it in the defensive posture John sported, and the wildness in his eyes. He found it in the way his cousin's hair was a little unruly instead of slicked back, and perfectly managed as it usually would be.

He saw it—he knew what he'd missed.

John was manic.

Or … his bipolar disorder was acting up, and he was on the cusp of mania. Sometimes, it came on really fast, and other times, it was a slow build up to a manic cycle that was sure to leave everyone in John's path untouched. To everyone else around John, it was easily noticed when he was slipping into one of the phases. To John, though? Well, that was an entirely different story.

It was a punch to Andino's gut.

Hard, fast, and *unforgiving.*

Guilt swept through him.

Because *yeah*—fuck yeah, he'd missed this.

How had he missed this?

He was supposed to be looking out for John; it was what *he* did. That was his deal—his one promise. He looked after John, no excuses.

How did I miss this?

Andino didn't have time to think on it for long.

"This better be fucking good," John grumbled. And then he noticed the rest of them. "What's going on?"

Lucian, John's father, spoke up first. "Have a seat, son."

John fidgeted with his jacket. "Nah, I'm good. I kind of want to know why I'm here, though. I don't like to be interrupted, you know."

"Yeah, I bet," Gio said under his breath.

John didn't miss it. "What the fuck does that mean?"

"John," Dante said, that warning coming back into his tone fast. "Show some respect, huh?"

"Yeah, all right." John looked to Dante, then. "I'm here—what's up?"

Dante got right down to business, and didn't even lead into it. "You didn't think to tell any of us that you were going to be having dinner with the Calabrese boss and his family last night?"

"I was invited." John shrugged. "Tell me how to refuse that without breaking the rules we live by, and I will do that next time."

"You still didn't tell anyone," Lucian pointed out.

"I didn't need to. It was a dinner."

"With the Calabrese boss. You know how the Marcellos feel about that family, John," Andino's father added.

John kept looking at only Dante. "I couldn't be disrespectful, and refuse. So, I went. It's over."

"You cannot trust a Calabrese," Dante replied quietly.

"I don't trust the Calabrese boss, or his shithead sons," John said, a heat coloring his words. "I remember what they did to my father's family."

Lucian cleared his throat. Bad blood never really washed out, Andino knew. And there was a hell of a lot of bad blood between the Marcello and the Calabrese families.

"Why didn't you answer my calls this morning?" Dante asked John. "You were fine with telling me you couldn't disrespect Matteo, and yet you made me call you ten times before you finally answered. What was so important this morning that you couldn't answer me, Johnathan?"

"I was busy."

Dante nodded, and relaxed in the chair—a lie if Andino ever saw one. "I know you took the Calabrese girl home with you, John. See, I found out about the dinner invitation, and thought just in case, you should have someone follow behind. I don't trust snakes like those ones in Brooklyn, and in no way will I allow a man of mine to confer with them without some kind of backup."

Andino *knew* the moment when it clicked for John—the very second when his cousin understood what Dante had just told him without actually saying the words. And like Andino figured, it immediately hit John right where it would do all kinds of damage. Not just damage to his cousin, either.

"You fucking had someone follow me?" John asked, turning to stone and hissing the words.

"I—"

"Someone tailed me?"

Yeah, okay.

Now was the time Andino had to step in. His cousin's gaze had blackened, and that defensive posture of John's had practically turned to offensive. That all spelled bad news if someone didn't diffuse the situation, and *fast*.

"John," Andino said, moving off the desk. "He thought it would be best considering how the Calabrese are sometimes."

John's gaze swung on Andino, and all that rage he knew his cousin was feeling suddenly slammed into him at full force. Maybe stepping in had been the wrong thing to do—if only because John needed to have at least *one* ally, and right then, he was looking at Andino like he was the fucking enemy.

Well, shit.

This wasn't good.

Not at all.

That guilt still swam heavily through Andino. He'd fucked up *big time*—missed his cousin's spiraling mental health, and now this. There was no denying how bad he messed up here.

It had always been him and John against the world—or that's how it felt a lot of the time. When the two of them didn't feel like they could trust anybody else, they could count on one another to do the right thing.

Except, that's not how this went down.

How could he fix this?

"Because I can't look out for myself or be trusted, right?" John asked. "That's funny, boss, considering the Calabrese didn't make any effort to hide fuck all about their intentions when they invited me to dinner. Except my own family does exactly that instead of just fucking asking me. But they're the ones I have to watch out for, huh?"

John laughed bitterly.

"It's not a big deal," Dante replied, "and it's not like you're making it out to be, John."

"Or is it exactly that, boss? Have you gotten someone to follow me before this time, too?"

No one answered John's question.

Andino could tell his cousin knew the truth, though.

"Why?" John asked.

"Andi mentioned you had an interest in the Calabrese girl," Dante said.

John's gaze flew to Andino in an instant—hatred staring back. "What, you ran to tattle on me like a fucking baby, or something?"

"No, I—"

"Screw you, Andino."

Andino stepped forward—he needed his cousin to know that what John thought wasn't actually the case. John's posture was the only thing that made Andino stay right where he was in that moment.

"John, they cannot be trusted, and you know that," Lucian said. "Not the men, and certainly not one of their women. No matter who she is."

"Fuck you all." John addressed all of them, but he only actually looked at Andino. "Yeah, fuck every single one of you."

• • •

Andino knew the exact moment when Haven noticed him during her jog—she almost missed a step when she came around the bend in the trail, but like the pro she was, never missed a damn beat. He came to this spot simply because he knew this was her turnaround spot. She always took her break here.

And frankly, he didn't have any other free time.

Everybody else was taking it.

Haven gave him a look—one that made him wink—before she dropped down to the bench beside him. Her heavy breaths took a minute to calm, and he gave her that time before handing over the vanilla latte in his hand like an offering.

"Really?" she asked, laughing lightly. "I'm exercising, and so you ply me with sugary caffeine?"

Andino shrugged. "Seems like a fair trade."

"For *what?*"

"Agreeing to meet up with me."

She nodded, and peered down at the cup in her hands. "To be fair, I was going to call today and see if you wanted to … talk, or whatever."

Good.

That meant good things for him.

"I might have called sooner," Andino said, sighing heavily, "but when shit hits the fan in my family, it tends to splatter on everyone in one way or another."

Haven arched a brow. "Gross."

"And yet, I didn't lie."

"I'm sorry."

Andino shook his head. "Don't be—this isn't your fault."

"I'm not even sure I know what *this* is, Andino."

Of course, she didn't.

She only knew a little.

His shoulders felt so goddamn heavy—too heavy to support the head that was meant to wear a crown that had never really felt like his. And yet, there he sat, doing exactly that. Or trying.

Trying, yes, and failing.

John's state reminded him of that.

Andino didn't even see Haven's hand come up until it cupped his cheek. Her soft thumb stroked his jawline with a gentle touch that made him want to disappear and feel nothing but that for the rest of his goddamn life.

Funny how that worked.

"You look sad," she whispered.

"Defeated, I think."

"Well, I don't like this look on you, so stop it."

Andino smiled a bit, and chuckled. Haven patted his cheek with a wink, and then dropped her hand back into his lap. For a long while, the two were quiet as they watched a couple of joggers pass them by in full gear.

At least, it wasn't snowing today.

Andino's thick, wool coat kept him warm from the mid-January air. Haven, on the other hand, didn't look bothered by the cold in her sweater and yoga pants. It was comfortable enough that she didn't even have gloves on, but at least she threw on a hat.

"I think what they say about me is right," Andino murmured after a while.

Haven glanced over at him with a little knot between her brows. "Who, and what do they say?"

"My family. I think they're right—my attention is not where it needs to be because I've been too busy elsewhere, and it's showing. I let things slip. I fucked up."

"Oh." Then, quieter, Haven asked, "Do you mean me when you say your attention is elsewhere?"

He really didn't want to answer that.

Because *yes*, that's what he meant.

Haven nodded when he said nothing.

Andino needed her to know, though ... "That doesn't mean I want to change what I'm doing—what *we're* doing, Haven. It just means I need to get my shit straightened out. Especially now ... for my cousin, and whatnot."

"Your cousin?"

"Yeah, John. You'd like him. He's quiet, and does his own thing. He's got some issues, but they don't make him who he is; they're just one part of him. He's uh, going through some shit, and usually I keep an eye on him to keep him out of trouble. He got mixed up with a woman—Siena

165

Calabrese—who comes from a family similar to mine. The difference is they're a bunch of snakes; bad people in general. So, he found trouble anyway. I haven't been looking out for him well lately. I figured he'd be okay since he was doing well, anyway. I'm supposed to be the one who takes care of him, you know. That's my job, and I fucked it up."

His unofficial job.

No one actually said he had to do it.

He just *did*.

"Andino," Haven said softly.

He glanced over to find her looking at him in that way of hers—all silent, contemplative, and yet *caring*. Even when they were still up in the air, and *not-supposed-to-be* … even when they were confusing, and trying to deal with all the things he'd never told her, but probably should have … she still gave a shit about him.

It stunned him.

All over.

"You have to take care of you, too," Haven said. "You have to look out for *you*, too."

"Sure."

"But do you really know that, though?"

Andino shrugged. "I have to look out for me, I know."

"Yeah."

"And John, too."

Haven laughed lightly. "I mean, if you *have* to."

"Nobody else does. Not the way he needs."

"But what about you?"

Andino met Haven's stare.

Didn't she know?

He was coming to learn …

"I think that's supposed to be you, Haven," he murmured.

It was the rest of the world that thought differently.

"Doesn't that …"

"It terrifies me, yeah."

Haven nodded. "Yeah, me too."

• • •

Andino knocked on the door of the small house in Queens, and shoved his hands in his pockets before taking a step back. He had all of one goal in coming here—to John's place—and that was to start righting some of this shit he'd let slide. He needed to get back in the right place with business and the family before too many messes piled up on him. There, he'd be entirely fucked. Right now, he had a chance to fix some of it.

Hopefully.

He was starting with John.

That seemed like the best route.

As for Haven and his family ... well, Andino's best bet for the moment was to keep Haven's presence as quiet as possible, and then deal with it when he no longer had a choice. *Somehow.* He was still trying to figure that bit out.

John first, though.

He intended to seem as least threatening as possible to John because if Andino's thoughts were correct on his cousin's current mental state, and John was already slipping off the edge of mania ... the slightest *idea* of provocation from Andino could send his cousin into a bad place. It wasn't even John's fault—it was just how his mania manifested.

It took far too long for John to even come and answer the door, and he didn't do it with any kind of grace or politeness, either. No, he swung the door open with a glare, and a sharp, "What in the fuck do you want?"

Andino kept his loose posture, and his hands stuffed in his pockets. "Thought we could talk, cousin."

John's gaze narrowed. "I would rather chew on glass, actually."

"Can I come in?"

"I don't think that's a good idea."

Andino sighed, and glanced away from his cousin. "Come on, man, let me in. Let's talk. You've got some things wrong, and I want to correct them."

John barked out a harsh, bitter laugh. "There's nothing to talk about, Andino. And really, *now* you want to fucking talk? Because lately, you've been just about everywhere but anywhere I fucking am, man. And that's fine—keep doing that."

"John—"

His cousin took one step out of the house, and forced Andino to walk down the steps. "No, you don't get to say *fuck all* to me right now, Andino. You sold me out to the family like a fucking piece of shit. You set me up with Siena the one time—acted like it was fucking *cool*, and then what did you do? Ran to Dante with the info like the good little underboss you are. Always following the rules. That's you. No worries; it's just business, right? That's all you're about. The fucking *business.*"

"That's bullshit," Andino snapped back.

He knew better than to move forward.

He knew not to provoke John like this.

Knew how bad it could be.

Still, Andino moved back up those stairs and never took his gaze off his cousin's all the while. He got close to John—too close, likely—and crowded him on the steps. He made sure his cousin was looking him right in the face, and not going to move the next time he spoke.

"You have *no idea* of the shit I am trying to handle, John," Andino said, pushing a clenched fist against his cousin's chest, "and that's *fine*. I don't expect you to know, man, but there's one thing you know better than to fucking forget—that's us. You and me; ride or die. I take care of you, and you do the same for me. No matter what. You thought this was different? You thought I sold you *out?*"

"You think I don't know?" John asked. "You still don't want to talk about her, do you? *Haven?*"

Andino stiffened.

His cousin had heard about Haven's involvement with Andino through the grapevine, not to mention everybody else's opinions regarding her and him.

John nodded, and sneered. "Is that what it is, then—you're trying to keep attention off you, and the shit you're trying to pull when they're not looking, so you decided to throw me under the bus by selling me out?"

What the fuck?

This was not John.

Not a *sensible* John, anyway.

This was John finding problems in every little detail. This was his cousin being paranoid and pissed and *wrong*. This was John stepping into mania, and unable to see reason or reality. And yet, *usually*, even in his worst moments, John allowed Andino in. He let him talk, or help.

Not this time, it seemed.

Coming here had been a mistake; Andino was sure of it.

Still, he thought he could *try*.

"When have I ever sold you out to them be—"

"Last week," John interjected. "You sold me out last week when they called me in for that meeting. And you can color it up or justify it with whatever bullshit you want to, but in the end, it's still going to mean the same thing to me. Fuck you, Andino."

Andino didn't even have time to react before John's hands stuck out, and hit him hard against his chest. All it took was one good shove that Andino wasn't expecting, and he was knocked off the steps entirely, and pushed a good three feet away from his cousin, causing him to slip on the step and spin as he fell. Andino barely managed to catch his fall before he landed face first into the pavement.

It was only the growls and barks muted behind glass that reminded Andino where he was, and who had just put their fucking hands on him that kept him from getting up and beating the hell out of John for that.

It was his cousin.

His *blood*.

His best fucking friend.

John wasn't John right now.

John was … not John.

Andino kept telling himself that even as he got up from the icy ground, and brushed his jacket off. He continued to repeat those words to himself even as his hands stung from the scrapes that now covered his palms. He glanced over his shoulder to find Snaps still trying to claw his way out of the Lexus's passenger side window in an effort to protect his master. Snarling, baring his teeth, and ready to fucking kill.

Damn.

He was glad he rolled that window up.

"Don't fucking bother me again," Andino heard John say from the steps. "I'll come to you when I am ready to talk, and not the other way around. After what you did, at least give me the respect of coming to you first, and not trying to push your shit on me when I'm not ready. Do you fucking understand me?"

Andino nodded, but still didn't look back at his cousin. He couldn't, or else the very small control he had over his anger was going to break, and he was going to do something he would seriously regret.

This wasn't John.

This was *not* John.

This was John in a bad place within his own head—nothing more. It wasn't John's fault. He couldn't control it.

"Yeah," Andino said, though it killed him to do it. "I got you, man."

He didn't go to Snaps until he heard the front door slam, and even then, he couldn't calm his dog down.

So was his life, lately.

One giant fuck up after another.

SIXTEEN

"It's way too cold for this shit," Haven muttered.

She struggled to turn the knob on her front door. *Finally*, her frozen fingers worked long enough to get inside the *very* warm house. A cold snap was moving through New York, and she wasn't having any of it. Except … she did deal with it every single day when she left her house to run, or even to jump into her vehicle to head to the club. Today, it was jogging.

Once inside the house, warmth instantly spread through her chilled bones, and she started to fell less like a block of goddamn ice, and more like a real human woman. It kind of felt like Valeria had probably turned up the heat a little bit, too.

Her relief came out in a long, grateful groan. "Oh, my *God.*"

"Cold?" Valeria popped her head around the corner of the kitchen entryway with a sly smile. She kept the same expression up even while Haven shrugged off her thick sweater, pulled off her cap and mittens, and hung them up. "I told you to buy a damn treadmill, Haven. At least for the winter."

"It's never *this* cold, though."

"Is it cold like this in Mexico, too, Ma?"

Valeria gave Haven a look, and disappeared back into the kitchen to indulge her ever curious daughter while Haven finished getting undressed. "No, we don't even see snow."

"*Ever?*"

"Not where I came from, anyway."

"*Cool.*"

Valeria's laughter filtered out from the kitchen as Haven headed down the hall. She entered the room just in enough time to see Maria stand from her chair where she was currently drawing something at her seat at the table.

"Will I ever get to visit there, Ma?"

Haven didn't miss the way her friend stiffened at the island. Valeria was smart, though—she had her back turned to her daughter so that Maria couldn't see how uncomfortable the simple question made her, and kept it that way even as she let a lie slip through her lips as though she had said it a thousand times before.

"One day," Valeria said. "One day, we will visit."

"Okay!"

Satisfied with the answer, Maria went back to her doodling. Haven, on the other hand, went to her friend. "You okay?"

Valeria kept her head down on the vegetables she was chopping. "Yeah, fine."

"You're sure?"

"She's going to ask, Haven."

True.

"But are you ever going to tell her the truth?"

Haven figured that was the better question. Although, frankly, it wasn't any of her goddamn business, and she shouldn't be asking. It wasn't that she was trying to pry for *herself,* but more that she was trying to prepare her friend for the inevitable.

Valeria seemed to understand.

"One day," Valeria echoed. "One day, I will tell her."

"You speak that lie so well."

Valeria laughed. "Yeah, *chica,* I know."

Assuming they were done with the conversation, Haven checked the oven to see what her friend was cooking up considering Valeria was prepping a salad, too. She found a casserole cooking, likely made from one of Valeria's special recipes.

"That looks—"

Riiiiiiing.

A familiar tune lit up the house; it echoed from the spot in the living room where Haven had left her phone charging before going on her run. She didn't even need to act fast to catch the phone as she knew who the caller was without checking the ID, and he didn't mind her calling back. She kept a special ringtone for Andino.

"Give me a sec," Haven said.

Valeria gave her a look from the side; one she didn't entirely understand. Haven didn't think on it for long as she was already out of the kitchen, and crossing the hall to grab her phone. She didn't make it in time before the call cut off, but before she could even pick it back up, a text message lit up the screen.

Lunch at my restaurant in Manhattan?

That was all he asked.

Haven typed back, *What time?*

An hour sound good?

Haven checked the watch on her wrist—she had to be at the club before three to start all the prep for opening, but she had some time to spare. Andino was so goddamn busy all the time that she really only got to see him occasionally, and never for very long.

She wasn't about to turn him down.

I'll be there, she messaged back.

His reply came within seconds: *I look forward to it.*

Haven found herself smiling even when she headed back into the kitchen. "Sorry, you'll have to eat without me for lunch."

Valeria frowned over her shoulder. "Really?"

"Andino invited me to lunch. You know I don't get to—"

"See him often, yeah." Valeria shrugged, and went back to her work. "Well, I'll make you a plate so you can have something when you get back from the club tonight."

"Thanks, Val."

Haven had already turned around, and was heading out of the kitchen to get ready to leave. She was still in yoga pants, and a sweaty shirt that needed changed. Plus, she had to do something with her damn hair. A messy bun was a nice look, but not when it was messy from running.

Still, her steps hesitated when she heard Maria say to her mom, "Haven's busy a lot, right, Ma?"

"Yeah, baby, she's busy."

"Oh—I miss her."

"Me, too."

• • •

Haven paid the cab, and thanked him for dropping her off on the wrong side of the damn street. Nothing unusual for New York cabs, though. She had just closed the door on the cab, and moved to the edge of the sidewalk to cross the street where Andino's restaurant looking to be busy with people going in and out was, when someone called her name.

"Hey, it's Haven, right?"

A bull of a man came from her left. She looked him up and down, and while he *seemed* familiar, she just couldn't place him. She only relaxed a bit because of the dog that was walking beside him—Snaps.

"That is my name," Haven replied. "And you are?"

"Pink," the guy replied. "Or, that's what they call me."

"Seriously?"

Pink shrugged. "It's a long story."

"Okay. Can I help you?"

"Just wanted to stop you and say hi—Snaps got excited to see you from down the way, too."

Haven smiled, and bent down to give Snaps a rub behind his pointed ears. The dog's tail wagged hard, and he huffed in her hands. She glanced up at the man quickly, asking, "Are you one of Andino's men, then?"

Pink nodded. "I am, yeah."

"Oh. Hello."

Haven's attention was back on a happy Snaps, then, but when she noticed the man hadn't replied to her or said anything else, she glanced up again. Pink wasn't looking at her, now, but rather, at something across the street.

She looked that way too—quieted suddenly at the sight of a familiar woman coming out of the restaurant with a wave over her shoulder.

Andino's mother.

Haven stood up, but by the time she thought to speak again, Kim was already gone in a town car that had pulled up to the side of the road. Kim never saw Haven, and probably had no idea she was even there at all. Had Haven kept walking across the road, she would have walked right into Andino's mother as she came out of the restaurant.

What were the chances that it hadn't happened? What were the odds that this unknown, strange man who worked for Andino would stop Haven before she could cross the street at just the right time?

Had that been ... purposeful?

"Well, I'll let you go see the boss, then," Pink said.

Haven nodded at the man—she couldn't find it in herself to be pissed off at him, frankly. He was just someone who was on Andino's payroll, and doing what he was told. It was with Andino that Haven had a fucking bone to pick.

"Have a good day, Pink." Haven gave Snaps one last scratch behind his ear, and told the dog, "And you be a good boy, Snaps."

She swore the dog smiled.

If only that made her happy at the moment. She was feeling a little too heavy for that.

Haven didn't bother to say anything else before crossing the street. She was quick to enter the restaurant, and bypass the girl at the podium who would usually direct Haven to whatever table until Andino was called out of his office to join her. She didn't even bother to search for him on the floor—she knew where he would be.

Sure enough, she found him in his office just beyond the kitchen. Andino was just sitting down at his desk—maybe more proof that he had walked his mother out of the business—when Haven darkened the doorway.

"Did you set that up?" she asked.

Andino glanced up—green eyes nailing into her with an intensity that might have taken her breath away at any other time. "I beg your pardon?"

"Your mother was just here, wasn't she? I saw her leave."

His face remained passive, but Haven wasn't stupid. It was only when Andino took great pains to hide his emotions externally that he was doing so with a purpose, and for a reason. Otherwise, he couldn't be bothered to try.

"She was here," he said. "So?"

"Pink—ring any bells?"

Andino leaned back in his office chair. "Haven—"

"Did you make sure I wouldn't run into your mother when I arrived here? Just answer the fucking question."

His gaze darted away from hers, and even if he hadn't admitted the truth in his next statement, that would have been enough to tell her what she wanted to know. "I don't need any more problems at the moment, so yeah, I made sure she wouldn't have any information to run to my father or someone else in my family at the moment."

God.

Yeah, that's what she wanted to know.

Not what she wanted to hear.

Those were two different things.

He was purposely keeping her a secret—hiding her from people who did not approve of his involvement with a woman that they didn't think was acceptable. That right there should have been enough for Haven to turn the hell around, and leave Andino right where he stood.

Instead, she found herself frozen to the spot.

And *hurting*.

"Why?" she managed to ask.

Although, really, she was sure she knew the answer.

"I told you—it might have caused a problem. Right now, I need to focus on handling one problem at a time before I go adding more onto my list."

"That's what I am, then. A problem."

"Haven, that's not what—"

"No, it's fine," she said, lifting a hand as if to wave him off. "You made your point—and place—clear, thanks."

She turned to leave the office, but barely even made it a step outside the doorway and into the kitchen before Andino was right behind her. His arm snagged her around the waist, and despite her spinning around to try and push him away, he held firm. He kicked the goddamn door closed behind them, too.

"What in the hell do you think you're doing?" she asked.

Andino didn't speak—no, he just crowded her against the fucking door, put both his hands flat against the wood on either side of her head as if to keep her barricaded in, and forced her to look at him. Haven knew damn well he could see how pissed she was in that moment. How could he *not*?

"If you didn't get the hint, that was me wanting to *leave*, Andino."

He nodded. "Yeah, I got it. We're not done talking, though."

"You don't have to be. I was done."

"No, you don't get to run every time something upsets you, Haven," he countered, inching closer with every word. So close, in fact, that his firm body molded entirely against hers. Every single breath she took had her chest pressing hard against his. His mouth was just a whisper away—enough that his lips ghosted over hers when he spoke. "You're *here*, aren't you? That's what I wanted. To have lunch with you today, and see *you*. My mother showed up, and in an effort to be able to have a decent lunch with you that wouldn't be interrupted by my family who can't mind their own goddamn business, I made sure you two didn't run into one another."

Haven pushed against him, but Andino stayed firm in his spot. "Because you don't want them to know about me."

"More like, I have other things to handle first."

"And so, it goes back to what I said—you don't want them to know about me, or us."

Andino glanced upwards as though he were searching for the heavens. "Haven, don't do that, baby."

"Kind of hard not to when *this* is what you do."

"And what did I do? Avoid a *problem*. That's all."

"Andino—"

"I wanted you to come here. I canceled a meeting just to get an extra few minutes with you while you would be here. Isn't that enough to tell you that I want you with me?"

Yes, in some ways.

And *not at all*, in other ways.

The bad overshadowed the good.

Didn't he realize that?

"Hey," Andino murmured.

Haven's gaze met his, and she wished she hadn't done that simply because the rest of the world ceased to exist when she stared at Andino. It was just them, the universe became smaller, and nothing else mattered.

How could he do that for her, but also hurt her?

"What?" Haven asked.

"Don't *ever* question what I want, Haven."

She blinked. "I rarely know what that is, though."

"You. It's *you*."

Damn him.

Damn him straight to hell.

"I'm still going to be pissed after this moment," she told him.

Andino grinned a little. "Oh?"

"Bet on it."

"Shame," he said softly.

Maybe it was.

Haven just didn't care right then. She had something else on her mind—something that always came up whenever they were this close, and alone. A need that coursed through her system, and threatened to drown her with the intensity every single time. A want that only he could fix for her.

Him, that was.

Haven closed the very short distance between them to kiss Andino. He didn't even hesitate to kiss her back in that familiar, rough way of his. He pushed her harder against the door while his tongue warred with hers. Those warm, strong hands of his were quick to dart beneath the skirt of her dress, and between her thighs.

She couldn't control herself.

Didn't want to.

She just spread her legs a little wider for him while she worked at the button and zipper on his slacks. Who cared that a whole restaurant worth of employees were just beyond the door behind her working? Who cared if they might *hear?*

She had one thing on her mind.

He seemed to be the same.

All of the breath in Haven's lungs came out in a harsh whoosh of air the second two of Andino's fingers found her cunt after sweeping beneath the gusset of her panties. There was no soft touches—no testing the waters, so to speak. Just his fingers filling her up as his thumb drove into her clit at the same time she finally got her hand wrapped around his cock beneath his boxer-briefs.

"Jesus Christ," Andino hissed.

Maybe she'd grabbed him a little too tightly.

Stroked him too firmly.

Who knew?

His hips jerked, making his dick slide through her hands just the way he liked anyway. Even as she stroked him harder, got his cock pulsing in her palm, and ready for her, he kept working those fingers between her thighs. Making her wetter—getting her body *hotter.*

"Fuck, fuck, *fuck,*" Haven breathed.

She was right there—ready to come, and *needing it bad.* And then he pulled his fingers away entirely; the loss of him was substantial.

Yet, Haven barely had time to think about it at all before she was lifted against the door. Her legs wrapped around his waist at the same time his mouth slammed against hers, and his hand was between her thighs once more. Only this time, it was to fit his cock where it needed to go—one hard thrust, and he filled her full again.

The sharp, fast flex of his hips, and the way his cock drove into her sent an ache shooting through Haven's bloodstream. But oh, God, was it good. It only melted in with the bliss she felt when he yanked his dick out from her body, rubbed the head against her slit, and then thrust right back in again.

She was so wet.

Slicking down her thighs.

Soaking his length.

Haven found herself a little too enthralled by watching the sight of him fucking her, even when his hand curved around her throat, and squeezed. All she wanted to do was watch him *fuck her so good*.

Every thrust of his body against hers sent her into the door—her back hurt from the force, but damn, she didn't even mind.

"Look at me and come," she heard him say.

Haven was still watching their bodies meet.

"*Look at me*," he growled, tipping her head back. There were those green eyes again, although a little deeper in color now, and swimming with the need for her. "Look at me, and *come*."

She did like to give him what he wanted. Even when it hurt her inside.

At least, that was one thing about sex with Andino—a good thing. He didn't hurt her like this; not unless she asked him to, anyway.

• • •

"Are you still pissed at me because of the other day?"

Haven *tried* to ignore Andino, but it was damn hard when his lips were grazing the back of her neck while she tried to make coffee in his kitchen. She could smell that woodsy cologne he liked so much surrounding her, and soaking into her lungs with every breath. All it took was the stroke of his fingertips moving her hair to the side, so he could kiss *that spot* behind the back of her ear, and she bet her fucking panties were ruined.

Because *yes*, she was still pissed at him.

She was also incredibly turned on by him.

"That was a shitty thing to do to me," she said.

Andino sighed—the pulse of his warm breath washed over the back of her neck, and reminded her of what it felt like to have his mouth doing that very thing to her pussy. *Jesus Christ, get a grip, Haven.*

"I told you—I didn't have a choice, and I have to handle one thing at a time."

"So, I come last."

"Haven—"

"Which means, you hide me from your family because I am your dirty little secret that no one can find out about. Totally okay for you to be fucking whenever you feel the need, but not at all good enough for you to be seen in public with me."

"Goddammit, that is *not* what I said."

Haven shrugged, still refusing to turn around. "That's how it felt."

"First of all, the restaurant thing was *three days ago, donna,*" Andino grumbled even as he moved away from her slightly. "Can't you let it go?"

"Not yet."

"Of course."

Haven shook her head. "You don't get it, Andino."

She didn't even realize what had happened before she was spun around fast to face him. His hand locked around her wrist, and he moved in close so that the only thing she was looking at was *him.* She fucking hoped to God that he could see the fire blazing back in her eyes.

If he thought he was getting laid tonight, he was *wrong.*

Frankly, Haven didn't even fucking know why she had come here today. Things were still tense after his little trick at the restaurant, and she should have just taken some time to settle her feelings about it all.

That would have been best.

Instead, when he called, she went.

He asked, she gave.

He demanded, she *did.*

That was them in a goddamn nutshell, and Haven wasn't even sure if she liked doing this with him now. If all it was going to leave her feeling at the end of the day was dirty and ashamed, then what was the goddamn point?

"I don't want to be your secret," she told him quietly.

"One thing at a time," he returned.

"Except, the problem with that is I don't know all the things you need to deal with before you can finally deal with us, Andino."

He sighed heavily. "Maybe I'm trying to deal with everything else so then I won't have to deal with us at all—it'll already be practically done."

"If by done, you mean chasing me entirely out of your life, then keep it up." Haven arched a brow, adding, "You're doing a fantastic job."

Andino's jaw tightened. "Come on, Haven."

"You *hid me* from your mother."

"For good reason."

"Yes, because they don't think I'm appropriate for you, and it seems you agree. Tell me not to have some kind of feelings about that again, Andino. Go on, I *dare you.*"

Because it would not end well for him.

That was a promise.

"Okay, stop," Andino murmured.

Haven glared. "I can have feelings about this!"

"*Stop.*"

He said it again, but even quieter and he came close enough that his lips brushed over hers as he spoke. It was enough to set Haven's insides off like a wild fire suddenly burning out of control. She wished she had more of that—control—around this man.

Or self-respect.

Maybe that's what she needed instead.

"You're not my *secret,*" he told her. "Nothing like that, but you have to let me handle my business first. Okay? That's all I am asking for, and then we'll deal with the rest."

"So, in the meantime," she dared to ask even though his answer might very well cut her up inside, "what am I to you?"

Andino smiled. "Important."

"Important?"

"Mmm. *Something.* But it's important."

Haven let out a heavy breath. "I wish that made me feel better."

Andino shrugged. "Listen, I have to handle other things—business, and my family. I will be doing that whether you like it or not. That is the one thing that isn't about you. Okay? It's not about you, Haven."

"You're making that abundantly clear, Andino."

"I beg your pardon?"

She patted a hand against his chest. "Very little in your life is about me—I get it."

Before he could try and respond, she turned back around, and finished making her coffee. A part of her was grateful when Andino moved away from her side, and another part of her wished he was still right there … giving her shit back to her just as much as she threw it at him.

Andino made a harsh noise in the back of his throat. "Fine, Haven. Listen, John is coming over—he'll be here within a few minutes. Be here, or go, that's up to you, but I'll be upstairs in my office. He knows where to find me."

Be here, or go.

Haven turned around just as Andino reached the entryway of the kitchen. "So, you want me here when he's here?"

Andino glanced over his shoulder, but even his stare was cold. "I never once said I didn't, my girl. We'll finish this conversation later if you're still here."

Yes, he hadn't said he didn't want her there, but she was still just something. And that was one short step away from *nothing.*

Haven was left alone with her thoughts, which honestly, was a hell of a lonely place to be, but she wasn't quite ready to have another verbal sparring match with Andino, either. Sometimes, one needed to recoup, and deal with their own shit first before bringing someone else's baggage into the mix as well.

She would do well to learn that.

It was only a knock on the door that drew Haven from her thoughts. She set her—now mostly—empty cup of coffee to the counter, and headed for the front entrance of the home. She expected Andino to come down and greet his cousin, but she didn't hear a single noise from him upstairs.

Maybe that should have been a hint for her—he *was* letting her open his home, and be in front of someone from his family. Didn't that mean something? He had all the time in the world to send her the fuck out of there before this person arrived.

Beyond the front door, Haven found a man and a woman waiting. The woman was tucked in close to the man—she was a pretty thing, but docile looking, too. Haven turned to the man, already knowing his name and a little about him from Andino.

"Johnathan, right?" she asked.

John nodded, a hint of a smile at the edges of his mouth. "It is. And you're Haven."

"I am." She glanced at the woman—unsure of who she was, and why she was there. "He didn't say you were going to bring someone with you."

Haven put out a hand to shake, and the woman offered hers as well.

"Nice to meet you," she said, "I'm Siena. You're Andino's wife?"

John stiffened.

Haven didn't miss it, and all she could do was give a bitter laugh and a wave of her hand in response. "No, see, I'm not appropriate enough to be a wife, Siena. I'm just ... something."

"Ouch," Siena murmured.

Haven smirked a bit. "It's a work in progress. Come in."

Yeah, a *work in progress.*

That seemed like a good way to describe this whole mess.

SEVENTEEN

Andino listened to the quiet murmurings downstairs, but couldn't quite make out what was being said. He figured John had finally shown up—if his cousin stopped to converse with Haven for even a couple of seconds, then that was a win for Andino in more ways than one. Sure, Andino needed to keep Haven's presence in his life quiet *for now,* but that only applied to a select few people. John was not one of them.

It was good for John to see Haven, too, especially after his cousin had thrown the woman in his face as a reason why Andino might have sold him out to their family. Keep the attention off himself, and on John instead, so to speak. Well, if she was *here,* and John could see her, then what was Andino hiding?

If his cousin was actually slipping into another manic phase of his bipolar cycles, then Andino needed to tread carefully. Measure his words, and his actions when it came to John. He couldn't even appear to be challenging John, or attempting to cause him harm—even if none of those things were the case.

John's mind would just … see it that way.

Make it happen, even.

And once Andino got this sorted with his cousin today—or tried, depending on John's mood—then he would deal with the very angry woman downstairs. That was, if Haven even decided to stick around long enough to chat.

One thing at a time, Andino.

Even though he'd heard his cousin approaching, Andino didn't look up from the paperwork on his desk when John knocked on the door. "You finally came around to see me, huh?"

"You finally decided to pull the underboss card and make me come see you," John countered easily.

Fair enough.

That was true.

Andino did that.

No shame.

Andino looked up to meet his cousin's stare from the doorway, but made sure to keep his posture and expression as least combative as he could manage. If he could get through this meeting with John without it spiraling into a verbal sparring match, then maybe he could judge just how bad his cousin's current state actually was.

"Had you given me a choice, I still would have come over eventually," John said.

"When would that have been?" Andino asked.

"Eventually."

"I sped it up, John. One of the perks of being the family underboss." Andino grinned. "Nobody gets to ignore my ass."

John laughed under his breath. "Yeah, lucky you."

His smile was quick to fade, then—was that was this was, *luck?* He wasn't sure he wanted to keep this kind of luck. "Well, the luck is debatable. Sit, John."

"I would rather stand."

"Why, are you going to fuck off if I say something you don't like?"

People in his life that he cared about—which weren't very fucking many—seemed to be doing that a lot lately. It drove him crazy.

John shot Andino a look—a warning if there ever was one. *Careful, Andino.* "I see Haven is downstairs. Siena is chatting with her."

Andino's gaze narrowed. "You brought her here?"

"I was with her when you called. I promised to spend the day with her since all I do is work my fucking ass off. I owe her time every once and a while, don't I?"

"Sure, John, but you know how they feel about—"

"I imagine, the same way *they* feel about Haven, no?"

Andino stiffened in the chair. It wasn't like his cousin to take easy shots like that—he made a checkmark on his mental list for John's irritability level. It was definitely a sign pointing in a bad direction. Sure, everyone had their bad days, but irritability for John was never a good thing.

"Point taken," Andino said.

"Yet, she's here, I noticed."

Good, that was the point, man.

"You sound like a broken record."

"Give me something to give a shit about, cousin," John snapped back just as fast, his hazel eyes burning with anger. "It's been weeks, and all I've wanted to do is break your face. So yeah, give me something right now."

Andino cleared his throat, trying to readjust his tone before he spoke again. "Maybe I'm taking a page out of your playbook."

"Which is what?"

"Doing what I want."

John laughed. "That's not going to be an easy road."

Andino smirked, and shrugged one shoulder. "No, definitely not. I didn't want to pull the underboss card to get you here, John. Honestly. I know you think I'm a fucking jackass right now, but I was fine with letting you come to me when you were ready."

"That so?"

"You felt like I crossed a line, and I get that."

Andino didn't miss the way his cousin's fists balled easily at that statement, or the hard clench of his jaw. John was very good at hiding his emotions—he'd perfected it into an art form over the years considering he battled constantly with an emotional disorder that he felt, made him weaker standing next to other made men in their business. Just the fact that John was struggling to keep his emotional reactions in check told Andino more than John ever could in that moment.

Sure, his cousin seemed level.

Acted *good*.

Kept his tone mostly calm.

All that told Andino was that John knew something was up with himself—his bipolar—and was currently trying to hide it, or ignore it. *Bad news again.*

"You *did* cross a fucking line, man."

"They already had somebody watching you, John," Andino pointed out, wanting to get his cousin to relax a bit. Nothing he said was a lie, though. That was the thing—he needed John to know he wasn't fucking lying, either. "I was approached because Dante had a guy trailing you, and he thought I might know something."

John was quick to sit, then.

Thank God.

Andino continued. "So yeah, Dante and your father came to me asking about the Calabrese, and whatever else. I thought if I tried to explain that Siena was really just a random encounter you had then they would leave it alone."

"You didn't think to give me a fucking heads up that they were trailing me like that?" John asked. "And why the fuck can't they just *trust me?*"

"I get the intentions were good, or that's how Dante meant for it to be, but I warned him then that he was crossing a line with you. That kind of shit messes with your head."

John wouldn't meet Andino's gaze then, but he really didn't need him to. He had already seen the things his cousin was trying to hide. Now, he had to decide what he was going to do about it, or if there even was anything he could do.

Dante had been clear.

Look after John—make sure he stays out of trouble.

It kind of looked like trouble was there.

Damn.

Andino had one last trick up his sleeve, though, and he sure as fuck hoped it worked. Or at least, worked until he figured something else out.

And … John would have to be agreeable.

Here goes nothing.

"I should have let you know, John," Andino said. "I'm sorry that I didn't."

John looked back at Andino. "They're never going to feel like I can handle this business without somebody babysitting my every move. It puts me on edge like nothing else. I fucking hate it, Andi."

"It won't be like that forever, John."

"Really?" John scoffed, quickly adding, "I've gone years without a major episode. I do everything they want me to do, and they still pulled this kind of shit on me."

"I know, but it won't be forever, John. Trust me on that. I'll fucking make sure of it, man. Anyway," Andino said, smacking his palms against the desk, and smiling, "the reason I had to pull the underboss card is because now, I am the one babysitting you."

John stiffened again.

Okay, babysitting might have been the wrong word, stupid.

"Excuse me?" his cousin asked.

It was now or never for this plan. Maybe ... Christ, *maybe* if Andino could keep his cousin relatively close for a couple of weeks, he could see if this phase in John's cycle would pass easily, or worsen in to something else that needed someone to step in. He was hoping for the former before the latter, but only time would tell.

"The boss wants me to keep an eye on you. Seems you're dodging your father, the boss, and even my dad."

"You know what they did," John said.

Andino waved that off. "Doesn't matter, John."

"It does fucking matter."

Frustrated.

Heavy.

Angry.

Andino changed the topic—anything to bring back the calm for John. "How's work?" Andino asked.

"Work is work," his cousin said quickly. "I've got my crew handled. Money is coming in just fine. All the Calabrese work is going fine, as it should."

"Good," Andino said.

"That's it? *Good.*"

"Yeah, why?"

"You're not going to push and question me on every fucking aspect of everything I do?"

"Nope." Andino smiled, and shrugged. "If you say shit is on the up and up with you, then that's what it is, John."

"I see what you did there," John murmured.

"Did you?"

"I'm bipolar, but not crazy or stupid."

"I would never call you those things, anyway," Andino replied.

"I know."

"And I'm not going to treat you like the rest of the men in this family do a lot of the time. I just want to make sure you're handling whatever you need to handle. Probation, work, and therapy. Anything else—who you're fucking, or the rest of that—is none of my goddamn business."

John cleared his throat. "You sure on that?"

Andino pointed upward. "As sure as the sky is blue, man."

"I still don't like it."

"Give them something, and they'll back off."

"But not about her. Not on Siena, Andi. They won't back off a bit."

"You're really messed up on this woman, huh?" Andino asked.

John smiled slyly. "How's that Haven thing working out for you?"

Andino smirked right back. "Yeah, I get it, John."

"But yeah, I am, Andi."

Messed up on her.

Andino knew that feeling.

Right now, he knew it too well.

"I guess nothing else matters, then," Andino said.

"Nothing?" John asked.

"I'm just here to help you, man."

John nodded. "All right."

Only time would tell, though.

Andino knew that, too.

• • •

Two weeks told Andino *a lot.*

More than he ever wanted to know, frankly.

John was not getting better—he was far worse.

Ignoring the mid-February cold biting at his throat, Andino tightened the collar on his jacket, and climbed the steps of a familiar home. He'd been tailing John for two weeks, keeping a low profile to make sure his cousin didn't know he was essentially babysitting him from afar, and then it came to a head.

It started with John's ... thing.

His girlfriend, Siena.

She finally thought something was wrong, too—Andino was quick to offer help even though he'd been watching John for a while and already knew that his cousin was slipping further into a manic spiral. And then yesterday?

Oh, Jesus Christ.

Yesterday, he watched his cousin beat a man to death in the back alley behind a billiards club. That was it for Andino—he cleaned the mess, and hid what John had done, but this was too much, now.

Andino needed help.

He couldn't handle John alone.

Usually when he entered his parents' home, the first person he would look for was his mother. He liked to greet her first, and make sure she had his attention for a bit before he went looking for his father.

Today, he went right upstairs.

He didn't even look for Kim.

Andino found his father reading a book in his office. Giovanni lounged on a leather couch that he'd kept for at least twenty fucking years—the damn thing looked twenty fucking years old, too with all its faded, roughed spots, and frayed edges. Yet, his father loved it for some reason.

Gio didn't even look up at Andino's entrance. "Afternoon to you, son."

"I have a problem."

His father's gaze glanced over the edge of the paperback thriller in his hands. "Go on."

"It's ... sensitive."

Gio rested the book on his stomach, all attention on his son, now. "I don't like the sound of that, Andi."

"Yeah—and I need someone who can help, but keep quiet."

"Since when do you have problems that are *sensitive?*"

Andino glanced away. "Listen, I know I'm not a fuck up, okay, but lately ... that's been a common occurrence for me. I'm just as surprised about it as you are."

"Relax."

Easier said than done, Dad.

"It's John," Andino murmured.

That *really* got his father's attention, not that he was surprised. John had always been like a second son to Gio, in many ways. John spent just as much time in this house with Andino growing up as he had in his own house. John was probably closer to Andino's father than he was his own, even if that was a sad state of affairs in that regard.

Gio sat up fully on the couch, and clasped his hands together over his legs as he stared hard at Andino. "What about John—I thought everything was good on that side of things? You were looking out for him like Dante told you to do, weren't you?"

"I *was,*" Andino said. "And I was also giving him a bit of leg room to do his own thing. You know, like he should be given considering he's thirty fucking years old, and knows how to be a proper made man like the rest of us."

"He's also fresh out of prison, dealing with a new therapist, trying to figure shit out with his life and parents, has Dante riding his ass, and—"

"I know," Andino interjected. "I know he has a lot on his plate."

And he did.

He'd just … forgotten for a time.

"Or are you distracted?" his father asked quietly.

Andino couldn't meet his father's stare, then. He looked at anything *but* Gio when he spoke again. "That's possible."

"Is it because of that wom—"

"Could we not? This is about John, not my personal life."

"I think it's about both," his father replied.

"That doesn't change the fact that I'm not talking about *her*."

"Why?" Gio asked. "Because as long as everyone's attention is on someone else—*John*—then no one is watching you, Andino? You get to fly under the radar, and do as you want with whoever you want? Is that it?"

"Is that seriously what you think?"

Gio chuckled dryly. "No, but other people might think it."

"I care about Haven. She's … not a toy for me."

He felt his father's eyes practically burning holes into him. He thought he could hear his father silently begging for him to look at him, but Andino didn't. He kept his gaze firmly stuck on the window overlooking the back yard. He had other things to handle right now—Haven was not one of them because she was the one thing he was sure of. It was everything else that was up in the air at the moment.

"Do you love her?"

Why did that question feel like a slap cracking against Andino's exposed nerves? Why did it hurt like someone had just stabbed a knife into his chest, and twisted until the blade came back out with a ruined heart on the tip? Why did it *kill* him?

He knew why.

Because somehow—between late nights, and counting tattooed stars, and just *her*—Andino found himself entirely fucked, and totally in love.

You know, with someone he couldn't have.

Or so they kept telling him.

"We're not talking—"

"I asked," his father said quietly. "Give me the respect of answering me, son."

"I don't owe you anything about that," Andino replied, "only her."

Silence answered him back.

Andino was grateful his father didn't push.

"All right." Gio cleared his throat. "One thing at a time, then?"

"If you wouldn't mind."

"How bad is John?"

Andino's chest ached. "Pretty bad—he's full blown manic at this point, but he's avoiding everybody, and not taking calls. Doesn't matter, though, because he's leaving a path of destruction wherever the fuck he goes."

"Like what?"

"Killed a guy yesterday. I cleaned up the mess."

Gio made a noise in the back of his throat. "Let's not repeat that to Dante."

Andino laughed bitterly. "Quite aware, yeah."

"Okay," his father said, standing from the couch, "we'll get this figured out, and quickly. Have it all handled before we take *anything* to the boss. You know how Dante is. I'll help you with getting him under control, and—"

"Getting who under control?"

Fuck.

Andino glanced over his shoulder to find his mother standing in the doorway. She smiled at them, and then looked to Gio.

"Something wrong?"

His father wasn't one to lie.

Especially not to Kim.

Gio smiled back. "Everything's fine, *Tesoro*. Like always."

That should have been another clue for Andino. His father would have his back no matter what—even to his own detriment. That's just what fathers did for their boys.

God knew he had the best father.

• • •

"Club's quiet tonight," Andino said.

Haven didn't pretend like she hadn't heard him speak when he sat down on the stool across the bar from her, but she kept her gaze on the cash she was counting inside the register. She barely even passed him a look when he first greeted her.

"Monday's usually are slow," she returned.

"You'd think that would be the night when people would want to go out, and get rid of their stress. The start of the week, and all that shit."

"Maybe."

Her quiet, but not *interested*, reply made Andino frown. "Hey."

Finally, she glanced over at him. He wished he could find some warmth in her blue eyes, but all he found staring back at him was coldness.

"Hi."

Andino nodded. "I'm sorry I've been busy. The last couple of weeks have been—"

"Don't worry about it, Andino. I'm not."

Ouch.

Her tone came out as sharp as a razor blade, and cut at him like one, too.

"Haven," he said.

He got nothing.

"*Haven.*"

Still nothing.

Fine.

Andino stood from the stool, put his hands on the bar, and launched his body overtop of it in one fell swoop. He landed almost soundlessly on his feet, and reached for Haven before she could even think to protest.

There were a lot of things he couldn't say to her right now. Some, he just wasn't ready to speak out loud, and other things ... well, he had to figure that shit out on his own. But he came to her time and time again because it was *with her* that he found some semblance of fucking peace in his chaotic days.

And he was sorry—fuck, he was so goddamn sorry—if she felt unimportant to him because that was so far from the truth, it wasn't even funny. Maybe he needed to work a little harder at trying to convey the shit he just wasn't ready to tell her.

Starting now.

Andino closed the distance between them, and practically handed his blackened, ruined soul over to her with a kiss. He was quite aware that she was working, and this was not the kind of thing she would usually do ... but it didn't matter to him.

All that mattered right then was the way her body felt tucked against his, how she grabbed his jacket to pull him closer, and the way she kissed him back. Those were the things that made Andino think, *this is worth it; it's far more than worth it.*

The longer he kissed her, the more she relaxed.

The better *they* felt.

All too soon for his liking, Andino pulled away, and then just as fast, dropped a soft kiss to Haven's forehead. Her work was forgotten about for the moment, and the club around them just disappeared while they dealt with them.

"I'm still a little mad at you," she admitted softly.

"I like a woman that can hold grudges better than even me."

She laughed. "Is that so?"

"Very much so, baby."

"I don't really want to keep being mad at you, Andino."

Yeah, he knew that.

She was due her feelings, though.

No matter what he was doing.

He wished he could tell her ...

Didn't she know?

How could she be his secret when the only thing he wanted to do was shout how much he loved her from the rooftops?

Except he couldn't.

Not right now.

EIGHTEEN

"You waited for me?"

Andino's head popped up at Haven's soft question. Leaning against his Lexus, she thought she might finally understand what people meant when they said *the devil you know*. In his long tweed coat, opened to show off the black three-piece suit with a matching silk, blood red tie and vest underneath, the collar flipped up to shield his face from the cold, and those green eyes on her ... this man was most certainly the devil she knew.

"I thought you might like to do something," Andino replied.

Haven, despite all the messy feelings she had about this man, couldn't help but smile like a stupid little girl who was entirely head over heels for someone she could never really have. Not entirely, anyway.

"Something like that?"

Andino shrugged his broad shoulders. "Lady's choice, baby."

"I actually promised to have breakfast with my roommate and her daughter in the morning. You know, because I've been so distracted lately, and all that. I haven't made very much time for them. I don't think staying out later than what I already have would be a good idea, all things considered."

He pursed his lips together, and then gave her one of those sly, sexy grins of his. "And what if I went home with you?"

Haven laughed. "Really?"

"Why not? I can even be out before morning if you need me to."

"Valeria wouldn't care as long as you didn't walk around half naked for her daughter to see. Oh, and you were quiet."

Andino's grin deepened into something *sinful*. Just the sight alone was enough to make Haven wet. She bet he probably fucking knew it, too—maybe he could hear the way her body reacted to him when he barely had to do anything at all.

He does have an ego the size of Texas.

"You're not saying yes or no," Andino murmured.

"I'm thinking."

"You're not still mad at me, are you? I didn't mean to make it seem like I was hiding you because you're *you*. I was trying to avoid—"

"I wasn't angry ... kind of," Haven said quickly. "But if you bring it up again, then yeah, I'm going to get back in that head space again."

And she was trying to let it go.

Sort of.

Haven peered into the Lexus. "Where's Snaps?"

"Spending an evening with my father and mother."

"Really, what like grandkids might?"

Because that was amusing.

And cute.

Andino chuckled. "Sort of, I think. Makes my mother feel less emotional about the fact she doesn't have any grandbabies yet. At least, if my dog is over there and not me, then she can go on and on to him about me knocking somebody up as soon as I possibly can instead of directly to me."

Haven blinked. "Oh, wow."

"You did ask."

She had.

And was regretting it.

"So, is that a yes on me coming over to your place, then?" he asked.

Haven hummed under her breath, and crossed the short distance between them in the empty, dark parking lot until she was right in front of Andino. He didn't waste any time before snaking his arms around her waist, and pulling her in close to his hard body.

Honestly, she liked it here better.

Staring up at him, Haven smiled. "Thanks for waiting."

"Things are better when you're around."

Were they?

She didn't dare to ask.

"Your mom and the grandbaby thing—is that because you don't want kids, or ...?"

"I want an army of kids," Andino said.

Haven blinked *again*.

Andino just laughed.

"Really, a *whole army?* Because that's a lot of diapers, and sleeplessness, and ... *college funds.* Eighteen years' worth spread over several different little humans that suck the life and soul out of you. Because that's what kids do, you know? You give them life, love them, and nurture them, and how do they pay you back? By puking on you at three in the morning when you've just gotten home from being on your feet for eight hours. And yet, when they wake up smiling the next day, all you can do is smile back and love them. *That* is parenting."

Andino shrugged. "I know—that's what I want. Just not today."

Huh.

And why exactly did that make her feel so fucking warm inside?

Goddamn him.

He made it terribly hard to stay angry—when she had every right to be exactly that with him even now—when he kept doing things that reminded her ... oh, yeah, she'd somehow fallen in love with him.

Stupid fucking heart.

"So, back to your place ..." Andino winked, and dropped a quick kiss to her mouth that really only left her wanting more. "Is that a yes, or a no? It's kind of cold out here, and I would much rather be doing something else entirely."

Sure he would.

So would she, really.

"Can you be quiet?" she asked.

Andino grinned—flashing white teeth and a promise of sin in a blink. "I think the better question is *can you?*"

She smacked his chest.

Andino's laughter filled the parking lot.

Heady, dark, and *wicked.*

But really, where was the lie?

He knew her well.

Maybe too well.

• • •

Heaven was Haven on her back, panties stuffed in her mouth, and Andino between her thighs. It was two of his fingers massaging her wet G-spot while he sucked on her throbbing clit like it was a small piece of candy he was trying to get every drop of sweetness from. It was sparks behind her eyes, and fire in her blood, and *bliss.*

Oh, God.

Heaven was *that* bliss.

She couldn't feel anything except the magic he was working on her pussy, and that was just fine to her. Instead of her soft bed, her body felt suspended. Floating high, and riding closer to the edge of an orgasm with every passing second.

In her head, she was screaming.

Begging.

Needy, and unashamed.

Outwardly, she was silent.

Or mostly.

The panties acting like a gag in her mouth were doing their job of keeping her quiet. Andino had been right about that—she wasn't able to maintain a respectable level of noise when he was making her come again and again.

How many times now?

Three ... four?

Jesus, what did it matter?

She was so close to coming again that she didn't even care how many times she'd come before this one. All that mattered right then was that she got to come again.

Andino's mouth left her sex just long enough for him to whisper darkly against her inner thigh while his fingers worked her aching pussy a little harder. *God*, he knew her body so well—maybe too well. Better than her, anyway. He could make her come like nothing at all, and now, she struggled to reach an orgasm by herself.

The asshole.

"Come on, come on," she heard him murmur. "Fucking give it to me. Christ, do you know how good you look spread out like this with those panties in your mouth? You're a *mess*, Haven, and I love it. *Fucking come.* Let me taste that pussy after you've come again before I give you what you really want."

His teeth bit into her leg, and Haven didn't even try to ease the way her fingernails raked lines over his back in response. The second his mouth was back on her clit, and that tongue of his started working its magic with a harsh beat that had her shouting behind the makeshift gag in her mouth, she was done for.

Spinning.

Flying.

Blissed again.

Haven felt the loss of him between her thighs before she'd even finished shaking her way through the orgasm—it was substantial to her nerves and body; every part of her screamed to pull him back in again, and have him close.

She didn't need to do anything.

He just *knew*.

Andino's hands found her face as he slid up her body—all the hard, firm lines of him fitting against her softer curves. His soul was on display when he kissed her; she was sure of it. Positive she could feel parts of him that he rarely even whispered about when no one was around to listen. She could feel all of that when he kissed her.

It was easy to get lost in that.

Easy to forget the world.

His mouth—still wet with her come, and tart with her flavor—was the best kind of distraction. She wanted nothing more than to keep him right there, kissing her forever. Nothing else needed to get in the way, right?

Andino was something else on his worst days, but in bed? There, he turned into something else entirely. Something far more sinful, and *wonderful*. Fast, sure hands, and a kiss that lit her body on fire. He never even broke their kiss as he rolled Haven to her side on the bed, lifted her leg to rest it over his shoulder, and fit himself between her thighs.

The size of his length was always a bit of a shock to her at first—no matter how wet she was, or ready she was … or *needy*, she felt him. She viscerally felt every fucking long, thick inch of him when he started to slide inside her cunt.

He took her slow.

Too slow, maybe.

Teasing and taunting.

"*Yeah*," Andino murmured above her, one of his hands locking her wrists against the bed while his other grabbed tight to her hip. She was pinned like that—stuck beneath him while he fucked her how he wanted until he chose to let her go. She didn't even mind. "I can *feel* how much you love that cock, baby."

He wasn't lying.

Every little bit he gave, her cunt was clenching for *more*.

She always wanted more.

Please, she wanted to beg. *Just fuck me.*

Andino chuckled like he could read her thoughts. She bet she was quite a sight being under him like she was, naked and gagged with her own panties. "A little more, Haven?"

She nodded.

A whimper escaped.

He gave her what she wanted—just a little bit more of him sliding into her pussy, but still not nearly enough. Why did he have such good control?

Fuck him.

She lost track of time as he kept playing that goddamn game with her. A little more of his cock, and then less when he'd pull right back out. Over and over until she was a trembling mess, and ready to shout at him.

Only then did he thrust in.

Only then did he fuck her the way she wanted.

Hard.

Fast.

Deep.

So brutal.

His hands kept her pinned down, and the gag kept her quiet. Every snap of his hips pounding into her body ached in the best way. Being silenced, it made her all the more aware of the sounds he made while he fucked her.

Husky words.

Sexy grunts.

More.

Her body felt overheated, and far too overworked. Every muscle screamed as it clenched in preparation for relief—it was coming again.

Fast.

"Fuck, yeah," Andino said, the words practically dragging their way out of his mouth through his gritted teeth, "show me what you've got, baby."

He fucked her until her throat felt raw from trying to hold back her screams; until her body was numb and she just couldn't come anymore; until he had to put her on her knees, and take her from behind because she'd used up every bit of strength she had.

And even then, the second he let out that quiet, deep *fuck* under his breath and pulled away from her, she rolled over and waited. Finally took those panties out of her mouth, and begged with raspy, soft words as he tugged on his cock above her with hard jerks of his fist around his shaft.

"Please, Andino."

She loved the way he looked when he came. Loved it even more when she was able to watch him paint her body with his seed. There was something raw about the way his eyes drifted over the milky white fluids spilled across her chest, and smeared along her ink.

Something beautiful.

Haven would miss that, she knew. When he broke her heart—because he would, that much was painfully clear about this thing between them— she was going to miss this.

She would miss him.

• • •

"Get up, and let me say goodbye to you," Haven heard murmured along the shell of her ear. Still half asleep, she managed a smile when Andino's lips grazed the spot that always made her hot, and shivering. It sent strong memories of the night before flooding her mind which only served to make her body heat up. This man didn't even realize the kind of effect he had on her. How could he? "Come on, get up."

His strong hands urged her to turn, so she rolled to her back. Unfortunately, she found he had already pulled on his suit from the night before, and even had his tweed coat slung over his arm, too. He was ready to leave, and she just wanted to yank him back in bed, and keep him there with her for a few more hours.

Who could blame her?

"You're leaving already?" she asked.

Andino grinned even as his brows lifted. "It's five in the morning."

Was it?

That was a big *nope* from her.

"What is wrong with you? This is too early."

Andino's husky laughter was only muffled when he bent down, and pressed a hard kiss to Haven's still tender lips. It hadn't just been her pussy that he'd put to use the night before, not that she was complaining.

"I don't want to make your roommate and her daughter uncomfortable," he said, pulling away from her far too soon for her liking. "And I have a big day today."

Haven abused her bottom lip with her teeth. "It's Valentine's day, Andino."

He was too busy adjusting the cufflink on his dress shirt to notice the way she fidgeted and waited for a reply.

"Yeah, I know—big party at my grandparents' mansion today."

"For Valentine's."

"They always throw a party whenever they can. The Marcellos like showing off."

"I suppose I'm not invited, huh?"

Finally, he looked at her again, and his face said it all.

Haven's smile was gone. "Yeah."

"It's just a party."

She knew that.

Except it was more, too.

"I just don't want to be used, Andino."

"When do I use you?"

It was starting to feel like it.

More often than she cared to admit.

"Be quiet when you leave, okay?" she asked, rolling over to put her back to him.

Andino's sigh echoed in the quiet room. "You're not my secret, Haven."

He kept saying that.

She didn't know if she believed it.

• • •

"You look rough. Bad night?"

Haven almost choked on the coffee when she took too big of a drink at the same time Valeria strolled into the kitchen. She coughed out half of a lung, and checked the clock at the same time.

"What are you doing up at five-thirty in the morning?"

Valeria raised a single brow, and shrugged before coming to stand next to the island. "Woke up when you tripped over the toy in the hallway, and didn't even try to be quiet about it."

So, maybe it wasn't Andino who needed to be quiet.

She shot her friend an apologetic look. "Sorry."

Valeria peered out the window where it was still dark. "A bit early for you to be going out to run or anything, isn't it?"

"A little."

"Wanna talk about it?"

Haven sighed. "Not really."

"You know, I saw his shoes and jacket when I got up to check on Maria last night. And while you were quiet … have to give you that," her friend said, "I couldn't help but hear something else, too."

Haven's cheeks pinked instantly.

Valeria laughed, and she leaned over the island a bit. Her hand came up to rhythmically smack the countertop with a fast, hard pace before she added, "The boy can sure keep a beat, though, can't he? A *long* beat."

"Oh, my *God*." Haven was sure her face was going to permanently turn red. "I'm so sorry."

"It's fine. I didn't hear much else, and I just turned the television on in my room. Maria's room is on the other side of the house, so …"

"That's the first time I've brought him home."

Valeria nodded. "I know. Don't worry about it. And besides, I mean, after a night like that, you shouldn't be standing here nursing a cup of coffee, and looking like someone kicked your puppy. What's up?"

A lot of things.

She could have just as easily brushed her friend's concerns off. It wasn't like her to share her personal problems because frankly, Haven wasn't the type to have that kind of issue to begin with. And yet, she'd had more in the time she'd been messing around with Andino than she'd had in her entire life before him.

She wanted to say it wasn't worth it.

The pain wouldn't be worth it.

Something else said it just might.

"You *can* talk to me," Valeria said.

"I know."

"Then talk."

There was a lot of things she could have said; how she felt, and the way things seemed to be shaking out for her and Andino at the end of the day. The inevitable end that she felt was coming, and soon.

Instead, Haven settled on saying, "I think I fell in love with a man who can't or won't love me back, Val."

Her friend sagged a bit against the island. "I'm sorry."

Haven shrugged. "I don't know how to tell him that, though."

Valeria nodded. "They have a way of doing that to us—men like him, I mean. They sweep into your life, and they're enigmatic. Electric, even. A complex walking, you know? Everything about them is something you know you should stay away from, and yet, the same things that scare you are the same shit that draws you back in time and time again. I get it, Haven. Really."

"That's what it was like for you, too?"

"Yes," her friend replied, "and no."

"Sounds complicated."

"It's all complicated when you love a bad man, Haven. It's when he starts to love you back that you need to be careful."

She wondered …

Did he love her back?

Did it even matter anymore?

"I don't want to keep being hurt," Haven said. Even if Andino didn't mean to hurt her, some of the things he had done still did exactly that. "I'm allowed to be the one who says that I don't want to be hurt anymore, right?"

Valeria gave her a look. "Who else is going to do it for you?"

NINETEEN

Andino nursed the glass of red wine he held, and let his gaze drift over the sizable crowd that had come to celebrate Valentine's day at his grandparents' mansion. Usually, he liked this type of thing—the wealth, respect, and standing. He liked everything that being a Marcello provided him, and he took great pleasure in knowing that other people recognized his privilege, too.

Tonight was … different.

Or it seemed that way.

His three-piece black on black suit with a matching tie and vest felt too snug—especially around his throat. The Cartier watch on his wrist was ticking down, and he felt acutely aware of the sound even if he didn't know what it was ticking down to. Every time someone else's gaze would drift in his direction, Andino was quick to look away. He didn't want to be stared at tonight; he didn't want to be here at all.

He would much rather be on the other side of New York indulging a blonde, blue-eyed woman with a masterpiece inked all over her body. It was fucking Valentine's day. It wasn't like he had ever had a reason to want to be with *someone* on that day before, but he did this year. He'd rather be *normal* with Haven for five more minutes and not the little Marcello king in waiting that he felt like tonight.

He'd never been more on display with his family than he was now— Andino was never more aware of that fact than now.

All eyes on him.

How well will you rise?

He could practically feel them asking that question of him in their minds. He didn't need to actually hear them say it when he could see it written on all their faces. Their expectations were all around him constantly.

Heavy is the head that wears the crown.

Wasn't that how the saying went?

It wasn't even the idea of being the boss that bothered him as much as it was the way these people wanted to concern themselves with *how* he became the boss, or how he chose to *be* the boss.

Andino cared nothing for that.

At all.

"You're looking lonely over here," his mother said as she slid in beside him. "And not talking to *anyone*, either. That's not like you."

God, he loved his ma.

He wished she wasn't so fucking observant, though.

"What's wrong, Andi?" Kim asked.

He gave her one of his most charming smiles—hoping it would do the trick, and divert her attention. "Nothing, Ma."

"Mmhmm. Try again."

Jesus.

Andino tipped his glass up, and polished off a good mouthful of the red wine. It gave him a couple extra seconds to think up some excuse as to why he was off on his own in a party full of people who usually adored him just because of who he was. "People watching, Ma."

Kim rolled her eyes. "Well, that's boring. And you're still lying."

She knew him too well.

"Thinking, Ma. That's all."

Kim glanced down, and swirled the wine in her glass before quietly asking, "Is this because of a certain young woman?"

Andino smirked. "We shouldn't talk about that—*her*—Ma."

"Why not?"

"You know why not."

Kim smiled sweetly, and arched a brow in challenge when she met Andino's stare once more. "Did you know I was engaged when I met your father—and *not* to Gio, I might add."

Andino cleared his throat. "I have heard the stories."

"I do know what it's like to go against the grain in this life, Andino. I know the consequences, and how hard it is to come out on top after it's all said and done."

"Ma, I have enough people telling me what I can and can't do with my life at the moment. Please, don't be another voice in that chorus."

Kim laughed softly. "Is that what you think I'm doing?"

"I know that's what you're about to do, actually."

"How so?"

Andino shook his head. "You know the rules—Dante put me where he did, and I have to follow along with his expectations regarding my personal life as to not be challenged after I take the seat. And … you did run to Dad the second you found Haven in my home. So, please, you've done enough. I don't need to hear your voice added to the chorus of control in my life, too."

"You're wrong," Kim said quickly, "but I suppose that's partly my fault since I didn't explain anything different to you, and you're left to make assumptions."

"Pardon?"

His mother shrugged as she sipped on her wine. "I told your father about Haven because I knew if that woman—if *love*—was the hill you were willing to die on for this life, then we had to be ready to die on it with you." Kim's gaze drifted to Andino's stoic face, and then she peered across the room. He followed her stare to find she was looking at his uncle, Dante. "And *some of us* ... well, some of us will need a bit more time, and some help along the way to see reason. I knew that, too."

"I—"

Kim held up a hand, quieting Andino. "You should try to put yourself in other people's shoes at times, Andi. Your uncle is not like your father, or even like his other brother. Dante is *Dante*. He's not as progressive, or open to change. He's stuck in a place where he's trying to maintain the status quo of what Cosa Nostra is ... the Cosa Nostra *he* knows. The one that was given to him. But he is not so stuck in his ideals that he would be willing to burn down this entire organization and family in the hopes of it remaining unchanged. Like I said ... he is not like his brothers, and he needs more time."

Andino didn't know what to say. His mother apparently didn't need him to say anything at all. The women in his life were always doing this to him, it seemed.

Stunning him.

Turning his world upside down.

Being *amazing*.

"But we all have an image and expectations to maintain," his mother added, "and so I hope you'll forgive me when I keep mine firmly in place until I no longer need to."

Yeah, he got what she was saying.

Kim nodded at the people gathered in the mansion's ballroom. "Go, and mingle. These *are* your people, and many of them, your family. Eventually, they're going to be the ones dying on your hill for that woman, too, even if it doesn't seem like it right now. Don't sulk in a corner—that's not the man I raised."

His mother didn't even wait for him to give a response. No, she simply patted him on the cheek with her soft hand, gave him one of *those* looks only a mother could give, and then she headed into the crowd of people again.

Well, damn.

Andino didn't get the chance to think about his mother's words, or do what she told him to. Something—or rather, *someone*—else caught his attention instead. It seemed like that was happening to Andino a lot lately.

His cousin cut through the crowd of people looking like a man on a fucking mission. And not a particularly stable man at the moment, if Andino was to trust that unusual gleam in John's eye.

Shit.

Andino quickly moved through the people to go after his cousin. John's mental state had been progressively getting worse over the last couple of days, and he rarely even picked up a call from Andino. His cousin had approached him recently rambling about a fucking file, and blaming him.

John was getting worse.

And fast.

Andino made it ten feet away from John when the man approached his own father. Lucian stepped away from the guest he was chatting with to greet his oldest, and only, son. "John."

"You didn't think to invite me?" John asked.

Lucian smiled faintly. "You didn't think to answer your phone?"

John shoved his shaking hands into his pockets, and his stare turned cold and hard. "Have you been talking to Andino, or something?"

Ah, shit.

Andino found his own father's gaze meeting his from behind Lucian. Gio shook his head subtly—it was enough for him to know that, *no*, his father had not updated Lucian entirely on the John situation, and what had been going on when no one was looking. Andino only needed to get a good look at his uncle to know the man suspected things were seriously up with John, but that wasn't the same as having all the details.

That was not going to be a fun conversation.

"Why would I talk to Andino?" Lucian asked.

John changed direction just as fast which was all too common when he was dealing with a manic spiral. Even the tone of his voice changed, and he spoke faster. "I don't know if it was you, or Dante, or who the fuck it was, but I don't need any of you sending me shit like you did last week."

Lucian frowned. "What are you talking about?"

"Don't play fucking games with me, Dad."

Lucian stepped forward, concern coloring his gaze. "John, are you all right?"

John stiffened, and his jaw flexed at that question. "Is that all any of you ever think about with me? If I'm okay, if I can handle myself, if my shit is taken care of? I am fucking *fine*, Dad."

Too loud, John.

Everybody looked their way.

"I only came here to make one fucking thing clear," John said.

Lucian put a hand up to stop anyone from coming closer—like he knew without having to look that at least one of his brothers were about to come to his aid. He was right, too. Dante had moved closer, but stopped at Lucian's raising hand.

"And what's that, son?" Lucian asked.

"Remember, it's not my loyalty in this family that ever needs to be in question."

John spun on his heel, and headed back for the entrance of the ballroom. Lucian gestured at an enforcer across the way, and pointed at his son—a silent order to follow John, which the man did without question, and quietly. How long he would be able to tail John was anyone's fucking guess, though. John was sneaky and sly like that, but especially when he was paranoid as hell.

Then, Lucian's sharp gaze turned on Andino as Giovanni joined his son's side. Anger, and fear swirled in the man's eyes, although his outward appearance remained stoic and calm.

So was the way of a Marcello man.

"What haven't you been telling me about my son?" Lucian asked quietly.

Like he already *knew* …

Andino looked in the direction John had gone. "It's a recent thing—he's not well."

"*Obviously.*"

"I was trying to keep an—"

"I don't give a shit what you were trying to do," Lucian snapped. "You're going to tell me everything, and you're going to do it now."

"We will," Gio said.

Lucian cursed under his breath. "You knew, too?"

"Andi came to me; I was trying to help."

"It's *my* son, Gio."

Giovanni nodded. "I know."

Except … Andino was Gio's son, and they all had to have priorities. Even if no one wanted to admit it.

"Someone start talking," Lucian said darkly.

"Yes, please do," Dante added, staring hard at Andino.

Well, this was going to be a long night.

Great.

• • •

Andino sent another text to Haven even as he pulled his Lexus to a spot in front of her house. Snaps jumped forward from the back to put his big paws on the center piece between the front seats. His tail went wild—knowing Haven was going to be around soon, and recognizing her house.

The dog did love her.

It amused Andino to no end.

His amusement was quick to fade when he noticed Haven didn't respond back to his text—like the last ten he'd sent since the night before, and over the morning. That wasn't like Haven at all which was why he just decided to come over to her place while he had five minutes to spare.

He couldn't be here long.

John had taken off the night before, but like Andino figured, the enforcer following behind had lost his cousin's trail the second they were on a freeway. That only served to put Lucian in a panic, which meant everybody else needed to be in the same kind of state.

Andino was going to look for his cousin just like everybody else—he figured John ended up in one of his favorite places. Somewhere that was comforting and familiar to him.

First, though, he wanted to check on Haven.

Snaps tried to follow Andino out of the car, but he was quick to make the dog stay. "You can wait, Snaps."

The dog huffed.

He just laughed.

Closing the driver's door, Andino rounded the car and headed for the small Brooklyn bungalow even as he checked his phone *again*. It wasn't like it buzzed or anything, but fuck, maybe the damn thing was—

"It's Andino, right?"

Andino's head snapped up to find a pretty woman closing the front door of the house before she came to stand on the front stoop. Even though it was cold out, she wore nothing but a sweater and jeans, and her dark brown hair had been thrown up in a messy bun. He recognized her, but only because he'd seen her once or twice in passing.

Valeria, he thought.

Haven's roommate.

They'd never had a real conversation—he thought he might have said hello to her once when he was at Haven's club, and the woman was helping out behind the bar. But beyond that? Nothing came to mind.

"It is Andino," he said. "And you're Valeria, yeah?"

"Most people call me Val," she replied, smiling faintly. "You don't need to worry about that, though."

Andino stiffened, and his steps slowed to a stop at the bottom of the stoop's stairs. "Something wrong?"

"Not that I know of."

"Good. Is Haven home?"

Valeria glanced away. "Not at the moment."

"Little early for her to be at the club, isn't it?"

"She's not there, either, although I wasn't told to tell you any of this."

"What's that supposed to mean exactly?" he asked.

"Does it matter?"

Yeah, it kind of did. Andino didn't like the way this woman seemed like she was trying to play word games with him. Either his girl was around, or she wasn't. And if she wasn't, then where in the hell was she?

What in the fuck was happening?

Andino checked the time on his phone again. "She's probably on her run, then."

"Not unless her run is twenty-thousand feet in the air."

"*What?*"

Valeria sighed. "Listen, Andino … I don't really know you, so I can't say whether or not you're a decent guy. I do know *enough* about you to make my own assumptions, though, so I'll leave it like that. Haven took a vacation because she *needs* one, not that you would know anything about what she needs, right?"

"I beg your pardon?"

Where did this chick get off saying something like that to him? She didn't know him, and he doubted she knew very much about him and Haven, either. Hell, *he* was still trying to figure out this shit with Haven.

"She headed out to see her parents for a week. She figured you would be around, and told me to let you know—"

"What?" he asked sharply.

"She wanted you know that she's going to worry about taking care of herself for a while," Valeria said, shrugging one shoulder and never breaking their staring contest. "So, take that however you want to."

"I don't want to take that at all."

Valeria nodded. "Yeah, I bet."

"So, she's just *gone?*"

And she hadn't let him know?

Why?

Valeria cleared her throat, and stared down at the porch beneath her shoes. "This is coming from me, and not her … but no one ever wants to be second best in someone's life, Andino. Especially not someone they love. It hurts too much."

He blinked.

Haven wasn't second best to him.

You did put her there, though. You did that—you had other shit to handle. You told her that again and again.

He couldn't ignore his thoughts screaming at him, even though he wished he could.

"So, yeah," Valeria added, turning to open the front door again, "she's taking care of herself for a while, and maybe in the meantime, you can get your shit figured out. Either way, she's going to be fine. I'm sure you know that about Haven. Everybody who knows her already does."

Valeria's final words hung heavily around Andino long after she went inside the house, and closed the door. He could hear Snaps barking behind him—still excited, and wanting to see his favorite person.

Andino didn't know how long he stood there dazed, confused, and feeling heavy in his fucking heart—it was only the shrill ring of his phone in his hand that brought him back to reality with a bang. He checked the caller ID before picking up just in case it was someone he could ignore.

It was the boss.

No one could ignore the boss.

Andino didn't even get the phone to his ear before he heard Dante bark, "*Where the fuck is John?*"

Fucking hell.

"I'm still looking for him," Andino snapped back. "Relax, and give me time to work."

"Time is up."

"What?"

"Just what I said," his uncle said darkly. "A warehouse was burned to the ground last night—a *Calabrese* warehouse. They're blaming it on John, and threatening action against him unless one of us finds him first, and keeps him out of harm's way. I'm trying to negotiate some kind of meeting right now. I need you to find John *now*, Andino."

Fuck.

Why could nothing go right?

"Listen, I know John is a little messed up right now … but burning a Calabrese warehouse? He's stuck on Siena Calabrese, Dante," Andino pointed out. "In a *big* way. He loves the woman. He's not purposely going to cause problems with her family that will force them to take her away from him. You know what I mean?"

"I don't think John did *anything*—the Calabrese are a bunch of snakes. We know that, but the problem is, does *John* know that when he's not seeing things clearly right now, Andino? You know as well as the rest of us do that when John is manic, he perceives everything differently. The last time he was like this, he almost fucking killed you. His *best friend*. Or did you forget about that?"

No, he had not forgotten.

Yeah, shit.

Good point.

"Find him," Dante ordered, "and I will call you back when I have news."

His uncle hung up.

That was that.

Andino looked back at Haven's house—once again, it seemed, he was going to have to put his problems where she was concerned to the back burner so that he could deal with someone else's shit.

Valeria was right.

He'd put Haven second one too many times. She probably wasn't even going to let him apologize for it, either.

Andino didn't blame her.

He deserved it.

• • •

Andino crossed the street quickly, and ducked into the restaurant that looked as though it was currently undergoing renovations. He ignored the murmurings of men all around him—waiting, and ready for bad shit to go down.

So was the way of their life.

The Calabrese waited on one side.

Marcellos on the other.

Andino didn't know how his uncle managed to get all these men—men who *despised* one another—into the same space without some kind of violence breaking out between them, but here they were. Peaceful, at least, for now.

How long it would last was anyone's guess.

He wasted no time finding his uncles and father. It was only once Andino was standing next to his uncle that he quietly explained what he knew at a level that no one but them could hear. "John is on his way—he sounds better."

Dante's expression gave nothing away when he asked, "How much better?"

Lucian and Andino's father were listening then, too.

"Better," Andino said. "Not as … out of it, or angry. Not like last night at the mansion, anyway. Better than he's sounded in days."

Dante let out a quiet sigh—relief.

Lucian, on the other hand, shook his head. "Don't get comfortable in that, brother. That's the thing about mania with John; it has crests and peaks. Ups and downs even when he's in the middle of it. He can be lucid and good for a little bit, but then he can get thrown right back into the worst of it with nothing more than a comment from someone else. It's fickle."

"But he's coming," Gio said, giving Andino a look. "Here, right?"

Andino nodded.

Giovanni shrugged. "Then, we'll get our hands on him. That's what we need—what *he* needs. Once we've got him contained, then we'll go from there and get him settled. He just needs some help. We'll give him that."

Andino tipped his head in the direction of the murmuring Calabrese men. "They were quick to show up here, weren't they?"

Dante scowled, and his gaze narrowed slightly. "They did—fucking snakes."

"They want something," Lucian murmured.

Giovanni nodded. "The Calabrese always want something. It's finding out *what* that becomes dangerous."

"Do you think ..." Andino trailed off, and passed his family a look. "Is it possible they're the ones antagonizing John lately? Did they make this happen, or make it worse somehow?"

No one answered him.

Andino understood why.

It was hard to say—John's disorder wasn't widely known in their circles, and definitely not outside of their people. The thing was ... the Calabrese family couldn't be trusted. The Marcellos called them snakes for a *reason*.

Andino wouldn't put doing something like this—manipulating or hurting John to get one over on the Marcellos—past them.

"Show time," Giovanni murmured.

Andino's attention went to the restaurant door where he could see John approaching. Well ... John and someone else.

"He was with her," Lucian said faintly.

Siena, that was.

Andino cleared his throat. "Yeah, shit ... I forgot to mention that."

Dante gave him a look. "You forget to mention a lot of things lately, it seems."

"One thing at a time," Giovanni said. "Right now, let's worry about getting John somewhere *safe*, and then we'll handle the rest."

His father said that like it wasn't a big deal.

No problem.

Right.

Because this wasn't going to be easy *at all*.

Andino knew that first hand.

TWENTY

The ringing of the phone echoed in Haven's ear like a backdrop to the beating rain pelting the window. She didn't know if it was normal for Florida to have this much rain nearing the end of February, but that seemed to be all it had done since she got here. Rain made everything a little drab, and heavy.

It was appropriate for her mood, though.

Bleak.

Tired.

Dark.

Finally, the call clicked through on the other end. Haven lost the daze she'd been in waiting for her friend to pick up while she stared out the window of her parent's Florida beach house. The voice on the other end of the call made her smile, even if her heart was all too heavy lately.

Funny how that worked.

One could smile through sadness.

"Still not using your phone, huh?"

Haven laughed. "I've just ... left it turned off, Val. This is supposed to be a vacation for me, remember? *You* practically threw me out the front door with my bag in hand, and told me to relax by taking time for me."

"Hey, it wasn't that bad."

"Pretty close."

Valeria let out a quiet sigh. "Are you at least enjoying yourself?"

"I'm enjoying visiting with my parents. I didn't realize how much I missed them until I was walking through their door, you know?"

"I do know," Valeria said quietly. "I miss my parents all the time, but I won't ever get to see them again. Not like you and yours, anyway. I'm glad you get to see them. And I expected you to enjoy visiting with your parents, I meant ... are you having a good time in *general*?"

Well, that question wasn't as easy.

"Yes, and no," Haven murmured. "I *really* needed a break from work. I've gone two years nonstop with barely even a regular day off every week. I like having a vacation from the club, and that whole thing."

"But?" her friend pressed.

Yeah, there was always a *but.*

That *but* was the part that was not so easy to answer. After all, Haven had been in Florida for quite a few days, and she still hadn't figured out what to do to fix this, or if she even wanted to at this point.

"I'm not the type to leave things unfinished, Val. You know that about me. I felt like I just left a lot of things hanging in the air back in New York, and it's weighing me down."

To say the least …

Mostly, Andino.

She didn't want to say his name out loud, though. It would only leave her feeling even heavier than she already did because there was so much about that man that Haven loved and adored, and then there were things about him that left her feeling second-rate, and unwanted.

She had worked too hard, and she loved herself too damn much to be anyone's second *anything*. At the same time, a part of her still wanted to try and give Andino the chance to fix what had gone wrong.

But would he want to?

Could he even *try*?

Those were the better questions.

"Well," Valeria said slowly, "at least you can check one thing off your list of worries. You don't have to worry about the club—Jackson has it all handled."

Haven grinned. "Yeah, I figured. I should let him have a bit more leeway, I think."

"You should; you could take more time off."

Didn't that just sound lovely?

And also, terrifying.

"A week or two is fine *for now*," Haven said, "and only because I really needed it. But if I start taking too much time off—"

"The club isn't going to fall into a pit of failure and despair, Haven."

She rolled her eyes. "So you say."

"So I *know*. And so do you."

Maybe.

A little.

Haven just didn't want to admit it, and also, maybe she was a bit of a workaholic. It was the only thing that kept her going a lot of the time, and it was the one thing in her life that gave her actual purpose.

That was part of the problem right now, too. She didn't have anything to keep her busy, or out of her own head. She was spending way too much time inside the loneliness of her mind, and trying to figure out the way she felt.

It was too much.

"He came the other day," Valeria said out of the blue.

Haven stiffened, and held a little tighter to the cordless phone. "Did he?"

"Showed up early in the morning asking for you."

"Did you tell him—"

"Not where you went, or anything," her friend was quick to say.

"Thanks."

"No problem, but …"

Yeah, another *but*.

Surprise, surprise.

"What?" Haven asked.

"He did look really taken off guard by the fact you were gone, and then kind of … sad."

Haven glanced out the window again—the rain had picked up, it seemed. Appropriate, considering her heart was heavier than ever, and her soul felt just as gray as the sky above. Love shouldn't make a person feel like this; of that, she was most sure.

Yet, she still did.

Love him, that was.

"I needed time," Haven murmured. "I couldn't just call him when I knew the first thing he would do was cloud up my thoughts and feelings."

Because hearts were traitorous like that.

They needed love to *live*.

Haven needed for love to not feel like a game, or worse, an afterthought to someone else. She couldn't have her love be something that Andino could do with, or without, depending on the day or his mood. She needed it to be *more* to him.

Something worth having, and *keeping*.

She didn't know if it was.

She didn't even know if he loved her back.

"Yeah, I know," Valeria eventually replied. "Well, Maria is just waking up. Call me when your flight lands today?"

"I will."

She'd been here long enough.

It was time to go home.

Haven still didn't know how she felt about that, either.

Yeah, she really was a mess.

Or a coward, her mind taunted.

That, too.

"All right, I'll talk to you when I land," Haven said.

"Sounds good."

A quick goodbye later, and Haven cradled the cordless phone on its base. Even though her conversation was done, it continued echoing through her mind for minutes after. Hindsight was always twenty-twenty, right? Wasn't that how the saying went?

Haven was seeing a hell of a lot clearer, now.

Instead of dealing with her problems, and giving Andino the chance to fix what had gone wrong between them time and time again, Haven chose to run. She wasn't so stupid or caught up in her feelings that she didn't recognize that little fact.

She had good reasons, though.

At least, that's what she thought.

Or maybe … just maybe … this had been Haven's shitty way of protecting herself from getting hurt again. There was a part of her that simply didn't want to be hurt by that man again, even if it wasn't directly. She didn't want to give him the chance to reject her, or shove her away.

So instead, she had done this.

Yeah.

Turning a bit, she stared at her cell phone that had remained dead for her entire stay in Florida. Not once had she turned it on—not even to check the voicemail, or something. She just knew there would be calls or texts from Andino, and she was trying to keep a clear head.

Maybe it was finally time.

Before Haven could overthink her next choice, she grabbed the cell phone, and turned it on. It took all of a minute for the phone to boot up, and then sync to all her unanswered notifications spread between emails, texts, calls, and voice messages.

Sure enough, there were about a dozen from Andino between calls and texts. He'd left two voice messages, too, it seemed. And then anything from him stopped after a certain date—likely when he'd gone looking for her, and was told she left.

She checked his last text message.

I really just need to see you—you home?

Haven stared at the words, and felt her chest grow tighter. He'd told her once that he believed *she* was the person in his life who was supposed to be looking out for him, but she hadn't really believed him at the time.

If it was true, then she'd fucked up.

Left him hanging.

Didn't even apologize for it, either.

She was going home now, though. She wouldn't be able to hide from him forever. Frankly, she didn't want to, either.

Haven hit the call button next to Andino's name, and put the phone to her ear. It took him less than a ring and a half to pick up.

"*Haven.*"

Pain colored his voice.

The relief was thick, too.

"Hey, Andino," she said, trying to keep a level tone. "Uh … I'm coming home today. I thought maybe we could meet up."

He didn't even hesitate. He didn't ask questions, or make demands. It only served to take away the heaviness resting on her heart, and crushing it.

"Anytime," he replied.

"I won't get in until late."

"That's fine."

"I'm sorry I didn't call."

Andino was quiet for a hell of a lot longer than Haven liked on the other end of the call, but she figured … well, she gave him silence for weeks. This was only fair, wasn't it?

"I never expected you to be a doormat, Haven," he finally said, "and certainly not mine. Don't apologize for needing space, or time."

Yeah, okay.

"Where are you going to be tonight?"

"The office at my restaurant—until at least one, anyway. There's a lot of shit going on."

"I can come to you, then."

"Please," he murmured. "I miss you."

Her heart hurt again.

The guilt compounded.

"I just …"

"What?" Andino asked. "Tell me *anything.*"

"If I matter to you—"

"You matter to me more than anything."

Haven let out a shaky exhale. "Then it shouldn't be a big deal to make me a priority. More often than not, I've felt like an afterthought, Andino."

"I can only apologize."

Apologize, she thought.

But not promise it wouldn't happen again.

Haven heard what wasn't said.

• • •

Haven listened to the cabbie chatter on from the driver's seat as he navigated the city streets. She was only half listening, and occasionally offered him a nod or hum to make it seem like she was conversing back. It wasn't his fault, really. Her distraction was her own.

Talking was likely the only thing that got him through the work day on a regular basis. It was going to be a late night for him, likely. It always was for cabbies in the city.

The phone in her pocket rang just as they turned onto the block for Andino's resturant. She hadn't even gone home to see Valeria or Maria yet. Pulling the phone out, she didn't bother to check the ID before answering.

"Hello?"

"Haven?"

Andino's voice made her smile.

"Hey, I'm about five minutes or so away."

"Shit," Andino mumbled.

All over again, that heaviness was back.

"What is it?" she asked.

"I had to leave—something came up with my cousin, John. His dad called me. He took off, and he's in a bad place. Remember when I told you that he got mixed up in some bad people?"

Haven's jaw felt stiff even as she said, "Yeah, I remember."

"Well, it's worse now."

"So, you're not even at your—"

"No, I'm a couple of blocks away right now."

Jesus Christ.

Haven didn't *want* to be angry. It might have even been a little irrational—she was willing to admit that. Still, she hoped maybe tonight could have been a turning point for her and Andino. She wasn't sure that it would be, now.

"Just don't go anywhere," Andino said quickly. "Wait for me, please."

Haven glanced out the window at the passing street. "I *want* to, Andino. I really do, but I'm not sure I should anymore. And it's more than tonight—it's a lot of things. So, maybe I need you to give me a reason why I should wait for you, okay? Because between us, I'm the one who goes the distance. I give; you take. It can't keep being like that."

"You should wait because I love you, and I would like the chance to tell you."

His declaration came out fast, sure, and *true*.

Haven still couldn't help but wonder … would it matter in the end? After everything was said and done, would *I love you* be enough for both of them?

Right now, it was.

"I'll wait," she whispered.

"Okay. I'll see you then, my girl."

The call hung up with a click at the same time the cabbie pulled to a stop in front of Andino's restaurant. The place was as dark as night, and obviously closed, but that wasn't the first thing to catch Haven's attention.

No, the first thing was the woman looking in the windows. Haven recognized her, but barely.

Siena Calabrese.

The woman Andino's cousin had gotten mixed up; the woman who came from *bad people*. Although, the one-time Haven had met Siena, she thought the girl was sweet, and kind. There wasn't very damn much that was bad about her.

"Thanks," Haven said to the cabbie, paying him quickly and stepping out of the vehicle. She was quick to cross the sidewalk, and climb the steps of the restaurant's entrance. "Siena?"

Siena spun around fast to face her—panic stared back from the woman. That screamed bad news to Haven.

"What are you doing here?" Haven asked.

"Where is Andino?"

Nice way to greet someone.

"He was here working in the office," Haven said. "But he got called out a while ago."

"Where is he *now*?"

Haven looked away, knowing she probably shouldn't tell this woman very much, even if she didn't have a lot to tell. Not because *she* personally thought Siena couldn't be trusted, but because she didn't know if Andino felt the woman could be trusted.

Therein lied the difference.

"Why?" Haven asked.

Siena's jaw stiffened, and her gaze hardened as she looked Haven over. "Let me guess, you're not supposed to trust me either, right?"

"Well—"

"I don't have time for this," Siena snapped, moving for the stairs. "John is in trouble."

"John?"

Siena hesitated in her next step, and looked back at Haven. "Yeah, John."

Haven could tell just by the way the woman said John's name, and the thick panic in her eyes that she loved the man. She was terrified, for reasons Haven didn't know, but she could see the love.

And Andino …

Well, he cared a lot about John, too.

"Andino is a couple of blocks away," Haven said. "I guess John's father called. He took off."

That panic in Siena's eyes only increased, a lot like the shrillness in her tone when she asked, "John did?"

"Yeah. Earlier."

Siena spun around to face Haven. "Please, tell them John is at my father's home."

"Why would I do that?"

"Because if you don't, Andino will never forgive you when they finally get John's body back from my family."

Siena spoke the words so surely that there was no question whether or not she was lying. Haven turned into a statue of ice right there on the stairs. A heavy realization slammed down on her, and while she had *known*, this made it all the more real.

Here was Andino's life.

Criminals.

Fear.

Bad people.

Siena took the stairs two at a time, and called over her shoulder at the same time. "I can't chase them. I have to help John instead."

Oh, God.

"Don't make me regret this, okay?" Haven called back.

Siena only laughed.

Bleak, and bitter.

Haven knew the feeling well.

TWENTY-ONE

"*Fuck*," Lucian snarled harshly.

The man was two seconds away from smashing his phone against the steering wheel of the car—Andino could tell. That might not end well for them, especially if John ended up deciding it was his father that he wanted to call.

Slim chance, given John took off on his father earlier, but still. It wasn't a risk Andino was willing to take, either.

"Try not to break the phone," Andino muttered.

His uncle shot him a look that *burned*. He didn't blame Lucian for his mood, or attitude. This whole day—maybe even the week, frankly—had just gone to shit with one thing after another. John's mania spiraled until it was too late to bring him out of it, and now bad things were fucking happening. As they usually did.

Andino wished he was surprised.

Right now, though, his only goal was to find his cousin, and bring him home *safely*. Out of the reach of the Calabrese family, who wanted to kill him, and without getting in trouble with the cops ... because that was a very real possibility, too.

"It just keeps going to *voicemail*," Lucian growled.

"My calls, too."

Lucian swore severely under his breath, and leaned back in the driver's seat. For hours—ever since John had taken off from his parents' house where everyone thought he would be safe and under control—they'd been like this. Searching, fearful, and *lost*. Andino went with Lucian, though he could have gone with someone else, because he figured it might make his uncle feel better to have someone who was close to John be with him.

That wasn't the case.

Lucian was pissed.

And scared.

Although, to a Marcello man ... being scared often just led to him acting like a gigantic asshole. No one liked to show their weaknesses like a hand of cards, so to speak. Someone was always willing to exploit what they thought could harm someone else in this business.

Lucian glanced out the window at the dark street. "Do you think they have him?"

"The Calabrese?"

"Who else?" Lucian asked. "He's been lost lately—too deep in his own head and issues to see how they were manipulating him. Nothing anyone

218

did helped him, and only pushed him away. Do you think he went to them because that's who he felt he could trust?"

"John is bipolar, but he's not stupid … and he's *not* crazy."

Lucian's jaw stiffened. "I didn't say he was. I *never* say that."

No one ever did.

Not in their family, anyway.

"I meant," Andino clarified, "there is no way in hell—regardless of the mental place John is in right now—that he felt he could trust the Calabrese family. He knows better."

"Then, where is he?"

That was the question of the hour, wasn't it?

Andino didn't get the chance to reply before the phone in his pocket buzzed with a call. Pulling the device out, he saw Haven's name, and instantly moved to get out of the car to take the call in private. His uncle shot him a look, but Andino pretended like he didn't see it. He'd just hung up with Haven a few minutes ago—why was she calling back so soon?

"Yeah," Andino said the second he shut the car door, "what's up?"

"I just ran into Siena," Haven replied, "and she said John is at her father's home."

It was like ice had been thrown all over Andino's body, and at the same time, someone drove a heavy spike of dread right into his spine.

"*Are you sure?*"

Haven was quick to say, "She was sure, anyway."

"Okay, thanks, I—"

"Have to go," Haven murmured.

Andino frowned.

God.

There was a lot of things he wanted to say to this woman. He owed her an apology; a real, true, honest fucking apology. She deserved so much more than what he had been giving her for too long, which frankly, wasn't very fucking much. She should be the most important thing in a man's life, especially when that man loved her. And he wanted to give her that.

Christ, yeah.

He wanted to give her it.

Andino just didn't know if he could.

"You should head home, Haven," he murmured. "I probably won't get back to my restaurant tonight. Another day, okay?"

He didn't even add in the apology.

She probably didn't want it.

Wasn't she sick and tired of useless apologies that never actually made a difference, or changed anything? God knew he was tired of giving them when he couldn't put his remorse to good use, and change the outcome for them both.

"I figured," she said softly. "I hope you find your cousin, and that he's okay."

"Me, too."

After a quick goodbye that was laced with her sadness, and his regret, Andino hung up the phone. He slipped back into the car to find his uncle looking at him.

"Well?" Lucian demanded.

"John's at Matteo Calabrese's brownstone."

His uncle blinked. "*What?*"

"That's the info I have."

"How—"

"Do you want to talk right now, or go get John?"

Lucian didn't even reply. He simply pulled the car out of park, and hit the gas hard enough to make the tires squeal. They were a ways away from the brownstone where Siena's father lived. Andino had never been to the place, but he knew *where* it was. Thankfully, the streets weren't congested this late at night, and there wasn't any cops hiding somewhere to pull them over. Although, Andino was sure his uncle blew at least four red lights, and there had to be a camera on one of them.

The car wasn't even at a full stop in front of the brownstone belonging to Matteo before Andino got out of the car. The wheels were still moving, and he almost tripped over his own goddamn feet in his haste.

He didn't care.

His mind was everywhere.

And nowhere.

John, John, John.

Had his cousin found death?

Had death found him?

Andino slipped inside the brownstone—the door wasn't even closed—and already had his gun drawn. He racked the Glock back, and stormed the front hallway just as a loud *bang* echoed from somewhere up above his head.

Shit.

The mantra in his mind shouting his cousin's name only became louder. Lucian was right on his heels even as Andino headed up the first flight of stairs. Neither of the two men spoke—there was nothing to say right now.

Their thoughts were bad enough.

What if …

What. If.

What if?

What if his cousin *had* trusted the Calabrese? What if Andino was just a little too late? There were so many fucking *what ifs*.

This was his fault.

His mistake.

He was supposed to look after John, and he hadn't done that. At least, not well. And if his cousin lost his life, then that blood was on Andino's hands. No question. He was never going to be able to forgive himself for that.

Ever.

He could hear a woman's voice talking as he climbed higher in the brownstone, but he couldn't quite make out what she was saying. Probably Siena. How long as she been here with John before they even arrived? Andino had just rounded the top of the third flight of stairs when that voice finally became clearer to him.

"Please, John, look it's *me* ..."

He picked up his fucking pace, then.

Andino came to a skidding stop in the doorway of what looked to be an office. His gaze darted all around to take in what he could.

His cousin, alive.

Siena, too close to a wild-eyed John.

A man, dead.

Bits of brain, and blood on a desk.

Andino blinked. "*Fuck.*"

It was the only thing he could think to say. Nothing else felt quite appropriate about the scene laid out in front of him.

A rival Cosa Nostra boss dead, and by his cousin's hand, it seemed. At least, if the gun in John's hand was any indication.

"Move back," Lucian snapped, pushing his way past Andino in the doorway. "Siena, move back from him *now.*"

The woman looked over her shoulder, wary and scared. She couldn't possibly understand, but that wild look in John's eyes meant bad things. He wasn't *here*—not really. He wasn't seeing her; he was seeing something else entirely in his mania.

The thin line between being manic, and sliding into psychosis.

Psychosis was a *monster.*

The last time his cousin looked like that, Andino stared down the barrel of John's gun. He'd not really been frightened, then.

He was terrified now.

"Move back!"

• • •

Andino glanced up from his coffee mug when his uncle came to stand in the entrance of the dining room. John's house was quiet, and dark. It belied the hell that they found only a few hours before. His uncle looked

221

worn—for the first time that Andino could remember, Lucian seemed like he was showing his age.

Stress could do that.

"She loves him quite a bit, doesn't she?" Lucian asked.

Andino lifted one shoulder. "Siena is very protective of John. She loves him."

Lucian nodded. "And yet, she is still—"

"A Calabrese, yeah."

"But maybe not *one of them*," his uncle murmured. "She shares their last name, and their blood, but she isn't like them."

"Little late to be coming to that realization, isn't it?" Andino asked. "Look at all that's happened."

Lucian shook his head subtly. "It's never too late to right a wrong, Andi. This life, and being a father, has taught me that."

Andino grunted under his breath, and glanced out the dark kitchen window. "So far, I've learned that this life does a lot of taking, but it doesn't do a lot of giving."

"It's called sacrifice."

"But for *what*?"

Lucian didn't seem to have an answer for that one.

His uncle joined him at the table, and the two were silent for a long while. Andino stared up at the ceiling where he knew his cousin, and Siena, were sleeping in John's room. Once they'd gotten John out of that brownstone, he'd gained a bit of lucidity.

That helped.

Not much.

"Do you think she's okay up—"

"She's fine with him," Lucian said. "Now."

Andino nodded, and went back to staring out the window. His mind was running a million miles a minute. Retracing every step he'd made these last few months, and all the errors that had come from it. Things he couldn't fix, or take back. Things that would likely irrevocably change his life, and his family.

The guilt, though, was a killer.

It weighed the heaviest.

Pulled him down.

Drowned him.

"Don't do that," Lucian said quietly.

Andino glanced at his uncle. "Pardon?"

"The guilt thing. I can see it. You don't wear it well."

Clearing his throat, Andino said, "If not guilty about all of this, then what should I feel?"

"John is not your responsibility," Lucian replied. "There is only so much we can do, and so far we can reach with him. The rest has to be his choice, and we can't make those choices for him, Andi."

Easier said than done.

"I've always looked out for him," Andino replied. "Ever since—"

"You were kids, I know."

"The one time I don't have his back, and he goes into a manic spell, kills a rival boss, and—"

"Andino."

He met Lucian's gaze. "What?"

"This isn't your burden to bear."

Andino knew his uncle meant the *guilt*.

But still …

"John's never been a burden," Andino said, "and if I don't look out for him, then who will?"

Lucian pointed a single finger upward. "Seems he has someone else doing that now. If not for Siena, tonight might have ended very differently."

True, but …

"I still fucked up."

"Andino," his uncle said firmly, "don't take this personally, but right now, this isn't about you. Don't make it about you to make it easier on John. It's what keeps him from choosing stability. When everyone else is so quick to offer excuses for him, or they take on the duty to care for him, it makes it easier for him to be blind to his own responsibility."

Huh.

Andino had never really thought of it like that. He didn't get the opportunity to continue the conversation further. It was the flash of lights outside the house, and several black cars pulling into the driveway that had both men standing from their seats. A simple look out the window told Andino that they were in for more trouble.

The Calabrese had come, it seemed.

Lucian held a hand up to Andino as if to silent ask him to stay put before the man slipped into the hallway. Andino did just that, and watched from the window as his uncle stepped outside to greet one of Siena's brothers as the man exited a car.

A quick conversation later, and Lucian reentered the kitchen.

"What do they want?" Andino asked.

His uncle looked upward. "Her."

Andino stilled. "We can't let them take her—she belongs with *John*."

Lucian nodded once. "I know."

"So, then she *stays*."

"And what, we get into a gun fight with a half of a dozen men? We let them storm the house? We—and *John*—dies? That's not going to work, Andino."

Yeah, *fuck.*

All he could think to say again was, "But she belongs with John."

After all Siena had done for his cousin, wasn't that fair to her?

She loved him. The same way Andino loved Haven. He knew it was true; he saw it every time Siena risked herself for John.

The only difference was … Siena and John deserved each other. Andino wasn't sure he deserved someone like Haven at all.

"She does belong with him, you're right." Lucian shrugged. "So, we'll have to get her back for him, won't we?"

That sounded simple.

It wouldn't be.

• • •

It took another two days before Lucian had been able to convince his son to voluntarily check in to a facility that would help stabilize John, and get him back on track. Andino stayed back, leaning against the side of his car, as he watched his uncle say goodbye to a very despondent John on the walkway of Clearview Oaks.

At least, the place didn't scream *psychiatric ward.*

It looked normal.

Because it was.

"This is killing Lucian," Andino's father muttered at his side.

"I can tell," Andino replied.

"John has to go in, and check in alone—of his own free will," Dante said as he came to stand on the other side of Andino. "Something Lucian needs to learn, I think. Let the man do this on his own."

Andino shook his head. "*Lucian* knows."

His boss shot him a look. "What's that supposed to mean, *nipote?*"

"It means, you don't need to keep stepping in on people's lives, and making choices for them when they *already know* what has to be done, and how to do it."

Giovanni cleared his throat.

Dante only arched a brow. "Is that so?"

"It is."

He wished his uncle would put the advice to use.

"Let's start with you, then," Dante murmured.

Andino stiffened. "That's not what I—"

"Oh, well. It's what you *said.*"

"I meant in general, not that we had to get in to specifics."

Dante shrugged. "Since you're all about letting others make their choices when they know what they have to do, and how to do it … I think it's best we do start with you."

Of course, he did.

His uncle continued on even when Andino stayed quiet next to him. "We have to make choices, now. *All of us*. What we're going to do from here, and how we're going to do it. John killed a rival boss, and the family of that boss is now in an uproar. Threatening war with our family—it's only a matter of time before the first person dies."

"I don't think he meant for that to happen," Andino muttered.

"Maybe not, but now we have to act. We have to protect our family."

"I know—"

"Do you?" Dante asked sharply.

"I do."

"And what would your call be, then?"

"Answer them with whatever they throw at us," Andino said. "Nothing that wouldn't be worth it, anyway. We can handle this. The Calabrese only want *power* from us—they're snakes in the grass, and nothing more. I wouldn't give them anything."

Dante scoffed. "Of course. You're so willing to rush into a violent street war with a rival family just *because* you know we can win it? What will be the cost, then? How many of our men will need to die because pride won't allow you to do what would probably be the best, even if it didn't feel right? My wife, or daughter? One of Lucian's children, perhaps? *Your* mother?"

Giovanni made a sound in the back of his throat, but stayed quiet on the other side of Andino. In fact, his father never even looked away from where Lucian was still saying goodbye to John on the walkway.

"That's the thing about wars," Dante said, "not that I expect you to understand, Andino, as we've kept the peace in this city for your entire life so that you never had to live through a street war with another family. But in war, *someone always has to lose*. And that loss doesn't necessarily mean in the grand scheme of someone coming out on top, or on the bottom. It means, each side will lose something and someone because that is inevitable."

Guilt compounded hard in Andino's chest. That duty—the responsibility of protecting his family, their life, and name—that he had been ignoring for so long was suddenly heavy and present on his head again, weighing down his shoulders.

He said nothing.

His uncle didn't seem to need him to.

"Heavy is the head that wears the crown," Dante murmured. "And it's always the man who wears the crown that sacrifices the most, Andino, so the rest of the people around him never have to. What are you willing to sacrifice? I asked you once … when push comes to shove, would you step up, or step back? Time's up, *nipote*. Step up with me, or step back."

In a way, it pissed Andino off that his uncle thought he wouldn't do what needed to be done. That he would think about himself before ever thinking about their family, and how to protect them. Andino had been protecting his family in one way or another his whole fucking life.

He didn't expect Dante to understand, though.

Andino knew what he had to do—even if it was to the detriment of himself, and his heart. Even if it would kill him, and someone else, too.

He knew how to make peace.

For now, anyway.

"You're doing that again," Andino said, "where you're trying to tell me to do something I already know I have to do, and how to do it."

"And what is it you have to do?" Dante asked.

"Make peace with the Calabrese."

By any means necessary.

There was really only one way to do that in their world when something like this happened. There was only one way to appease the rage and violence before it spun out of control. There was one single thing he could give to feed the snakes so that they didn't come back to bite them.

Because even if Andino hated that he was in this position, he was really the *only* Marcello man who could possibly offer something good enough to a rival family that they would hold off on starting a war. He was the only one with any sort of position that still had an open spot at his side in his public and private life that needed to be filled—the next boss, still without a wife, and now, stuck between a rock and a hard place.

No one was going to be *happy*.

At least, not the Marcellos.

Not Andino.

Not Haven.

Duty called.

It waited on no one.

TWENTY-TWO

Noon—meet me on the trails.

Haven hadn't even needed to ask *which* trails Andino meant. The same jogging trails where they had first crossed paths.

It felt foreboding.

Something bad was on the way.

She didn't have any particular reason to feel like that, but in her heart ... it was there that she knew. Like they were coming back to this place where they first said hello so that they could maybe say a goodbye, too.

It was his first text in days, so maybe that was why she was left with this dreadful feeling making her throat tight, and her heart ache.

Haven's phone still burned a hole in her pocket long after she'd gotten that text from Andino earlier that morning. She'd responded confirmatively, but he'd not said anything more.

Here it was, five minutes to twelve, and he still hadn't shown his face. Haven was *trying* not to let that bother her. Just like she'd been trying ever since she returned home from Florida to get back to some semblance of normal in her life.

Jog.

Work.

Home.

It might seem boring to someone else, but it was comforting to her. Like this, she knew that no matter what happened, she could still maintain the normalcy of what had once become her life before the hurricane that was Andino Marcello rushed into it without any kind of warning.

"Haven."

She looked up from the white snow blanketing the ground to find Andino was only ten feet away. He didn't move to sit beside her on the bench. There was no Snaps by his side with a stick in his mouth like usual. No latte in his hand for her. He didn't even take his hands out of his pockets, or even really look at her. He was too busy staring down the trail as though he were waiting for someone to stroll down to their spot.

Oh, yeah.

She *knew*.

"I'm sorry," he said quietly, never turning to look at her entirely. "Sorry that I did a lot of things wrong, and I'm sorry that there's a lot of things I can't do differently. I'm *most* sorry that I can't be what and who you deserve."

Haven blinked.

227

Was that what he thought?

She'd just wanted to be *something*.

Something more than nothing to him.

"I knew you were going to break my heart," Haven said.

Andino looked at her then—all forest green eyes blazing, and his face passive. "Did you?"

"I just ... felt it."

And she didn't want to sit around, and let him keep breaking it, either. If this was done, then she figured, they needed to let it be done. There was no reason to linger, and allow it to hurt them even more.

Or ... *her*.

She didn't want to hurt more.

Haven stood from the bench, and brushed the few snowflakes off her coat with shaking hands that she tried to hide by shoving in her pockets. Despite what she *knew* she should do—leave, and let it be done—her soul screamed for her to stay right there.

It was such a fucking contradiction.

She *hated* it.

"What changed?" she asked. "A couple of days ago, you told me you loved me. You didn't even give me the chance to say it back, Andino."

His gaze met hers again. "Would you—say it back, I mean?"

"Of course, I would. That's why the first thing I did when I came back was to call *you*. I know we could have done things differently, or that things could be different on both our sides if we just figured it out. But it didn't matter to me, either. I just wanted to feel like I was something important to you, and not an afterthought in your life. Not something you used, and *discarded*."

Like he was doing right now.

That *killed* her.

Haven wasn't even sure Andino knew that, and if he did, she wasn't sure he cared. Andino's stiff posture, and blank expression remained. It was like nothing she said made any impact, and Haven wasn't sure what to do with that.

"We're never going to be together," he said, the words barely a murmur carrying through the wind. "Not now; not after everything. You're not appropriate for my position in my family, and I can't keep being selfish."

Ouch.

A slap might have felt better.

Haven refused to let him take another shot at her, although really, she wondered if his words were simply meant to send her running. Not that he actually meant them. Either way, he achieved his goal.

Giving him one last look, Haven said, "It was good, though, wasn't it?"

Andino smiled faintly. "While it lasted, sure. Have a good life, Haven. It's what you deserve."

Haven was all the way to the mouth of the trail that would lead her back home when she finally looked over her shoulder again. Still holding back tears she refused to let anyone see fall because she was not weak; a man would not make her weak.

Still, she looked back.

She had to know.

Just to *see* … to know if he was still there, or already gone.

She expected one thing.

She found another.

Andino was still staring at her, but he'd lost that blank slate of nothingness that had been his expression before; pain stared back now.

Loss.

Haven recognized it if only because she was sure that was the same thing reflecting back from her, too.

He didn't want her to go. He still let her leave.

Why is he such a good liar?

Why?

ABOUT THE AUTHOR

Bethany-Kris is a Canadian author, lover of much, and mother to four young sons, one cat, and three dogs. A small town in Eastern Canada where she was born and raised is where she has always called home. With her boys under her feet, a snuggling cat, barking dogs, and a spouse calling over his shoulder, she is nearly always writing something ... when she can find the time.

Find Bethany-Kris at:
www.bethanykris.com
www.bethanykris.blogspot.com
www.facebook.com/bethanykriswrites
www.twitter.com/bethanykris
www.instagram.com/bethany.kris
www.pinterest.com/bethanykris

Sign up to Bethany-Kris's New Release Newsletter here:
http://eepurl.com/bf9lzD.

OTHER BOOKS

Andino + Haven
Duty
Vow

John + Siena

Loyalty
Disgrace

Cross + Catherine

Always
Revere
Unruly
The Companion
Naz & Roz

Guzzi Duet

Unraveled, Book One
Entangled, Book Two

DeLuca Duet

Waste of Worth: Part One
Worth of Waste: Part Two

Standalone Titles

Effortless
Inflict
Cozen
Captivated
Dishonored

Donati Bloodlines

Thin Lies
Thin Lines
Thin Lives
Behind the Bloodlines
The Complete Trilogy

Filthy Marcellos

Antony
Lucian
Giovanni
Dante
Legacy
A Very Marcello Christmas
The Complete Collection

Seasons of Betrayal

Where the Sun Hides
Where the Snow Falls
Where the Wind Whispers
Seasons: The Complete Seasons of Betrayal Series

Gun Moll Trilogy

Gun Moll
Gangster Moll
Madame Moll

The Chicago War

Deathless & Divided
Reckless & Ruined
Scarless & Sacred
Breathless & Bloodstained
The Complete Series

The Russian Guns

The Arrangement
The Life
The Score
Demyan & Ana
Shattered
The Jersey Vignettes

Find more on Bethany-Kris's website at www.bethanykris.com.

www.ingramcontent.com/pod-product-compliance
Lightning Source LLC
Chambersburg PA
CBHW030821020726
47499CB00006B/2012